FEVER

NICK MANCUSO

Chloeeee! 8/29/19
Thanks for coming down,
reading this and all the
good book recs.

–Nick Mancuso

PRAISE FOR NICK MANCUSO

"To say that all is not well on Staniford Drive in leafy Dorset, CT, is an understatement. In Fever, Nick Mancuso orchestrates a symphonic tale about the relationships among a group of neighbors during one rainless summer. Grief, isolation, sex, rage, and above all, racism fuel the page-turning action that leads to an unthinkable crescendo at the novel's end. Writing with something like x-ray vision, Mancuso looks not only into the perfectly appointed homes of the neighborhood at the center of this story, but into the broken hearts and troubled minds of the people who inhabit them. There is no way to read this irresistible novel except at a fever pitch."

— RACHEL BASCH, AUTHOR OF THE LISTENER

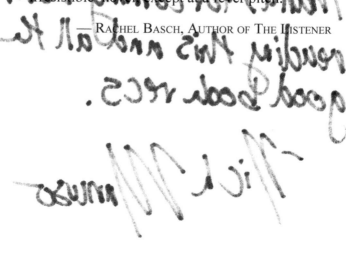

"Fever takes us deeply inside of the underbelly of a suburban neighborhood during the last hot month of summer. Nick Mancuso's ability to reveal how neighbors can alter each other's lives irrevocably is both moving and frightening. These pages crackle with heat and a frenetic pace."

— KAREN OSBORN, AUTHOR OF CENTERVILLE

CHAPTER 1

TUESDAY, JULY 29

NEIL

8:47AM

APPROXIMATELY ONE MONTH before he would be lowered into the ground during a small, sparsely attended funeral service, Neil Testa's mother called to tell him his father had died. When the phone rang, he'd only been up a short time, having woken up late, fighting off a slight hangover.

He'd slept fitfully, dreaming of Vanessa again, as he seemed to all the time now. Sometimes he'd wake up and forgotten she'd left years prior, and eyes closed, smiling, still wrapped in the cocoon of his dream, he'd imagine her putting the coffee on downstairs. Not that morning, though. Instead, he recalled some fight they'd had, slammed doors and exhausted stalking off into the night. He woke with a pulsing, aching, headache, and called in sick to work.

When the phone rang, he was staring out past his television, out into the gloom of a rainstorm. The ground needed it; it'd been so dry the last few weeks, and the lawns on Staniford Drive looked terrible. It didn't fit with the neighborhood. Didn't fit with the whole town of Dorset, Connecticut really. When he was growing up in the suburban town just a few miles eastward of New Haven, his street, Staniford Drive, was a cul-de-sac of four large McMansions, and one little rundown cape on the corner. The McMansions looked like they'd been stamped out, one after another surrounding a smooth pool of new pavement, with sloping green lawns rolling to a thick dark curb. Under normal circumstances, the lawns would be green and mown in careful diagonal rows, the style uniform, and the pattern running from edge to edge of each lot (all done by the same company) as if the whole street and all of the houses sat on the same roll of diagonal green fabric. This summer, though, was the hottest and driest; they'd only had half an inch of rain.

When the call from his mother came in, he was staring blankly at the wide aquarium of his television, with some talking heads around a glass table, recapping football. He was sprawled wide, his lanky arms and legs open, over the weathered brown leather couch. His light brown hair was sticking up at all angles, and his tired grey eyes were gazing almost unfocused on the TV. He reached down casually and scratched his testicles over the flannel pajama pants and rested his hand on his knee. His phone buzzed across the coffee table, the display bearing the word 'Mom' in a big sans-serif font. He looked at it a second, at the photo of the earth below her name, its surface swirled with clouds, before sliding the green arrow over and moving the phone to his ear.

"Hey, Mom."

"Neil, it's Mom." She sounded tired, exhausted.

"I know; it says your name when you call—"

"Listen, please." He heard her draw in a sharp breath. "Honey, Dad is . . . Dad is gone." He sat upright quickly and reached for the remote, knocking it to the carpet as his feet swung down off the table. He dove for it and hit the power button quickly.

"What? What do you mean?"

"I mean he died this morning." She sniffed, and he could hear the sadness creeping in, like darkness over the trees, the shadows long.

". . . what, when, how long ago?" The words didn't come easily. His throat felt dry suddenly, parched, and his voice squeaked a little. *He couldn't be gone*, he thought. He'd just talked to him a few weeks ago.

HE REMEMBERED THE LAST TIME HE'D SPOKEN TO HIS father.

"Hi, Dad."

"Neil? It's your father."

"I know. It pops up your name when you call."

"Oh." A silence followed on the line.

"So, what's up? How's the weather?" Neil nudged.

"Oh, it's fine, you know, very humid. I can barely leave the house now. I've got the air conditioning on all the time."

"Yeah, it's been hot here too," Neil said, scanning the brown grass.

"How's my lawn?" His father asked as if intuiting landscaping negligence from a thousand miles away.

"Vibrant and alive," he lied, knowing his elderly father wouldn't be up from Florida to take in the burned desolation that was his lawn and the others on Staniford Drive anytime soon.

"You know, we still haven't gotten the paperwork tied up, so don't get your grubby hands on repainting just yet," his father snarled suddenly. For a second, his father's tone surprised him. Neil forgot momentarily that his father was suffering from Alzheimer's Disease and had relocated to a special memory-assistive community on the gulf coast with his mother. Neil had no idea what a memory-assistive community was or why it was helpful to his father's fading memory. This time, his father had forgotten that he'd signed the house over to Neil and his then-girlfriend Vanessa five years prior. Neil steadied himself and steeled his tone to reply.

"Dad, you gave me the house five years ago." There was a silence on the line.

"Neil?"

"Dad?"

"I . . . I got confused. Sorry about that."

"It's okay Dad," he said, sighing for a second.

"So, how's my lawn?"

"It's fine, Dad. It's fine." There was a scuffling sound, and his mother's voice sounded on the line.

"Neil? It's Mom."

"Hey, how's Dad?"

"We're having a tough day over here. I noticed his asking you twice about the lawn."

"Yeah, he got confused for a second. What did he need?"

"I don't know why he called. I'm sorry to bug you."

"It's okay," he sniffed.

"Are you okay?" she asked, her tone sounding harshly interrogative.

"What? No yeah. I think I picked up a cold at work," he lied, pretending the heat he could feel around the corners of his eyes wasn't real.

"Well, rest and fluids. Get a little sun when it comes out again." He nodded and then realized she couldn't see his gesture.

"I will."

His mother ended the call.

NEIL CAME BACK TO THE PRESENT AND RESTED HIS HEAD in his hands. He could feel himself shaking but fought to stabilize it. His mother was speaking words he couldn't hear. How could he be gone? How could his spirit have vanished? Neil remembered how he felt when his father was diagnosed with Alzheimer's seven years ago, how tearful and worried his father was when he and his mother returned from the doctor, how his father told him gruffly and kept wiping his eyes. He'd thought he knew what grief felt like then, as if his dad had died there, in that moment, and now just his corporeal remains had dissolved. Neil inhaled a sharp breath. His phone in his hand felt sweaty.

"I went into his room just now, he still wasn't up, and he was in bed, asleep, but stone cold. He must've passed away at some point in the night." Neil recalled their new arrangements of separate bedrooms in their condo. His father's disease had gotten worse in recent months, his confusion frequent, and he'd been waking Neil's mother up in the night, panicking about who she was and why she was in the bed beside him, growing hostile, anxious, even bordering on dangerous. His mother had gently and quietly moved to the guest bedroom.

"Oh my god, Mom."

"I felt for his pulse, but he'd been gone a long while. He was so cold." She gave a sharp inhale at the end of her sentence.

"Are you okay?" he found himself saying, now standing up and peering out the window at his burned grass, looking around for no reason, as if to hope his father would appear, standing at the end of his driveway, gesturing a wordless exasperation, arms outstretched, at the state of the lawn. He smiled slightly at the image of his father's heavy mouth, shaking jowls mouthing the words '. . . the fuck did you do to my lawn?' and then breaking into a smile.

"I'm startled. I just . . . I didn't . . . I didn't expect it. We'd had a pretty good night last night, he was great at dinner, and . . ." He heard her devolve into whimpers. "I almost slept in his room with him, and I'm wondering if I had . . ." She sniffed, her voice straining. "I would have caught him and, maybe gotten him help in time."

"Mom, you couldn't have. There's no way." He heard sirens on the other end of the phone.

"Honey, I have to go, the ambulance is here, I have to go. I love you, okay?"

"I'm flying down," he said quickly.

"Okay, let me know." And she was gone.

He rose from the couch, feeling as if he was in a fog. Moving slowly to the window, he rested his forehead on the cool glass and closed his eyes. Long breath in, ragged breath out. Gripping the edge of the window frame, Neil steeled himself against the structure and opened his eyes again.

Across the street, a moving van had pulled up at the house from which only last week a frumpy realtor took down its for sale sign. The van sat for a moment, the driver likely waiting to see if the rain would stop, Neil reasoned, and behind it pulled up a silver Audi A5 convertible with a canvas top. A young black woman emerged; pretty, nice body, wearing a t-shirt and yoga pants, covering her head with her hands fruitlessly. She dashed to the driver side of the moving van and waved a *c'mon* to the driver. Neil couldn't see who the driver was from the glare, but he imagined whoever it was shaking their head. She gestured again, this time stopping the useless shielding of her hair, and put her arms out, palms facing upward as if to show it wasn't raining *that* badly. The door to the moving van popped open, and a tall black man emerged, looking around and smiling broadly at the woman and shaking his head. She gave him a wave as if to dismiss him and walked around to the back of the van. Even in the rain and from across the street, Neil could see she was beautiful.

Diversity like this was unheard of in Dorset. Hell, in

his entire life there, he'd only seen a handful of black families in town, and never before on Staniford Drive. *Why'd they want to move here of all places*, he thought, looking out to the other houses on the cul-de-sac.

Aside from the run-down little cape on the corner, each McMansion was marginally different, while still being structurally the same. They were all colonials with at least four bedrooms and vinyl siding in various neutral colors: taupe, yellow, white. They all had big arched second story windows looking onto the foyer over the glass-paneled door. They all had rock paths to the driveway. Some, like his, had an in-ground pool in the backyard and a deck. Every house had an almost strategically placed copse of trees halfway down the lawn, planted on a neat pillow of mulch. When Neil's parents gave him ownership of the house, he was still with Vanessa then, and thought living in a house without a mortgage would set them up to raise kids successfully in the place he was raised. How moronic that seemed now. Looking out the window he wondered what the point was in even staying.

He watched the rain again for a moment. The couple across the street had conjured a large sheet of plastic that they would cover furniture with and then carry each piece up the stone front steps and into the house, tilting sideways through the open, glass inlaid door. These people he'd probably never even meet looked nice. They laughed and smiled at each other, big wide smiles. They pranced around in the rain, as if to embrace the fact that they would get soaked anyway. They were the sort of fun-loving young people the neighborhood needed, a breath of fresh air among the stiff fifty-plus neighbors, and he found himself watching her movements, carefully, her curves prevalent in her yoga pants.

He sighed heavily once more and then moved away from the window to book immediate flights to Florida.

CARLA

11:38 AM

ACROSS THE STREET in the doorway of their nearly identical house, Carla sat down, her behind smooshed against the wood parquet in the foyer and untied her neon pink sneakers, the laces clotted with mud. The rain fell harder during the last hour; the scant few boxes were rushed inside, sopping sodden cardboard now, the duct tape wet, loose and flapping.

Phil, her husband, stood in the doorway of the foyer. The yoke of his gray T-shirt was soaked, his head covered in droplets, rivulets running down his temples, past his dark eyes, to his scrub of stubble. He smiled at her. She smiled back. Finally untangling her laces and gingerly pulling the soaking shoes off and setting them by the door, she reached her hands out to him. He stepped forward, clutched her fingers in his, and lifted her off the floor. He was so much bigger than she was, she thought as he pulled her into a standing position, the top of her head coming just up to his sternum.

"That it?" he asked, looking to the stack of boxes by the door.

"For now," she said. "There's still five or six smaller ones of books toward the front of the loading bay, but they can wait. I don't want to risk it with the Great Flood out there." She reached behind her head and squeezed out her black ponytail to a splatter of water onto the wood.

"I'll get them. We've got to return the truck anyway," he said, moving to the door.

"C'mon, they can stay for now. We'll get them in a few. C'mon, show me what you did." She peeled her soaking socks off and tossed them in a ball by her sneakers. Phil moved to the archway to the kitchen and gestured for her to follow.

"Through here," he said, moving quickly through the kitchen with the cherry cabinets, past another pile of damp boxes. "Quickly, because I haven't done anything in here." She smirked at this, and he led her around the corner to the annex by the garage. He moved swiftly ahead of her and pulled the door to the room ahead closed.

"What's this?" she asked as he stood in front of the door.

"I present, the home office of Dr. Carla Bishop, Assistant Professor of Political Science, Yale University." He swung the door open with a flourish and stepped aside for her to walk through. For a moment before she stepped through the door, she was flush with a rush of affection for this man, and all of his wonderful attributes. She crossed the threshold and smiled. He'd moved her writing desk to the center of the room, her chair scooted behind it. The curved corner bookshelf, presently devoid of books. Her potted palm by the two windows and her brown divan under the windowsill. She panned the little space with the white walls, and on the wall beside the door, he'd mounted her diplomas, Bachelors from Princeton, MS and Ph.D. from Northwestern. She was positively overcome.

"I haven't done the desk drawers or anything, I wasn't about to do that. I just figured you'd need a place to get settled, get adjusted, you know."

"Oh babycakes," she said using a pet name they'd originally coined to make fun of overly affectionate couples that'd somehow been incorporated into their lexicon over the last eight years. "I love it. You didn't have to unpack this first. We haven't even finished the truck."

Phil shrugged at this. "Of course I did. I caught you reading email in the truck. I figured I'd better get your office up or you'd go stir-crazy without a place to work." She chuckled a little and ran her hand over her desk, the cherry wood smooth and even colored. In time, she wouldn't be able to even see the fine surface again, it'd be stacked high with books, and her enormous monitors and laptop dock would occupy most of the space. She imagined herself here, late at night while he slept upstairs, scrolling through old documents. This would do just fine.

He was right about the space, of course. In their eight years together, he'd boasted that he'd been developing a map of her brain, and he could project exactly where her thoughts would go from one place to another, thick grooves tracing topic to topic. She never believed it, except right here, right now, when the whole impetus for their buying of the house, their tight one-bedroom not allowing for spare bedrooms or an office was in front of her. This was what she'd wanted to do so badly, had halfheartedly carried in boxes of dishes and cutlery, jars of spices and an artisan cookie jar, all of it seeming like the appetizer for the entrée: setting up her office. Carla had felt like digging through the truck, picking and finding just the boxes and pieces of furniture pertaining to her office and pulling them out and setting them up. Phil must've prioritized her office boxes, picked them strategically, been making trips to her office first, before other more critical spaces.

"What's the story upstairs?" she asked, turning to him. He squirmed a little.

"Everything's up there, but I kind of didn't put the bed together or the drawers back in the dressers. The mattress is against the wall." She laughed at this and moved past him, out the door to the kitchen.

"We need a place to sleep, you boob," she said, reentering the foyer and turning up the stairs. She reached the first landing, the stairs banking up and to the left. Phil had tracked wet footprints up the hardwood, and around the corner. She pretended she didn't notice.

"But I know your priorities!" he called from below after coming up after her, his shuffling socks making light noises on the blonde wood of the stairs. She closed her eyes for a moment. She'd come to love that sound, she knew she would, the almost wood-block like 'plink' of his feet against the treads. At the top of the stairs, she ran her hand along the railing that looked out over the foyer, at the brass chandelier that hung from the ceiling. That'd have to be changed out with something more contemporary. This house, at last, even with its echoey emptiness was theirs. No more rented one-bedrooms in Wicker Park. No, they owned this.

She reached for the brass handle to the first door and opened it onto a small bedroom with two windows facing out the back. Boxes piled on the desk in the middle read "P-Office." She turned around as he reached the top of the stairs.

"You didn't even unpack your own office. That was so nice of you, honey," she said, turning back to him.

"That's because I don't have a job," he said, his eyes downcast. She crossed the space to him and kissed him on his scruffy cheek.

"Yet. You don't have a job yet," she said with an affectionate pat on his behind.

"You know how many law practices there are in Fairfield County? I bet you'll be in final rounds of an interview by the last week of the month," she said, throwing out what she rationed to be a fairly accurate projection.

He nodded in a way that seemed to her to be more to himself than anyone else, and he stepped away from her toward another door on the hallway. He pushed it open without ceremony, and she stepped into their carpeted bedroom. New construction smell greeted them, and Carla wondered how long the house had smelled like wood dust, even if it was built just two years ago. Crisp white painted walls were light and airy, and a bowed out bay window looking directly onto the street magnified even the dim light of the day into the room. Their sleigh bed leaned against the wall in pieces, their mattress propped opposite. Like an uneven stack of books, the dresser drawers sat perched on top of one another.

"I love the light in here," she said, trying to cheer him up. He nodded slightly and picked up one of the drawers to slide it into the tallboy by the bathroom door.

He turned into the bathroom, faced away from her and reached up with his hands, the tips of his fingers folding over the edge of the molding around the door-frame. For a second, she swore she saw his muscles in his arms tighten, as if he was going to do a pull-up on the molding, and his shirt shrugged up, showing off his smooth lower back. An idea formed in her head as she as she glanced out the window. They had to wait out the rain somehow.

She reached around either side of the mattress and dragged it down from the wall to the floor, dropping it with a thud at the last second, and Phil jerked his head to her.

"What are you doing?" he asked, lifting the next drawer from the stack and sliding it into its slot. She climbed onto the mattress and pulled her tight shirt off over her head. She beckoned him over. He smiled a little bit. This would do, she thought.

"Now?"

She nodded and reached behind herself, unclipping her bra and laying down on top of the mattress. He moved over to her and pulled his own shirt off, revealing his wide chest with his patch of curly black chest hair and defined pectorals, his shoulder muscles straining and pulling. She smiled. Her husband was a handsome man. He leaned over her and kissed her slowly. She put her hands on his face, and he reached down and shimmied her yoga pants and underwear off. He kissed slowly down her chest, under her breasts, and stopped. He climbed up off the low mattress on the floor for a moment to look in the bathroom.

"What are you doing?" she called after him.

"Just going to gargle really quick, my breath is awful. I packed it somewhere in these boxes."

"Don't bother with it, come back here," she called, sliding her hand between her legs again to keep herself occupied while he rummaged. He stuck his head around the doorway.

"Is this counting as a try?" he asked, looking serious and climbing back down onto the springy mattress. She nodded as he worked down below her smooth brown stomach and carefully kissed her. She shivered for a second and wondered if she'd remembered locking the front door. She closed her eyes and lifted her legs, compressing her knees to her chest. He moved in careful, deliberate strokes, two fingers, his lips and tongue moving in synchronization and she felt the swelling inside. Between sharp breaths, she whispered an invitation and then his gym shorts were off, and they were on their sides and he was in her mouth and she could taste the sweat on him. She moved beyond that, quickly as he returned to work on her, and she wanted nothing more than the main event.

He positioned himself between her legs. She'd missed the feeling of his girth inside her, the stretching of muscles that hadn't been in the last week with the stress of orchestrating the move and the various components. She'd missed him.

As she moved slowly, pushing back into his strokes, she thought about the last visit to their doctor back in Chicago. He'd produced a complex schedule of times when they needed to have sex in order to align with her body rhythms, to hit her optimal fertility. The doctor, a Jewish white man, had been someone she'd strangely connected with. Normally she'd preferred the probing and examinations to have been by a black doctor, but Dr. Levin was patiently friendly. When he'd discovered she too was a doctor, albeit of philosophy, there was this unspoken recognition between them, the occasional subtle nod. Phil remarked on it in the car on the way home after the appointment.

"What was that about? You two got real comfortable fast."

"It's a doctor to doctor thing. You wouldn't understand," she said, teasing him. She'd instantly regretted it. He scoffed loudly and she wished she hadn't made that joke.

He said nothing and looked out the windshield, driving back to their apartment. She wasn't surprised he disliked this concept, seeing a doctor to remedy their ultimate goal of having a baby. After trying for a year, Phil confessed he felt weird about it, like it was somehow his fault, but after examinations and tests and lab-work on each of them, there was no reason as to why they couldn't, so the aged doctor with his diplomas on the walls beside his desk, just like hers, rigged up a schedule and told them to be more aggressive about it.

"Jo and I had a hard time trying to conceive a century ago." He chuckled at his own age and somehow this dumb joke made her smile too. "It took us three years, but, then, we got lucky," he said with a smile. She leaned back then.

"Three years?" she said with a look of horror. He nodded solemnly, then, reached across the desk and turned a picture frame around to face them. The picture showed Dr. Levin and his gray-haired wife standing by the dusty brown cavern of the Grand Canyon, their arms linked with five college-aged girls in sunglasses and bright sneakers.

"Are they all yours?" Carla asked, studying the photo. Dr. Levin beamed with pride and nodded.

"Sarah was first, then two sets of twins. The last pair just went off to NYU so you can understand why retirement is probably never in the cards for me now." He laughed again and then stood up, reaching his hand out to shake Phil's first, then hers. "Stay with it, you're healthy, smart people, don't lose faith. Persevere!"

She thought about his words as Phil built to climax, his breathing shallow and faster, and she thought a wordless prayer to whatever gods that be, that this time, it'd catch, that the biological force that jolts the magical system to join up, the basic elements to create life, that this time it'd work. She held this in and exhaled the prayer in a long breath as Phil's muscles went limp on top of her and he groaned.

AMANDA

6:58 PM

THAT NIGHT, after the rain stopped, Amanda Holbrooke, the neighbor to the immediate left of Carla and Phil stepped out into the muggy night for a run. She tapped her rubberized fitness tracker three times and started off a jog down the street and around the cul-de-sac.

Amanda ran whenever she felt stressed. The expense of sweat helped relieve the rumbling of her thoughts and the pressure that built against her temples. She stopped, before taking a left onto Cliff Road at the entrance of Staniford drive. She wanted to make sure that her husband Gavin's car was long gone, off to drinks at the tavern in town with his friends from the police force. She hated bumping into him when she was out for a run. He always shattered her solitude with a volley of questions from across the passenger seat, his car slow-rolling alongside her chatting about everything else at home. She hadn't had the heart in the twenty years of their marriage to say anything; it wasn't all that often, but half the time she felt like calling at him through the lowered window, "Do you mind? I went for a run to get away from home for a little while."

She'd wanted to go for a run since before dinner time. The night was hot. It had rained earlier in the day for just a little while, and she'd prepared fresh garden salads for her family and had just set the table. Gavin wasn't home yet. She listened intently as the sound of his Porsche came around the corner and down Staniford Drive, sometimes with Guns 'n Roses blaring from the speakers so loud, the sound diluted into a dull throbbing, not unlike a headache. Tonight however, it was just the rumble of the engine she heard pulling up, then the sound cut, a car door closed, and he came in the door to the kitchen.

Gavin Holbrooke was a big man, wide, tall, his shoulders broad and hands thick and meaty. She liked that about him, he was so much bigger than she was, and years ago when their passions were more active, she loved how powerful he felt. He could pick her up off the floor without strain, could lean her against the wall and take her standing upright, all without getting tired.

They met when she was a senior at UCONN and still naturally blonde. She'd run a red light and Gavin, a police officer at that time, pulled her over to issue her a ticket. She figured she'd need to flirt to get out of it, but when she'd seen his dark eyes and thick hair, she smiled, and he smiled back. Somehow it worked. They stayed there, her car pulled over the side of the road, him leaning over, chatting to her for over an hour before he glanced at his watch and she remembered she'd been pulled over. She hesitantly reminded him of this, and he chuckled, reminded her to watch out running stoplights, and wrote his number down on a blank ticket for her.

They went out a week later, and their chemistry was magnetic. Amanda was sick of the men in college then, the bravado and the swagger, and Gavin seemed self-conscious and modest, having come from a poor family, his father making vulcanized rubber at Uniroyal in Naugatuck. Despite having earned a position as a police officer, his career path remarkably distilled at the ripe young age of twenty-three, his modesty was refreshing. She felt this swelling of affection two years later when they married on Long Island Sound.

Today, Gavin owned a security company, Vanguard Communications, which provided paid security services to VIP among others, as well as installed complex security camera and alarm systems on businesses and some wealthy homes. Their own house had one such elaborate system.

Twelve Staniford drive, its security aside, was the largest colonial on the street, with a large square backyard fenced in, wisteria vines curled through the top links of the fence, surrounding a large kidney-shaped pool with a rock waterfall. They also had a pergola attached to the back of the house, the patio elaborately placed stones and wrought iron furniture. From the table, where Amanda had her coffee every morning in summertime, it was like their own fenced-in utopia, with the high fences topped with shrubbery against the forest out back.

. . .

IN THE DOORWAY, GAVIN GROANED AND PUT HIS HANDS behind his back and leaned back, cracking what sounded like forty vertebrae. After another moan, he crossed the space to her where she was tossing the salad for dinner and kissed her once on the cheek. She smiled knowingly.

"I think I want one of those stand-up desks," he said, moving into the living room and twisting his torso this way and that to loosen up the muscles in his back and his arms. It was strange to see him stretching like this; Gavin kept to a strict exercise routine in their basement gym.

"Oh?" she called.

"Yeah, I think sitting down all day is killing me. I feel so slumpy."

"Newsweek did call sitting at work all day the smoking of our generation," she called from the kitchen. She heard him scoff.

"I wish I didn't do anything all day but sit and read fuckin' Newsweek," Gavin called back on his way to the stairs. She rolled her eyes at this and sprinkled a handful of diced almonds over the salad. She'd also read an article about how bad for the environment growing almonds was, but somehow using them now felt earned, like she deserved it.

"Dinner's on when you're ready. Yell for Kyle," she summoned from the island counter as she went for the wine rack in the fridge and took out an Italian pinot grigio. It would go perfectly with the salad she'd made. She pulled the foil seal off in one swift move, crumpling it and tossing it in the garbage bin in one of the cabinets of the island beside the sink. What did he think she did all day? She thought as she clamped the bottle in the opener and pushed the handle down, the sharp pike drilling down into the soft meat of the cork, the screw cutting through the fibers. She pulled back on the handle, extracting the cork with a pop and set the bottle down. She did four loads of laundry today, went grocery shopping, prepared dinner, went through the basement and disposed of three different boxes of Christmas decorations, discarding moldy, stained electric candles for the windows and half-working strands of lights. They'd need new ones for this season, and the thought put her stomach in knots.

She poured herself a glass alone, knowing better than to presume Gavin would want wine with dinner, and moved to the sliding door onto the pergola. The wine had a sweetness to it, a definite citrus flavor that surprised her. The pool looked tranquil out there, and she caught her own reflection in the glass of the slider. She still looked young and perky, she thought, and those weren't crow's feet in the corners of her eyes—the glass was just smeared. Her hair, professionally dyed blonde twice a quarter when she had the money for it, was pulled back into a tight ponytail, not a hair out of place. She finished her glass of wine and turned around, wondering where her husband and son were. She set her glass down with a clink on the counter and left the kitchen to the living room onto which the upstairs hallway looked. She started up the stairs. At her bedroom door, she stopped and listened to the hush of the shower from their master bathroom. He'd be at least

another fifteen minutes. She continued down the hallway, running her hand along the railing. She stopped
outside her son, Kyle's room and pushed the door open.

Kyle sat on the bench at the end of his bed, his eyes
glassy and fixed on the forty-eight-inch television on
which he was playing a first-person shooter. He wore a
headset over his ears, microphone hovering just below
his lips, his eyes darting back and forth over the landscape on the screen, which moved smoothly and too
quickly, and it made her dizzy. Kyle had her blonde hair,
long, as was the trend, bangs swept to the left over dark
brown eyebrows and tiny dark eyes, his father's. His
voice had just dropped, and that unfamiliar baritone
seemed to have crept into everything, even his diction.

The computer-generated landscape on screen looked
like a crumbling middle-eastern city, and she watched
her son's assault rifle march in file with several US
Army soldiers in desert camouflage. For a second, she
couldn't look away. This scene was all too familiar, with
all the on-the-ground news footage from Iraq or
Afghanistan these days, the question as to why her son
was willingly playing this dangerous real-life scenario
evaded her.

"Chuckles go left, behind the water tank. Billy, take
position behind us and pick off any hostiles," he spoke
quietly, seemingly to nobody, like he was talking to
himself. "Ethan, stay with me, let's go." That name she
recognized. Probably Ethan Carlisle, a neighbor boy
Kyle had been friends with since second grade. Amanda
watched as the virtual soldiers followed her son's orders
and for a second, she imagined him actually deployed in

Iraq or Afghanistan, a draft reinstated, and her baby boy, the only child they had, shipped off to fight the barbarians in the middle east somewhere.

She still hadn't been noticed by her son.

"And go, go, go!" he shouted into the microphone, and the soldiers, on her son's command, fanned out across the landscape. Kyle and the soldier she figured was a representation of Ethan (albeit looking nothing like him) moved ahead and from a building came a spray of gunfire, flashes of light. She jumped slightly, and a spray of blood came from Ethan's avatar's head, and she covered her mouth. Kyle laughed and spoke into his headset again.

"No joy today, big man, it's back to the ranch for you. Chuckles, cover me with the sniper, I'm going in."

The sign on the building was in Arabic, likely correct, she reasoned as to the disturbing realism of this particular game and watched her son's gun proceed toward the building then crouch lower. He pulled a trigger or pressed some button or something and unleashed a volley of rounds into the vacant window of the building. Shots returned, and he jumped to the left. She was riveted.

He started to back away from the building and in the doorway a man emerged; an Arabic man, a crude stereotype of a terrorist, his arms wrapped tightly around himself. Suddenly Kyle shouted: "We've got a suicide vest, I repeat, he's got an IED. Ethan, how close are you?" She watched horrified, Kyle was backing away faster now, his gun trained on the man intent on running at him, closing the distance. He fired his gun and clipped the man, but he kept on running toward, closer, closer still, and she gasped. Kyle jumped suddenly turned his real head and noticed her, no doubt wondering how long she'd been there. Suddenly the virtual terrorist reached Kyle's gun in the lower right-hand side of the screen, and there was a sudden explosion. A rupture of gore and flames and a red filter fell over the screen, words in a typewriter font hammered out across the header. *KILLED IN ACTION.* The game prompted him: *Respawn? Y/N.*

Kyle pulled one ear of his headset off and turned his head to her, setting his controller on his lap.

"What's up, Mom?" She felt shaky. How was he so unfazed by the fact that his avatar was just killed by a suicide bomber? She cleared her throat.

"D-dinner's ready." She listened for the shower two rooms over, but it was off.

"Dad's out of the shower. Let's go." Kyle, perpetually appeasing and friendly, nodded and pulled his headset back on.

"Hey, I've got to run. Be back on later on." He clacked some buttons and the console's main menu came back up. He reached for the clicker on the end of the bed, looking like an absolute anachronism next to the high-tech controller he discarded onto his duvet and powered the massive glowing window to other worlds off.

DOWNSTAIRS AT THE TABLE, AS HER SON SAT DOWN AND reached for the salad tongs, he spoke.

"Mom, what night is the garden party?"

She scanned her memory, thinking of the annual Staniford Drive garden party at which she always supplied her locally famous mojitos.

"Saturday afternoon. Are you actually gracing us with your presence this year?" she said, distracted, remembering she needed to buy the supplies, the rum, limes, and mint.

"It's my last one before I ship off," he said, and for a moment, she imagined him actually shipping off to war, and felt a tightening around her heart. She knew what he meant—shipping off to UMass in the fall—but he must've appropriated that lingo from the game. She shivered slightly.

The supplies though, she needed to go get them, enough to make mojitos for forty people for a few hours. She rose from the table, called out her husband's name from the kitchen doorway, and went to her purse on the counter. In her wallet, she unzipped the money pocket, and reached in and counted fourteen dollars. That was all she had left. She knew what she had to do and gulped. She could feel a headache thumping against her skull.

Fuck, she thought, *I need to go for a run.*

ETHAN

7:14 PM

ACROSS THE STREET, right at the mouth of Staniford Drive in the little blue cape, Ethan Carlisle took his headset off, Kyle having signed off seconds ago, his own interest in blowing terrorists away rapidly waning. He clicked the TV, smaller than Kyle's, off, and rose from the couch in the living room. His house, the little house he shared with his mother Jennifer, his father long out of the picture, was the smallest on the street. A simple three-bedroom cape, no pool, set back from the street on the corner of Staniford Drive and Cliff Road.

Ethan barely remembered his father. His mother and father had a bad divorce when he was four, and his father never argued for custody, so Jennifer took sole responsibility. Allegedly, the child support payments came in every month, on time, with no messages transmitted.

Ethan left the living room and proceeded around the corner and up the stairs to his own bedroom. He pushed the door aside and flopped down on his bed. He retrieved his phone from his pocket and began to scroll through Facebook, flipping with his thumb. He stopped on a post by Mike Powell, one of the more popular senior students at Dorset High. Mike's post was clear; the varsity lacrosse team roster had just been posted on the high school's website, and Mike had been appointed captain.

Ethan had been waiting for this. He sat upright on his bed and clicked the link to the school website and entered his username and password. In Dorset, the lacrosse team was everything. For the last decade, the varsity team had won every state championship and the trophies glimmered in the front lobby of the high school. Ethan himself had been on the junior varsity team, had done fairly well in years past, but last season, somehow, he'd choked in the final game. The surrounding audience in the aluminum stands groaned when he shot and missed. It was the goal that would have put them over the edge, and he missed it by a lot.

In the car on the way home, his mother didn't say anything, her own disappointment palpable. Ethan had felt guilty because ever since he was little, lacrosse was his primary focus. He could remember his earliest games, he was ten, played on foggy fields early in the morning in April. He'd rip the ball through the net, the netting of his stick launching a satisfying whipping sound as it fired. He'd lived for it, and every night after school for as long as he could remember was practice or a game. His mother had often used it as a prideful point about her son, eager to prove something against the waves of blistering judgment of her single parenting.

The link opened and he scanned the list. It was listed by position, and he scanned downward, searching, searching. Nothing. *Where the fuck is it*, he thought, scanning again, double checking the list. At the bottom he caught sight of his name and exhaled heavily. He was okay. He saw his name and read closer.

Ethan Carlisle, Team Manager.

"What the fuck," he said, reading it again. "Team fucking manager?!" The team manager was the position they gave the fat kid who wanted to be involved, the excluded, the social outcast. He yelled and threw his phone across the room. It impacted the wall with a fatal-sounding crunch.

"Ethan?" his mother called up the stairs. "Y'alright?" she said, the sound of the TV on behind her.

"Yeah, just caught my finger in the drawer," he lied. He couldn't tell her. After years of her driving him to practice and rooting him on, this would mean more to her than to him. He got up from the bed and gingerly crossed the room, pausing before he lifted his phone from the carpet, and turned it over. A thick crack like lightning had struck down across the screen from the top right corner where the device collided with the sheetrock. "Fuck, fuck, fuck," he whispered, rubbing the glass with his thumb, hoping to rub the crack away, fruitlessly. He groaned loudly and fell back on his bed, fuming. Holding his phone up to the light, he pressed the lock button and it unlocked, still responding to his touch. He opened Facebook again and watched as the comments dribbled in onto Mike's status. People who hadn't even played on the team last year piled on in, celebrating their placements.

This was it. He wouldn't play again. If he didn't make the team for senior year, he'd never have a shot at playing in college. He'd lost the chance for a sports scholarship. He'd have to spend senior year outside of the circle of popularity that surrounded the lacrosse team. For a minute, a creeping dread of college costs crept over him. Could he afford college without a lacrosse scholarship? No, no, he couldn't worry about that now.

Ethan wasn't surprised, if he was being honest. Lacrosse was everything in Dorset; it was all that mattered, and he'd wanted to be a part of it so badly. But when he whiffed last season, the coaches dismissed him outright. They needed the fifteenth trophy in the lobby, and he'd cost them that. For a second, Ethan realized the absolute frivolity of it all, how fucking stupid the worship of these silly games was. If he hadn't been playing since he was little, he wouldn't have cared so much, so fuck his mother too, for making him like this. He rose from the bed and paced from left to right in the tight bedroom. He clicked *like* on the status and tossed his phone back down on his bed, gingerly. Almost instantly, his phone plinked. Someone new had commented on the status. When he saw who, his insides locked up. Mackenzie Gornick.

Mackenzie Gornick was one of the most beautiful girls he'd ever seen. She had long blonde hair and gray-blue eyes, and high tight cheekbones. He'd known her since kindergarten, but lately, she'd become more beautiful. She ran with the popular crowd and was even tangentially friendly with Ethan—they volunteered together for their high school's community service requirement, they knew each other's names, were friends with each other on Facebook and even had each other's numbers. Her post was short, but it cut him deep. *Congratulations Everybody! Go Lions!* He almost spat. She was both congratulating him and not. For a second, he imagined his routine internet pornography-based fantasy of Mackenzie, topless, her breasts round and bouncy like the sort of stuff he'd seen online. She'd lovingly take him in her mouth. Of course, he didn't know what that actually felt like. He came back to reality, to the lit screen of his phone.

That was the other thing that nagged at him now, his persistent virginity. Aside from the occasional make-out with someone at a lacrosse party, Ethan was still a virgin, and he allowed himself his fantasy of losing it with Mackenzie Gornick. That would never happen now for sure. He put his face in his hand and rubbed his eyes. She'd never have sex with the team manager. She was likely only interested in Mike because of his mighty captainship of the team. He cursed high school and all of its elements and scoffed loudly.

He needed to talk to someone.

Kyle was out, and he could never admit to him how much he cared about this, especially when Kyle was hardly the athlete, didn't understand lacrosse in Dorset. Plus, Kyle already graduated and probably didn't care. Ethan scrolled through his phone selected his friend Chelsea and texted her. She responded instantly. Chelsea was an avid student of art history and had early acceptance to RISD to study design. She and Ethan had become friends after they'd broke four petri dishes seated beside each other in a biology lab course in sophomore year.

Can you fucking believe this? she wrote back.

I honestly can't, he replied bitterly.

Want me to come over? We could go to a movie or something, she offered, but he could sense the half-heartedness in her voice. Even she didn't want to see him.

Nah, it's fine, my mom just put dinner on anyway, he lied.

I'm sorry bud. That sucks.

This town is too fucking obsessed with this, he fired back.

Yeah, sports is so stupid, it's designed for mass moron consumption, she said. He nodded to nobody and stood up. He wanted to do something, anything to get his mind off this. He needed a little stress relief, maybe something chemical.

He looked next door to Neil's house, but the windows were dark.

CHAPTER 2

TUESDAY, AUGUST 5

NEIL

3:37 PM

THREE DAYS AFTER THE FUNERAL, and just twenty-four hours after returning to work, Neil let the plastic handset fall back into its cradle. He leaned back in his swivel desk chair, the mesh backing cradling his spine. He pivoted and peered out the window beside his desk. Below, a dense cluster of skyscrapers, downtown Hartford, stood surrounded by an apron of trees and suburbs. Hartford was weird like that, he thought, such a bustling little urban center, surrounded a thin halo of abject poverty and outer still, the wealthy suburbs. He glanced for another minute; down below, a window in a nearby office building had opened and a ream of paper had blown out the window, the white sheets whipping about in the sunlight. As the sheets floated down leisurely, the sunlight caught them, whiter than any snow he'd ever seen. His windows didn't open. Up on the ninth floor, there was no summer breeze to whisk a ream of copy paper out the window, just low throb of the air conditioning.

The paper was whiter than the draping on his father's casket.

The day after the service, he'd tried to stay, tried to argue he should stick around and help out as much as he could. But after offering, his Aunt Isabelle pulled him aside to encourage him to fly home, and assured him that his mother would do much better if things could return to as close to normal as was possible.

The funeral (unlike his would be in just four weeks) was massive; distant aunts and uncles had flown in, and his mother's sister Isabelle had flown down from Westchester, eager to be as helpful as she could after his father died. The service was lovely, exactly what his father would have wanted; a long Catholic Mass, with the casket in the center aisle, arguably the best seat he'd had in Church in a long time.

Neil sat beside his mother, who surprisingly, given the situation hadn't wept much. But when she leaned over to whisper that his father had picked the song the choir sang, he could smell Jim Beam on her breath, and for a second, he was jealous. She almost keeled over onto him as she hissed in his ear, but he pushed her back gently, and Aunt Isabelle stabilized her.

During the service he'd willed himself to cry, hoping he could muster even one tear. No such luck. He felt like everyone was staring at him, expecting him to cry, wondering if he would, as if his tears somehow validated this event. It wasn't that he was mad at his father, but to Neil, his dad had died four years ago. When the diagnosis came. This shell, this ragged bag of bones and organs wasn't anything other than a vessel his father had vacated ages ago, and just now had shut down. Sure, he reconciled with himself, he was mourning his father, and maybe a little more than on a regular day, but still. At that moment in Mass, trying everything, rubbing his eyes, he couldn't bring himself to cry. At least not until the flight home a day later.

On the way back, trying to watch a movie on his iPad, "Shane" was up next in his Netflix queue, and he'd suddenly stumbled on the realization that that film was the last movie he'd watched with his father. At Christmas, it was on TV and he and his father sat in the TV room, as his parents called it, and watched the black and white film. Thinking of that tinny whine of, *"Shane, come back!"* Neil had been overcome with a sudden wave of trembling. He rose from his seat quickly and, crashing through the aisle to the bathroom, sliding the door open, and locked himself in.

The tears came fast and hard; wracking sobs, they shook his body silently, and he swore his strength to hold in the pain was rocking the plane the way his shoulders were shaking. He was in there a while before a flight attendant knocked, he wiped his eyes and said he'd be right out. He'd returned to his seat and closed his eyes, forcing himself—willing himself—to sleep.

After landing at Bradley and exiting through the gate and out to the parking shuttle, he rode silently. The air conditioning was off in the shuttle. The old bald driver was sweating and had the window down. It must've been broken. The heat off the tarmac soaked through everything, and Neil found himself rolling up his sleeves as he retrieved his bags from the rack by the driver and walked through the admittedly cooler parking garage to his car. He slid in and immediately dialed the air conditioning up and took several deep breaths of the arctic air as if he'd just emerged from underwater.

NEIL STARED OUT THE WINDOW, DISTRACTED, HIS HEAD in his hands, barely thinking of the sales forecast he needed to write, having secured a commitment from a customer just moments prior. This wasn't protocol; company best practices recommended that he immediately update the forecast upon the conclusion of the call, how many connectors, which model, which plating, unit price, and delivery date.

He worked for Unilectro, a connector company that manufactured and sold the ports that thousands of servers needed, in business development. His desk phone rang.

"Hello?" His boss' name, Al, was on the display.

"Hey, would you mind coming down here? Wanted to talk to you quick." He agreed and stood up, retucking his shirt and straightening his tie. Was this the news he'd been waiting for so long? Was he going to be promoted? In his five years at Unilectro, he'd never been promoted, never been noticed by senior management. His performance, even he'd admit, was mediocre at best, but his years of service had to have been worth something. Plus, he realized as he ironed out wrinkles in his shirt with his hands and tightened his tie, his father had just died. There had to be some sympathy.

Thinking of the salary that came with the position, he realized he could save more and sell his parents' house and move. He could move somewhere with more young people, somewhere where he didn't grow up, somewhere where he could be his own person, and stop living in the snakeskin of his parents' former lives.

He picked the jacket up off the back of his chair and swung it over his shoulders. It was go time. This was it. He'd get the strategic sales gig. This is what he'd wanted. He'd spoken to Al about it for some time now, arguing the case that he knew the product line and the customers and was ready to get out there. He'd been stagnant long enough.

He strolled down the carpet, waving to the occasional coworker, smiled weakly at Julie from HR, cute little Julie with red hair and green eyes. She looked up from her computer, distracted, and gave a halfhearted wave. Neil entered Al's monochrome office, and behind the desk, Al sat. Scott, another coworker, was seated in one of the guest chairs across the surface.

"Gentlemen." Neil spoke with delicacy, and Al nodded to him, and Neil took one of the chairs.

"How are you?" Al asked, leaning low over his desk and looking into his eyes. He felt a shock in his spine. Al was asking about how he was holding up in the wake of his father's death. He nodded.

"I'm doing okay."

"Well, you know, take whatever time you need,

we're all behind you," Al said with a weak smile. Of course Al was saying this now, Neil thought savagely, he'd already come back to work.

"So, I wanted you both here so I could tell you in person," Al said, moving papers around on his desk as if they were relevant to the conversation. The stacks were enormous, disorganized, the sheets poking out at different angles, stacked unevenly. Neil had to peer over a stack of reports. It didn't matter if he'd finished his forecast, he realized in that moment. Al would never read it.

"Senior leadership and I have decided to promote, you, Scott, to the position of Senior Strategic Sales Manager, and you, Neil, will report to him so you can spend some more time studying the process up close." He must've noticed Neil's face, because he continued speaking. "Think of it as shadowing him, so you're ready for a future promotion," Al said with the conviction that this was a common sense idea. Scott nodded along enthusiastically. He must've been told already. Neil's ears were buzzing, his head hurt. He was getting passed over? He looked at his shoes, reaffixed the blank look on his face and looked up at Al.

"Great," he said without thinking.

"We can go out on calls together!" Scott said, nudging him on the shoulder like they were friends. *We are not fucking friends*, Neil thought angrily. Scott had started eighteen months ago, and eager to befriend the nearby other thirty-something came by Neil's desk every day for a month to see if he wanted to get lunch. Three weeks in, Neil realized he wouldn't stop until he consented, and four weeks in, he finally accepted. The kid was three years his junior, was he being passed over for this? On top of everything else, they were telling him this right after his fucking father died?

"Fantastic. Alright, great. That's perfect. Thanks gentlemen," Al said, mirroring Neil's lexicon. *Don't do that*, he thought savagely. *Don't pretend we're all fucking chummy here. You just bent me over your fucking desk and fucked me.* He burned inside. He grimaced through gritted teeth and rose from his seat.

"Perfect. We can get started with some travel for next month," Scott said, turning to him as they moved to the door. "So, I prefer to fly into LAX, but if it's got to be Burbank that's fine too, whatever tickets you can find are great," Scott said, thinking he was being perfectly friendly and easy. *Now I'm booking his fucking travel.* Neil walked out of the office.

"Just email me your shit," he said, the last word blasting out of his mouth like the flash from a gun muzzle in the dark, much more angrily than he intended to be. Scott nodded and banked off to the left.

Back at his desk, he looked at his watch. 4:35 PM. Time enough to get the fuck out of here. He was over this, and wasn't going to fucking stick around. He undocked his laptop, slid it under his arm and made for the elevator.

HOME, INSIDE HIS FRONT DOOR ON STANIFORD DRIVE, Neil slammed the door and tore his tie off, throwing the discarded strip of silk to the floor.

"FUCK!" he screamed into his house, the hard *K* sound reverberating off the ceiling and walls of the foyer. He kicked off his shoes as angrily as he could; one skidded to the end table. He ripped his buttoned shirt off, struggling with each button, one last difficult one on the bottom proving too insistent for his shaking fingers. He pulled the shirt and undershirt up off of his head and threw it too onto the stairs. He unbuckled his black leather belt, and stripped off his pants, the silver buckle clattering to the floor as he dropped it. He tore his socks off, each one, balling them and throwing them. He stood naked in his foyer, his heart pounding in his chest, his jaw set, his breathing heavy. *Fuck all of this*, he thought, kicking the shoe as he walked through the foyer arch to the living room. On the wet bar was the Jack Daniels and he unscrewed the cap, the fire burning down his throat, sloshing angrily in his empty stomach, over his mouth. He wiped his chin with his forearm. Good. Good.

Fine, he thought. Tomorrow, he'd write an email and quit. Tomorrow he'd show Al who was in charge. He wasn't going to become somebody's fucking admin. Never again. He'd never visit that stupid beige office in that stupid beige city. How dare they fuck him like this, especially after losing his father. Didn't that count for anything?

When he finished chugging the bottle, he dropped it into the trashcan in the kitchen where he heard it crack on the floor tile under the bin. Grabbing the next bottle, tequila, he pulled the heavy wooden stopper out and dropped it on the carpet in his living room. He drank from the thick lip of the bottle, the sour sting different from the Jack but still the same. He slid open the slider door to the pool, still completely naked and looked out to his backyard, fenced in with high privacy fences, and wisteria curling around the top. He wouldn't be seen. He didn't care. He slid the door open and proceeded onto the pool deck, the stone warm under his bare feet, warmed by the sun all day. He walked toward his pool, setting the heavy-bottomed tequila bottle down beside it, and dove in, headfirst.

The water was cool on his balls, strange, the sensation of the water between his pubes, the electric feeling of swimming naked. He broke through the surface and swam to the side and took another long draught from the bottle before swimming back out into the deep end. He swam past discarded leaves and dead bugs, mosquitos grounded, grass clippings blown in from the landscapers, and ducked under the water and held himself there.

In the muffled silence under the water, he wondered, what would it be like to just drown himself here. For a second, he relished the prospect, floating, motionless, his body eventually bloated. He'd be found by the landscaper next week, plenty of time for his body to decay in the water and chlorine. Realizing he could hold his breath no longer, Neil emerged from the water with a gasp and swam to the side. He drank from the bottle again, finding a sweetness in the liquor and turned around, floating on his back.

The clouds were wide across the sky, purple bands graduating to pink off in the distance. Since the rain just yesterday, the earth had dried up like wrinkled skin, shriveled, and the forecast said it was expected to remain hot. Neil floated on his back, staring up at the sky as the water moved around him, his breathing slow and steady as waves of drunkenness washed over him, numbing him into nothing.

CARLA

5:04 PM

JUST ACROSS THE STREET, Carla drove home slowly in her Audi convertible. She had the top down; the wind felt good in her hair. The sun had begun its descent, still bright, still hot, just moving slowly across the sky. She sighed as she turned off Cliff Road onto Staniford and glided down the smooth macadam toward their house. Across the street, she wasn't sure who lived there, someone had parked in a hurry, their black sedan was parked diagonally across the driveway, like they'd almost skidded in the driveway. She shrugged with a smirk and moved her cat-eye sunglasses up onto her head.

While the semester hadn't started yet, she'd been besieged with new employee on-boarding, committee meetings she'd been suckered into joining by conniving elder professors, staff meetings, curriculum design seminars and so on. Despite having no classes yet, she figured she'd be driving into New Haven every day this week. She pulled carefully into the driveway, careful to park perfectly beside Phil's bright blue new Ford SUV, in sharp contrast to the awful parking job across the street. She wouldn't, no, couldn't, be one of those people.

Inside the front door, she heard Billie Holliday playing from the living room and she proceeded through, stepping around boxes to find Phil on his knees, his head in the television cabinet.

"Hey," she said, setting her light summer jacket down on the arm of the couch.

"Hey," he called from inside the cabinet, and he pulled back, dusting off his hands. "I think I got it, no cable guy needed!" he said triumphantly.

"I've heard that before," she said with a smile.

"No really, I'm getting good at setting up DVRs. If this whole lawyer thing doesn't work out, I'm going to work for Comcast." She reached for the remote.

"Try it out," he encouraged, standing to the right of the big widescreen TV, motioning to the screen. She turned the TV on and changed inputs. The DVR menu appeared, and she smiled as Phil gave a little bow.

"Thank you, thank you, I'd like to thank the academy, and the installation guy from our last apartment . . ." He crossed the space to her and pulled her into a hug.

"I missed you so bad today," he said with a smirk.

"I can't honestly believe that. Look at all you got done today," she said, motioning around the living room, the TV now set up, the couches in place, the paintings unpacked and leaned against their intended walls. The bookcase reassembled and books unpacked and on their respective shelves.

". . . and our bedroom, too, shy of unpacking your clothes, which I left for you because whatever I place will be invariably moved," he said. There was a sudden big booming ring through the house, and they looked at each other.

"Was that our doorbell? Is that what it sounds like?" she said to him as she leaned back from their embrace to look through the glass on either side of the door. Figures were shadowed behind it, and Carla broke off their hug, and they moved to the door together.

"Are you expecting anyone?" she whispered as they moved through the foyer.

"Of course not, I don't know anybody," he said as they reached the door, and Carla unlocked it and swung it open.

On the threshold, were two people, middle-aged, a man and a woman. The woman had tight, curly, springy blonde hair, and was wearing a pink polo and a white tennis skirt, holding a plate of brownies. Her nose came to a little point above pink lipsticked lips. The male had bristly gray hair and also wore a polo, a dark blue one, over khakis and held a bottle of white wine. They looked surprised at seeing Carla and Phil, a look Carla knew too well; they had no idea their new neighbors were black. She smiled at them warmly, and they both shook off their looks of surprise and fixed smiles on their faces.

"Hi there," the male called, a little too boisterous, and thrust his hand out to Phil first who smiled and shook it.

"I'm John, John Gornick," he said, shaking Phil's hand vigorously.

"I'm Nancy, welcome to the neighborhood!" she cried and reached for Carla, switching the brownies to her left hand, who shook her right.

"I'm Phil, and this is my wife, Carla," Phil said, and she wondered why he'd bothered to specify their relationship, as if another adult living in the house wearing a wedding band answering the door in suburban Connecticut be anybody other than a spouse.

"A pleasure," Nancy said, shaking Phil's hand now. "We wanted to drop by and bring you a bottle of wine and some brownies to welcome you to the neighborhood," she said with a big smile, clearly holding back her discomfort. Carla smiled back and turned to Phil briefly.

"Of course, come on in!" she said, standing to the side as the neighbors entered, looking up into the foyer and around. "I'm sorry we've barely unpacked," she said, avoiding Phil's gaze. "No, no, of course, we didn't mean to ambush you," the husband, said, looking around at the mountain range of stacked, staggered boxes. Carla scooted past them to the island counter, lifting a box of cake-tins with Phil's handwriting on it down to the floor, and sticking it in a cabinet. She'd get to it later. As she stood up, she suddenly realized it didn't matter; there were still boxes everywhere.

"Here, we've got the patio set all set up, let's go to the pergola," Phil said, moving across the foyer and through the kitchen to the back-door slider. He slid it open and gestured out onto the patio where birds tweeted from nearby trees against the sunset shot sky. She followed.

"Thank you, this house is just so cute," the woman said, scanning the space as they went, Nancy wearing what Carla interpreted as a thinly disguised look of disappointment. They stepped clear onto the patio and sat down on the new black plastic woven furniture. They'd been delivered earlier in the week, and one of the legs of the table still had foam taped to it.

"Honey, get some glasses and a corkscrew," Carla directed as they sat. Phil moved to the slider and replied, "As soon as I find them."

"I'm sorry, we haven't unpacked a thing, I've been working non-stop since we moved in," Carla said as Nancy and John settled into the chairs across the round table from her.

"Oh sure," Nancy said.

"What do you do?" John said, leaning back.

"Oh, I'm a professor at Yale," Carla said calmly, throwing the line away, trying not to relish this. They seemed impressed. "What about you?"

"Insurance," John said, clearly bored. Nancy put up her hands.

"Homemaker." And she shrugged, as if to say *guilty*. Carla nodded. Phil reappeared with four dripping red wine glasses—they must have been dusty—the wrong shape for this pinot grigio. She smiled at him anyway as he set the glasses down. He uncorked the bottle and looked around.

"What did I miss?"

"We were just chatting," Carla said, looking to change the conversation.

"So, what do you do?" John asked, and for a moment Carla wondered if he had any more questions other than that.

"Oh, I'm between jobs currently," Phil said, still smiling, and in that moment, Carla wished he hadn't said that. Nancy's eyebrow raised and Jim looked over at her.

"Phil's a civil rights attorney. He bravely surrendered his job when I got my gig at Yale and we moved here, but he'll find something soon. You have a couple of leads already, right hon?" she said, quicker than she intended, but she had to save face. He nodded, a complete lie, but Nancy nodded along.

"Of course," Nancy said. Carla wondered if that was her catchphrase. Between *so what do you do?* and *of course* this was shaping up to be a very rich conversation. Phil poured the wine into the wrong styled glasses and handed each one out, ending with himself.

"These brownies look fantastic," Phil said reaching forward and lifting the saran wrap on the paper plate.

"Oh, it's nothing special, just a box, you know," Nancy said offhandedly with a wave and looked out to the lawn surrounded by the high fence.

"Well they coulda sold me," Carla said, smiling at Nancy.

"Damn shame that rain didn't do anything for the grass," John said to Phil as if the lawn was something they were supposed to be talking about. He sounded frustrated, set his glass back down on the table, and leaned back, crossing his arms. "We're in drought-like conditions, according to the news."

"It's been a hot summer, no surprise there," Phil replied, pulling out the chair between Nancy and John and sat. Carla already wondered if these people had anything interesting to say or if the tired corpse of this conversation would be relegated to the weather and jobs. She began thinking of reasons to end the conversation, but couldn't come up with anything.

"So, what inspired you to move to Dorset?" Nancy asked, reaching out to slide her wineglass around a little the wine swirling around without picking it up. Wow, a big swing of a question, Carla thought.

"Oh, well, we're trying to have a baby, and the schools were a big draw, and it's within commuting distance of New Haven, it's perfect." Nancy clapped her hands together at this, and John reached his hand out to Phil.

"Oh, I'm so happy for you!" Nancy said, beaming. "When our daughter was born, everything changed, and we had to move from Glastonbury to here." For a moment, Carla wondered what difference between one yuppie white suburb like Glastonbury was versus Dorset, but she withheld judgment.

"Thanks," Carla said, smiling, and wondering if— no, hoping—someone was growing inside her in this very moment.

"So, you two *have* to come to our garden party this weekend!" Nancy cried, as if suddenly remembering.

"A garden party?" Carla said aloud, and she visibly

watched Phil roll his eyes, blessedly unseen by either Gornick.

"Oh yes, it's a Staniford tradition," she said, her tone as cavalier as if explaining what a Christmas tree is. Carla wondered what other *Staniford Traditions* there were; parties with zero other black people, she presumed.

"John and I host everyone in the neighborhood in our backyard, it's like a block party, and everyone goes. It's Saturday afternoon, you have to be there."

"Oh damn, we have so much going on next weekend," Phil lied feebly.

Carla set her brow and smiled. "Oh, I don't know Phil, we can probably move our trip to IKEA to Sunday." He couldn't contradict her now, but she'd pay for that later. "We'd love to go. What should we bring?"

"Oh good!" Nancy clapped again. "There's everything, just everything, food, Amanda's famous mojitos, music, last year we even got John here to dance," Nancy said with a stupid *oops!* look on her face. John rolled his eyes and repeated his no doubt practiced line:

"I can neither confirm nor deny these allegations."

Carla tossed him a chuckle so he could feel the line wasn't wasted. Phil crossed his arms.

AFTER SHOWING THEM OUT FORTY MINUTES LATER, Carla closed the door with a friendly wave and turned around to face her husband.

"Why would you agree to go to that?" Phil fired.

"C'mon, stop being so sensitive. We don't know

anybody here. If we want to make friends, this is a great opportunity to," she said, moving past him, avoiding his eyes.

"Yeah, I'd love to go hang out with a bunch of white people, let's drink culturally appropriated mojitos, and have chips and dip, come and see the latest attraction, the local unemployed black man," he scoffed and turned toward the stairs.

"First of all," Carla began, raising a finger as he started up the stairs. "Mojitos are delicious," she called the joke after him to break the tension. He scoffed down at her from the railing at the top of the stairs.

"You're so obsessed with being accepted that you can't even take what I'm saying seriously."

She heard the door to his still-packed office click shut.

AMANDA

AMANDA POURED herself a glass of wine at the island counter. It'd been a few days since she'd checked her wallet and found she had fourteen dollars left.

Despite having only thirty miles to empty in her car, she needed to make it last. This was their system—rather, this was *his* system—and she begrudgingly lived with it. On alternating Sunday mornings, as if a ritual from some religion of frugality, Amanda would find on the island counter in an envelope, her handout of the biweekly period's allowance, $150 in cash, and would have that to spend on food for the house. Usually, she had to put a request in ahead of time for an "overbase" as Gavin called it, for special occasions: anniversaries, Christmas, and so on. She'd forgotten to request an overbase for the garden party on Saturday, and she'd done a big grocery shopping trip just the day before. Still, she had to plan her strategy delicately. There was no way she could buy even just the amount of limes and mint needed for the big punchbowl of mojitos at the party with fourteen dollars.

She drank deeply from the glass and set it down with a clink. Gavin would be home any minute, and she knew what she had to do. In a way, she thought, she didn't regret what would happen.

Gavin's car pulled in the driveway. For a moment, she was surprised at the regularity of his return home. The same sounds, at the same time, every day. The same tires on the driveway and the same slow sound of the garage door rising. The same double beep from his car when he locked it with the remote. The same steady steps up the stairs, the trudge, the stop at the table on the landing to rifle through the mail briefly, before the trudge continued. She looked up as he entered the kitchen. She set her wineglass in the deep-bottomed sink.

"Hey," he said, tossing a few letters on the table, looking up at her. Amanda looked at her husband, his strong forehead, his broad shoulders and was able to see how attractive he was, how handsome he was, slightly golden in the recessed lighting, his hair almost scraping the ceiling. She understood how she could have fallen in love with him so many years ago.

"What?" he asked, smirking slightly, smiling at her.

"You're still so handsome," she said aloud, more to herself than to him.

"What makes you say that?" he said, his hands on his hips. She loved when he did that. Traditionally a motherly gesture, it made him seem wider, bigger, taller. It made his shoulders pull backward in his dress shirt. If he flexed, she imagined he would tear the cotton open. She walked around the island counter and took his hand. She pulled out the kitchen door and through the living room, to the stairs. He went along with her. Up in their room, with the door closed, he whispered one half-hearted rebuttal.

"What about Kyle?"

"We have thirty minutes," she said, undoing his belt buckle, bracing herself for what she'd initiated. She crouched low on the carpet, using her hand against his knee to steady herself, and she took him in her mouth. He groaned at this, and she closed her eyes. They moved onto their bed, their wide, low bed, and she slid her jeans off. He positioned himself behind her, and they moved together in short, swift strokes. She closed her eyes. *It won't be long now,* she told herself as she heard his breathing build to a climax. She knew he was finishing. When he was done, he withdrew from her, and she rolled over, wiping her bangs out of her eyes. Gavin flopped down beside her on the bed and planted a stubbly kiss on her cheek.

"What a way to get home from work," he said with a pant and a breathless chuckle.

"Sorry to just jump you like that," she said, putting on her sultriest tone. "I just couldn't wait, I've been thinking about you all day." He sighed contentedly at this, and sat up, struggling to undo his dress shirt. Tearing it off and sliding off the bed, still panting, he stood and pulled his socks off one by one.

As he undressed, still breathing heavy, she wondered if now was the time to ask. She opened her mouth and let a single breath escape before she realized it would be too obvious what'd happened. *No, best to wait*, she decided. She clamped her mouth shut.

"What?" he asked.

"That was . . . great," she lied. He beamed at this, now naked, and moved to the bathroom door.

"Happy to oblige," he said before stepping in. She heard the sudden rushing of the shower. "You could join me in here if you want," he called from behind the glass door.

"I can't. I have to go get dinner on so Kyle doesn't suspect anything," she called back over the steam. He called an "alright" and she headed down the stairs.

Pleased with herself, still smiling, Amanda boiled some quinoa on the range and scooped out the grainy seeds inside four green bell peppers. She smiled at this. Gavin always ate more than a normal serving; he needed twice the usual portion sizes and she felt warm inside at her knowingness about this. She checked the chicken breasts in the oven—still needing ten minutes—and sautéed the mushrooms and kale in a saucepan. Cooking, she'd realized some years back, relaxed her. It had a quieting feeling, a way of making all the clutter and noise of her own head silence, although, maybe that was the wine. She retrieved the glass from the sink and poured another glass of the pinot grigio from the fridge door. He'd have to be in a good mood now, she reasoned. Nothing like some sex and a big dinner.

While she cooked, she projected her number. She needed at least a hundred and fifty dollars—that would probably cover it, and she'd even offer to return whatever leftover she had. She heard a car pull in the driveway and looked out a window in time to see Kyle's silver BMW convertible slide in beside his father's Porsche. She imagined him doing the same sorts of things Gavin did when he arrived home, beeping the lock twice, the trudge up the stairs, the inspection of the mail, even though she knew he'd never stop and check the mail. All his mail came in plink sounds to his iPhone. This was a generation that'd never know what it was like to open the mailbox and find a surprise.

She thought about sending him old-fashioned letters in the fall once he was away at college, so he'd have something tangible to hold and read when he missed her. She knew her son; underneath that lacquer of masculinity was a gentle and delicate boy in there, emotional and fragile. She knew he'd miss her, worse so, how she'd miss him. She almost gulped at the thought of being alone in the house with just Gavin for most of the year. Oh sure, they'd still have summers, but still, come Labor Day, the balance in their house would be radically upset like a see-saw once Kyle left, even more than it was now. She shook off this feeling as Kyle entered the kitchen and tossed his backpack down on the floor by the slider.

"Hi Mom."

"Hey honey," she said, setting the spoon down and rounded the island counter to pull him into a reluctant hug. "How was work?"

He shrugged, looking at his phone. He'd recently begun working for the summer at a local accounting firm, a client of his father's, filing and whatnot, as a sort of pre-college internship. He pulled his tie off, just like his father. She returned to the range. The shrug wasn't unexpected; she never really knew what was going on in his life anymore. That didn't bother her. Did she tell her parents everything, or let alone anything, when she had been his age? She doubted it. Still, she wondered what his life was like beyond the confines of Xbox in his bedroom, or his afternoons in the pool or at his job.

She stuffed the peppers, baked them for a few minutes, pulled the chicken, and plated it. She deployed the meal across the kitchen table as Gavin entered the room, crossing behind Kyle's chair, putting both his hands on the kid's shoulders and shaking him. He uttered a "Hey Dad," without looking up, and she joined them at the table.

"How's the office?" Gavin said proudly, and for a second, Amanda thought about how strange it was to be asking that question, as if they were all working adults.

"It's fine, kind of boring, but I'm getting used to it. I got a chance to talk to one of the partners today which was great," he said, still engrossed in whatever was on the display of his phone.

"That's m'boy," Gavin said, clapping him on the shoulder again, and Amanda smiled demurely. It was go time.

"Everybody excited about the Garden Party?" she asked, cutting her chicken and looking at both of them.

"That this weekend?" Gavin asked, a mouthful of chicken. Her pulse began to quicken. Here it was.

"Saturday, yep!" she said excitedly. She reached

over and put her hand on her husband's bicep, feeling it briefly before she spoke. He smiled.

"Speaking of which, can I get an overbase on next week? I need to get the stuff for it."

The reaction was immediate. Gavin's face fell into consternation and Kyle's head snapped up.

"How much?" he said coldly.

"Oh, you know, just a hundred bucks or whatever. I just need to buy rum and limes and mint. I'll return whatever's leftover," she said quickly, nonchalantly, she hoped, looking back down into her plate, still smiling, trying to recover this. He chewed slowly.

"Where did the rest of the money go?" he asked, measured and calm.

"You know, I just . . . I had to do a big grocery run, and honestly, I forgot. I'm sorry." She gave an oops look, and scanned the table, looking to Kyle, whose eyes tracked back and forth between them.

"Why the fuck did you spend so much?" he spat.

"Well we eat a lot of food, especially with a growing boy," she said, smiling still and gesturing to Kyle, now more man than boy. "I've watched him eat a box of cereal at a clip!" The joke had been intended to break the tension. It did not.

"What'd you buy all this health food shit for, anyway? What even is it? Kale and quinoa? What are we, fucking rabbits?" Gavin said, pushing his plate away angrily. It clattered against the serving dish. His honesty stung about the dinner she'd made.

"Oh come on now," she said, her pulse quickening. This was going poorly, she needed to defuse this situation now. "I thought we were trying to eat healthier, boys," she said in the friendliest, most matronly chiding tone she could manage, now cutting her chicken and looking down to hold back tears she felt coming.

"Well, that's where all your money went," Gavin said angrily, sitting back and crossing his arms. "We don't even want to eat stuff like this, right, Kyle? Where's our steak and potatoes. Is that so fucking hard? It doesn't even take that long to cook."

For a moment, she was above the scene. She was hovering above the kitchen, like she was watching from one of the craters of the recessed lighting. *He is so fucking stupid*, she thought. *A baked potato alone takes a fucking hour*.

"So, I really can't have an overbase? What if we take it out of next week?" she pleaded.

"Not when you make stupid calls like this, nope." He slid back from the table and stood up. "C'mon Kyle, let's go to Burger King and get some real fucking food." Her son rose silently, avoiding her eyes, which felt hot and tight. In that moment she wished he'd have stayed, but she imagined he too was as terrified of Gavin as she was.

She didn't even believe he'd actually do this. He would never leave a perfectly good and healthy dinner on the table for a greasy, disgusting burger wrapped in paper. She didn't even have words for this, she was speechless and numb as her husband and son left the kitchen, and she heard a car start outside.

ETHAN

7:35 PM

ACROSS THE STREET, Ethan watched Kyle and his father climb into the Porsche sedan and pull out of the driveway. For a moment, watching from his bedroom window, Ethan rippled with jealousy of their father-son bonding. Retreating from his window to his bed, he kicked up a cloud of dust motes in the golden light from his reading lamp. He hadn't left the house in twenty-four hours. Feigning a stomach bug and claiming he needed sleep to get out of his part-time shift at the nearby supermarket, his mother had left him relatively alone, popping in occasionally to make sure he was alright, and offering to get him things.

He lay there, as the hours ticked by, watching the red LED of his alarm clock move from 7:37 to 10:00 PM. Eventually, he heard his mother turn off the news downstairs and come up to her bedroom, shutting the door. He sighed. He wanted to forget everything about the stupid lacrosse team list. He wanted to get drunk, really ragingly drunk. He climbed out of bed and pulled on a pair of sweatpants. He retrieved his school back-pack from under his dusty bed, long unused since school got out in June. He went to his Lego-brick shaped plastic bank and pulled out a wad of cash and stuffed it into the front pocket of his hoodie. He clicked the light off and arranged his pillows so it looked in the dark like he was sleeping. He carried his sneakers with him, padding along the hardwood floor past his mother's room, down the stairs which thankfully didn't creak and out to the back door.

The night was warm, and a low breeze carried the scent of a fire from somewhere, charcoal and burning wood, and he wondered where he'd find it. He couldn't see any smoke against the stars. He imagined another family, a perfect one, different from his own, crowded around their brick backyard fire pit, the little kids singing songs and roasting marshmallows while the parents smiled knowingly at each other.

In the yard, he headed down the sloping lawn and into the copse of trees behind his house. He moved quietly through the forest. The sound of acoustic music played from somewhere else, and he kept walking through the darkness, stopping and hiding behind a tree while cars passed, their yellow headlights on the road just beyond the woods. When he came up on Neil Testa's backyard, the lights from the house were dark, but an eerie green glow emanated from the backyard. He had to have been home. Ethan approached the wooden door in the side of the privacy fence and knocked, surprised to find it swinging open. He peered inside and spotted Neil, sitting, wrapped in a towel on his deck furniture, looking down at the pool. There was an empty bottle of tequila next to his chair.

"Hey," Ethan said. Neil's head moved slowly up, slowly taking him in. He nodded first, as if agreeing to speak and then spoke slowly.

"Hey."

As Ethan approached, around the side of the glowing green pool, he could see Neil's eyes, glassy and frozen. He was wasted.

Living so close, Ethan often came by to buy pot or booze from Neil. The deal was always in cash and always friendly.

"You okay, man?" Ethan said, approaching him slowly.

"Fine, you know," Neil said slowly. Upon closer inspection, Ethan could see he was drenched, the hairs on his chest were wet, and his nose dripped onto the towel he was wearing.

"Went for a swim?" Ethan said, pulling up a chair beside Neil. Neil nodded noncommittally. "Good idea. It's a hot night," Ethan said.

"You can go in if you want. I'm done, though," Neil said slowly.

"Uh, no thanks, I didn't bring my suit," Ethan said, gesturing at his sweatpants and hoodie. Neil seemed appeased.

"So." *This is awkward*, Ethan thought. "So, do you have any booze you're willing to sell?" Neil looked confused. He looked down at his towel, then at his hands, stretching out his fingers slowly and then balling them into fists. Suddenly he looked up at Ethan.

"What?"

"Booze. Can I buy some booze?" Ethan said, his eyes narrowing. He'd seen Neil stoned before, he'd seen him drunk before, but he'd never seen him this absolutely wasted. He was wrecked. If he was too tanked to do this now, he'd come back later, tomorrow maybe. Suddenly, being home sounded like a great idea. He stood up, and Neil stood up suddenly with him.

"Sure, of course." He moved to the slider and Ethan followed him into the living room in the dark. Neil made wet footprints on the white carpet in the moonlight, and Ethan followed him along to the liquor cabinet. On the floor in the foyer around the archway, Ethan spotted what looked suspiciously like a heap of clothing in the center of the foyer, and he briefly wondered if Neil was completely naked under the towel.

At the liquor cabinet, standing to the side of it, Neil flung his arms out each way.

"Ta-daaaa," he announced lazily, his sounds slurring.

"Great, what can I have?" Ethan said, reaching around the bottles in the dark, trying to figure out what was what.

"Anything, friend, anything," Neil said, now leaning against the wall, his voice sounding drowsy. He yawned.

"Thanks," Ethan said, picking up a mostly-full bottle of Fireball, a handle of Skyy vodka and a half-empty bottle of Captain Morgan. He slid these into his backpack and turned to face Neil.

"How much will it be?"

Neil shrugged and motioned for him to follow him

back outside. By the pool again, they sat, and Neil motioned to Ethan's bag, who opened it, and Neil pulled out the bottle of Fireball, unscrewed the cap, dropped it onto the cement of the patio and drank from the bottle. Ethan stared at him as he chugged, wiped his mouth with the back of his hand, and handed the bottle to him, gesturing for him to do the same. Ethan obliged, cringing only slightly at sharing the mouth of the bottle with him, and took a long drag from the bottle, setting it down on the table between them with a clink. The cinnamon whiskey burned on the way down, but it was good to taste something, anything other than bitter disappointment. Neil reached for the bottle and hit it again, setting it down with a clink.

"You want some pot or something?" Neil said suddenly, as if coming to his senses, the words all running together.

"Nah man, this is good," Ethan said, and Neil nodded.

"Sometimes, life just sucks, you know?" Neil said out of nowhere, and seemingly telepathically, as if he knew what Ethan was feeling at that very moment.

"Yeah, I do," Ethan said, shaking his head, looking down at his knees, his right one jiggling.

"It's like you want something so fucking much and then it doesn't pan out. You know? It's just like fuck you, you're somebody's admin now." Ethan wasn't sure what he meant by the last part there, but this sounded like something Neil needed to say. He listened.

"Yeah, I get that."

"I mean, like, you're on this one track, right? Like

you're just straight killing it. You're doing it, you know? And then, everything comes to a screeching halt, and you're working for this asshole." Ethan nodded like he understood, he did, again, until the last part.

"Yeah, that's got to be frustrating."

"You have no idea. It's like, so fucking stupid." Ethan didn't have anything to add to this. He nodded along. It didn't seem like Neil needed a reply anyway. He seemed too distracted, too drunk, too wrecked to even realize he was talking to someone.

"So, how much do I owe you for this?" Ethan asked, picking the metal cap to the Fireball off the patio, screwing it on and sliding the bottle into his bag. He stood, reaching into the front pocket of his hoodie.

"Nothing my man. This one's on the house," Neil said and chuckled with a slight hiccup.

"No way, I can't just take this, c'mon, how much?"

"Think of it as a birthday present," Neil said, rising and smiling. Ethan didn't bother to correct him that his birthday was in February, not that Neil would know that, but he nodded.

"You sure?"

"Of course I'm fucking sure, bro," Neil said, reaching out and putting his hand on Ethan's shoulder. Ethan felt weird about this gesture, that his older neighbor, wasted and probably naked, was making physical contact with him. He yearned to escape. Neil patted him on the head, his eyes looking past him, looking out beyond.

"You're a great kid, kiddo," Neil said, patting his

head, and Ethan stepped away, unsure of what to say to this.

"Uh, thanks. See you around, I guess."

"Yep," Neil said, returning to his seat. Ethan slipped away quickly, moved around the side of the pool, and out the wooden door in the fence. He took one last look at Neil, sitting back down, staring back into the pool, just like when he arrived.

CHAPTER 3

FRIDAY, AUGUST 8 — SATURDAY,
AUGUST 9

NEIL

FRIDAY NIGHT, after the news of his new assignment working with Scott, and now almost a full week after his father's passing, Neil arrived home and dropped his keys into the bowl by the door with a clatter. He hadn't quit, of course. He couldn't justify going without an income, and after storming around, he did feel at least marginally better.

The decorative gold bowl was one of the remnants of Vanessa before she left some years ago. She'd decorated this house with him, spent hours poring through the stacks at Bed Bath and Beyond in North Haven, finding a matching duvet (he called it a comforter) and choosing lampshades that represented an ambiance the house needed, apparently. She'd done over the whole house, even intuitively, he remembered, she drove him to the Yale Art Gallery to peruse some of the work there, taking careful notes of what he seemed drawn to. A large art-deco print of a woman with wavy hair in the ocean, the waves equally sized and equidistant from one another, hung over the table, and for a moment, his eye was drawn to it. He pulled his eyes away, in spiteful rejection of her exit forever ago. While now at least four years old, the styles probably weren't popular anymore, but they made it kind of felt like she was still there, and that was how he liked it. He kicked his shoes off and left his phone on the table.

He passed the bar cabinet on the way, looking at the new bottles of vodka and rum he'd bought after discovering his missing the other day. He wondered if he'd drank them in the binge and destroyed the glass somehow, as it wasn't in the trash. His stomach rumbled.

Neil moved into the living room and undid his tie and dug into the fridge. There was a leftover soy-sauce-soaked stir-fry meal from last week which looked wholly unappetizing.

From the foyer, his iPhone toned an echoing bling, the sound of a text. He returned to it. There was a message from Sarah, a woman he'd been texting with as a method of distraction.

Are we still a go for 8PM at the Omni Hotel bar?

He'd met her online through a website created for the purpose of connecting married people who wanted to have affairs with other married people. He'd been using an alternate name, Ben (his middle name actually) pretending he was married and bored in his relationship. She'd left her details unshared. She could probably tell he was making it up by how much detail he'd provided, as she'd revealed nothing about herself other than her name and some mild chatting. The messages had slipped quickly down into a sultry conversation about her sexual interests, which, ironically, included performing oral sex and "rough stuff." He was intrigued, even if she was making it up. She even began sending pictures; a close shot of her nipples and one finger touching her lower lip, an image from up a skirt. He wondered if they were actually photos of her or random ones from the internet.

He responded in the affirmative, walking back to the kitchen, and set his phone down on the counter. He pulled the slimy leftover stir fry out and tossed it in the microwave for two minutes. In that time, he found his laptop on a side table in the living room and carried it to the kitchen counter where he opened it. He opened the browser and navigated to one of his most visited websites after Google and Gmail, a porn aggregator, letting users post anything, scouring the net for free smut. He scrolled through the hottest videos being "watched now" and selected one of an orgy. In the video, some poor girl was positively besieged with men, the ambient moans and groans provided the soundtrack as he ate, his eyes fixed on the pulsing movement of flesh.

Turning the volume up, Neil retrieved his reheated stir fry, and sat down to eat and watch, other sounds drowned out by auditory and visual carnality.

NEIL ARRIVED AT THE PENTHOUSE BAR OF THE OMNI Hotel in New Haven, overlooking the city, the Yale campus, and the lights in the harbor as big cargo ships maneuvered into slips by the working waterfront for the night. Early, he pulled down on the cuffs of his dress shirt under his jacket, opting against the tie, better off to look relaxed, casual for this sort of thing he found. Finding a seat at the bar, he ordered an old fashioned, his father's favorite then, quickly deciding it was too painful, and he didn't feel like crying in public, he caught the bartender's attention again and changed his order to a rum and Coke. He looked down the step and across the dining room out to the city. It was kind of idiotic to have this swanky of a restaurant in New Haven, he thought. It didn't fit. It wasn't like there was a skyline of other skyscrapers, like in New York or Boston. New Haven's skyline was pretty short, four and five story buildings made up the area with the green quad of Yale in the middle.

The elevator dinged its arrival, and he looked over instinctively. A woman entered, with long dark red hair. It was her. She scanned the bar and caught him, sitting alone. He smiled, and she walked over to him, slinking in her dress.

"Ben?" she asked, with all the effervescence of a person on a blind date.

"You must be Sarah," he said, reaching out for a friendly handshake. She shook his with both of hers.

"So great to finally meet you," she said, sliding onto the barstool beside him. She was smooth; everything about her movements was smooth, like she was a liquid, poured over the leather of the stool. As she turned to the bartender, he caught a glimpse of her left hand, no tanlines from a missing wedding band. She was good. She'd done this before.

"So, what do you do?" she asked him, again, bubbly.

"Insurance," he fibbed, and shrugged with a smile. "Like everybody else." She nodded knowingly and chuckled.

"Who are you with?" The question and implication itself loaded. Who are you with? A wife? A husband? A partner?

"Aetna," he lied. "You?"

"BCBS," she said quickly without looking away. He reasoned that was probably true, who else instinctively would use the acronym for Blue Cross/Blue Shield?

"So, you ever been here before?" she asked, turning on her stool, leaning on the bar as her martini arrived, a thin slice of lemon peel floating on the perfectly clear surface.

"No, never," he lied again, playing along.

"Oh, the views are just breathtaking," she held the word breathtaking a while, exhaling, said in a way that made scenic New Haven sound like Paris or Rome. He had to fight the urge to roll his eyes.

"So, is your name really Sarah?" he asked quietly as the bartender moved down the bar.

She reached out for her drink, grasping the rim with the pads of her fingers, and looking at him, sipped from the glass.

"What is this, your first time?" she asked, her tone deepening to a hard layer of ice under the mist of a joke. He smiled at this, unsure of how to proceed. Time to raise the odds, he thought. Seeing as he'd already blown his cover, what could he lose?

"Alright, big-shot," he said with a smirk. "What do we do now?" Her glass clinked onto the bar as she set it down empty. She was fast.

"We go for a drink somewhere else," she said, standing up, fixing her dress as she stood.

"We could go back to my place," Neil offered. "It is all the way in Dorset, though."

"That's fine. I'll just follow you." She was already on her way to the elevator, and then they were in it, standing against the back wall, holding the handrail and looking at each other as the metal box plummeted nineteen stories to the street.

Outside in the hot night, he took his jacket off and rolled up the cuffs of his sleeves and bleeped the headlights of his black Toyota sedan. She nodded and crossed the street.

All the way home, he kept checking for the metallic blue of her headlights. She followed him closely, out of the city, onto 95 North, up to the exit for Dorset, and down the back roads, across Cliff and turning left onto Staniford. He pulled slowly into his driveway, and she parked behind him. He opened the garage, and popped his own car door, to the sound of the garage door rolling up.

She exited her car and looked around.

"This is lovely," she said of the neighborhood as she followed him inside.

Just inside the door, he stopped and pushed her against the wall. She felt thin, light, her arms were stringy with muscle though, she pushed back, and he grazed her neck with his lips. She smiled at this.

"So what do we do now?" he whispered.

"Haven't you ever heard of foreplay?" she whispered back. "Go make me a drink," she said the last word through her teeth, he could hear her tongue click against the roof of her mouth. He released her, and moved to the living room and she followed, taking off her shoes. Was she already that comfortable here?

"This house is lovely," she said, moving about in the darkness.

"Oh, thanks, it wasn't me," he said, immediately realizing he probably shouldn't reference his wife, however fake she was.

"Where is, the decorator, anyway, if you don't mind my asking?" Sarah said, taking in the massive art-deco print in the foyer.

"Who?" he called from the bar, struggling with the gummy cap of the vermouth twisting free with a crack.

"Your wife," she called back.

"Oh, Vanessa," he said before he could stop himself. "She's on business in Seattle." He felt a sudden pang of regret. *No, no, no time for that now.* He re-centered himself on the illicit pictures Sarah had sent.

"Perfect," she said, moving back to the living room. Outside just beyond the glass of the sliding door, the swimming pool glowed green. "Oh, you have a pool?" she said, turning to look at him, her hand on the slider handle.

"I do."

She heaved it open as he lifted the drinks, two

rough, warm martinis, and followed her out onto the deck. He set the drinks down on the little end table, tossing the empty bottle of Patrón from the pool deck onto the soft carpet of the living room with a thud.

"Look away," she said playfully as he covered his eyes with his fingers, peeking between them as he watched her unzip her dress on the side and slink out of it, shimmy her underwear off, then unclasped her bra. She dove headfirst into the water. *Great form*, he thought, the splash little for her trim figure. He briefly remembered watching the Olympics with Vanessa. Every few years she'd get excited, and there'd be wall-to-wall swimming coverage for days. He shook his head, *no no, no time for that now*. In the water, she rubbed her eyes, washing her running makeup off, and turned in the water to face him.

Even distorted under the shifting water, she was gorgeous. He approached the side of the pool and set one glass down beside the water. She swam to the side and rested her arms on the deck, reaching for the drink.

"Can I join you?" he asked, kicking off his shoes.

"It's your pool."

He unbuttoned his shirt and pulled his undershirt off. Off came his socks, his pants, the buckle clattering against the cement pool deck, and walked, his bare feet on the warm floor, naked, and sat down on the deck, his behind scraping a little against the cement. He sunk his legs and feet into the water, his knees hanging over the edge. He lifted his drink and took a long drag. She moved toward him, her eyes on his nakedness.

"That's enough foreplay, I think," she said, touching

his hairy thigh with her hand, and then, taking him in her mouth, just above the lapping surface of the water. For a second, he remembered when he and Vanessa used to have sex, remembered when they'd book hotel rooms with Jacuzzi tubs, their bodies barely in the water, the excitement keeping them warm enough.

CARLA

THE FOLLOWING DAY, in the heat of the mid-afternoon, Carla and Phillip began their walk across the cul-de-sac to the Gornick's garden party. That morning, she'd made a massive bowl of white sangria. The glass punch-bowl, a wedding gift, unpacked ahead of its porcelain brethren, was washed and filled with wine, rum, vodka, and pounds of floating fruit. She carried it steadily in her hands, her fingers holding the deep grooves in the thick glass. Phillip walked ahead of her, and opened the door to the garden, the side door in the fence. They were greeted by quite a crowd already assembled.

The yard was enclosed by a high wooden fence, much like the other yards on Staniford. Dated salsa music wafted over the crowd from speakers mounted in the corners of the fence.

John clearly had spent the morning stringing up big bauble Christmas lights and hanging folding paper lanterns across the yard. Tiki torches had been lit atop the fence posts, and the air smelled faintly like citronella. A number of guests were there; all white people, of course: women in bright sundresses and sandals, the men in tight polo shirts in equally bright colors over light summer khakis. For a moment, Carla almost felt frustrated that Phil had chosen a darker, seasonally inappropriate pair of pants, and wished he could be like one of the other men here. Wished he would conform. Nancy shrieked when she set eyes on them.

"Look at the two of you, you clean up so well!" she cried, unaware of the implication, of which Carla smiled through. She caught a subtle eye-roll from Phil as he bent down to embrace Nancy before shaking John's hand.

"I brought sangria, I hope that's alright. I wasn't sure what to bring," Carla mumbled, and Nancy gasped, leaning back positively surprised.

"Look at you, you trendy thing, punchbowls *are* back in! Of course, of course, here, we've got the fun stuff on this table here." She walked her to a folding table by the wooden fence with a bright lime green tablecloth, beside a dozen or so bottles of white wine. Carla set it down, rubbing her tired wrists as Nancy poured her a brimming glass of chardonnay.

"What a pour!" Carla cried as she took the cold glass, her ring clattering on it with a chuckle and Nancy laughed too. Her laugh was big and overzealous, as if needed to be heard by people in the back row of an old theatre.

"Where did you get this dress, it's just lovely!"

Nancy said, holding her at arm's length, as if she was a favored grandchild.

"Oh, I just got it at the outlets yesterday afternoon, I zipped up after work," she said, starting to feel at ease as she sipped from the overfull glass, knowing the waves of comfort from the wine would soon wash over her.

"Really? I can't believe it! It does not look like an outlet dress. You positively can't tell anyone, they'll never know!" The swelling sensation of being accepted quickly deflated. She walked across the crunchy grass to Phil, trapped in a conversation with John. Phil looked like he was contemplating suicide.

"Sweetheart, c'mere, John was just telling me about what happened with the trash company." He reached for her lower back and pulled her to his side. She struggled to repress a smirk.

". . . so I told the guy, you listen here, whatever the fuck I put out, you haul it the fuck away. I'm the customer, you're the fucking trash collector."

"Good thing you said something," Phil said. She knew he was being facetious, but only she knew him well enough to tell. John wiped his forehead with his hand.

"Christ it's hot." They nodded and Phil began batting his chest with the collar of his polo.

"So then he calls me again and—hang on, I need to go say hello to Bill and Rhonda. Be right back," John started and turned away from them walking toward the gate and another entering white couple.

"Pretty sure I was going to die in that conversation if

I heard about how he roughed up the trash collector for another minute. Fuck it's hot." She nodded and looked around.

"Think we should mingle?" she asked, looking up at him. His forehead was shiny; it was hot for sure.

"Why else are we here?" he asked, resigned.

Carla moved across the lawn toward Nancy, who was chatting animatedly to a couple, a hulking big man, and a tiny blonde woman. Nancy stepped aside to welcome them into the conversation.

"Oh, where are my manners. Amanda, Gavin, this is Carla and Phil," she said of the blonde woman who feebly shook Carla's hand, and then of the man whose shake was also loose. Judging by his size, Carla wondered if he deliberately shook with less force because he knew how strong he was.

"A pleasure."

"They just moved here from St. Louis, wasn't it?" Nancy tried.

"Chicago," Phil corrected. "Close enough." The blonde woman chuckled at this, and Nancy smiled, and for a second, Carla was thankful Phil was so engaging.

"They just moved here, as Carla is starting to teach law at Yale in the fall." Carla fought to avoid rolling her eyes.

"Oh Bill and Rhonda are here! I have to say hello! Welcome!" Nancy called, throwing her hands in the air as she moved away from the quartet and moved to the couple still stranded by John near the gate.

"He's the lawyer, actually," Carla said now faced with the couple. "I'm a political scientist."

"Where do you practice?" the man called Gavin boomed, all but ignoring Carla, crossing his arms and facing Phil.

"Oh, uh, not, anywhere yet," Phil said, his words trailing away.

"What do you mean?" Amanda asked, promptly covering her mouth and what Carla assumed was a hiccup. *C'mon Phil, nail this one*, she wished.

"Well, we moved here for Carla's new job, and so I haven't found a new position for myself yet." *Not bad*, she thought. Going forward, she decided, he'd say he's consulting, or at least *own* that he was looking for a new job. He'd find something soon enough, she reasoned. He was so smart and so talented.

"Are you looking?" Gavin fired, his words like a spray of shotgun fire. Phil nodded and shrugged.

"Yeah, uh of course," he said, visibly deflated. Carla raged inside. Who the fuck were these people?

Gavin gave what sounded like a *hrmph*.

"I mean, it's also probably been helpful to be able to get the house all unpacked and what not." The blonde woman, Amanda spoke, nodding around to everyone. *I can rescue my own husband*, Carla thought savagely. She went to sip from her glass to find it empty.

"I need a refill. Anyone else? Great," she said quickly, not waiting for an answer before she stepped away from the group back to the bar, where she reached for the chardonnay, but it was gone. Carla scanned the other bottles, picking the one with the oldest vintage and pulled the foil off the top of it. She reached for Nancy's elaborate electronic corkscrew. Glaring at it for a second or two, she wondered who the fuck even has an electronic corkscrew instead of a normal one. She jammed it on the top of the bottle and pressed the button. In her hand, the cylinder buzzed and rumbled and clicked, and when she pulled it off, the cork fell out of the device. She poured herself a Nancy-Gornick-sized pour and turned back, bumping into someone, her wine splashing over the rim of the glass, sloshing onto her fingers.

"Oh, shit, I'm so sorry," she said, looking up from her hand to the face of a woman she hadn't seen before. She was in her late forties with light brown hair, pulled back in a ponytail. She had kind gray eyes and wore a white checkered shirt and white jeans.

"Oh, not at all," the woman said, reaching behind Carla for the table and grabbing a wad of napkins. "Did it get on your dress?"

"No, no, just my hand, oh, thank you," Carla said quickly as the woman patted her hand dry with the napkin. For a second, she was surprised this woman would even touch her, but she just seemed to snap into a problem-solving mode.

"I'm Carla, by the way. Oh, no that's fine, I'm fine," she said as the woman stopped drying.

"I'm Jen, I live over there." She pointed in the direction of the street. Carla put her right hand, which was dry, out, and Jen laughed a little and shook it. "It's so great to meet you," she said what sounded honestly. "I hate when that happens, white wine gets so sticky," Carla laughed at this too. Jen suddenly looked around furtively, and reached back to the table and grabbed a jug of ice water. She turned her back on the party and said quietly, "Here, put your hand out." Carla, feeling confused turned her back to the party and stepped closer to this woman so to obscure what was happening, transferred the glass to her right, and held her left hand out. Jen poured the cold water onto her hand over the grass as she flexed her fingers and gave it a little shake, and then twisted her wedding rings to clear any stickiness under them.

"I'm *sure* I wasn't supposed to do that, but I hate that feeling," Jen said quietly.

"Thanks so much, I was just going to try and find a bathroom," Carla said as Jen set the jug back down on the table and looked around furtively again. She shook her left hand again, and used another napkin to dry it.

"Oh, you'll never find one in that house, the layout makes no sense," Jen said, throwing a thumb over her shoulder at the building.

"You're a lifesaver," Carla said with a smile at this kindness.

"Oh, pssh, I'm a mom," Jen said with a flick of her hand, and Carla felt a pang of sadness, how much she wanted to be able to say that, ready in any situation to help, not totally useless and quibbling with her husband. She managed out a pained dry laugh.

"Do you have any kids?" Jen asked, and Carla shook her head.

"We're trying, my husband and I," she said, pointing across the party at Phil who right now was listening to John with his hands on his hips, his eyes cast upward at the cloudy sky.

"That's amazing," she said with a genuine smile

again, and Carla for a minute wondered why she wasn't visibly uncomfortable with her, why wasn't this neighbor being condescending?

"Well, I'm rooting for you. This is a great place to raise kids," she said, and Carla nodded. That's what everybody said here.

Over by the pool, Nancy broke free from her conversation and headed towards them with an over-emphasized wave.

"Oh Jesus," Jen said quietly looking back at the table.

"What?" Carla asked also quietly, her eyes cast downward.

"C'mon, here, c'mon," Jen said and she beamed toward Nancy, a wide toothy smile on her face, and Carla decided she very much liked this woman.

"Just going to get some nosh," she called toward Nancy, and Carla watched as she did an over emphasized stomach rub. They stepped clear of the table well before Nancy could get to them, and crossed to the table of food some forty feet away.

At the food table, Carla let out a little relieved chuckle. "Thank you," she said looking up at her new friend, and poking at a piece of cantaloupe from a tray with a toothpick.

"No problem. Nancy is honestly really sweet, but every year she does this event and becomes unbearable. She's a real winner," she said with a scoff, and took a sip from her own glass of white wine. That was the first time Carla had heard that phrase used like that, a real winner, and she filed it away for later use.

"So what do you do?" Jen asked, turning to her.

"I'm a new assistant professor at Yale," she said smiling and looking down.

"No way! That's amazing," Jen cried. "At your age? So impressive," she said, and for the first time in days, she felt relieved her surprise wasn't at her race.

"Oh, thank you, I mean, I'm . . ." for a second Carla struggled with the words, but Jen shook her head.

"No, no," Jen began. "It's basically impossible to get a tenure track role in higher-ed anymore, I have a handful of friends who've been relegated to lifelong adjuncting. It's literally no way to live. You should be so proud. What do you teach?" Carla's face felt hot, this woman was very kind, and very engaged in this conversation.

"Political science, but my research has mostly been on like elections, media, and the parties," she said.

"What a time to be a political scientist though, and this fall with the midterms? I'm jealous of your students," she said earnestly, and Carla wondered if she was a liberal, and ventured a guess to presume she was.

"Oh well, when I have an interesting lecture planned you should come down and sit in," she said with a wave. Jen's eyes lit up.

"I would *love* that," she said. "I'm such a news junkie, I can't handle it. I'm excited for the fall, I just love it." Carla smiled at her wonkiness; Yes, indeed, she liked her a lot. "So what's gunna happen in November? I hate to pick your brain like this, but nobody in this neighborhood actually ever wants to discuss politics, unless it's some garbage they heard on

Fox," she said, confirming Carla's assumption about her affiliation.

"I think the Republicans'll hold the house because of all the gerrymandered maps," she said, tipping her own hand, liberal to liberal, and she thought for a second Jen smiled at this. "And the senate, I'd say it's a tossup, but probably not in our favor, because we gotta hold a lotta seats. Shaheen, for one," she said, suddenly noticing how the wine and the excitement of her favorite topic had made her slang slip, *we* as in Democrats, *gotta, lotta*, but for a reason, she felt safe here, felt like Jen could understand. Jen nodded along.

"Yeah that's my big worry," she said looking down. "I'm so glad to have another bleeding-heart liberal here among this nest of country-club republicans," Jen said gesturing around. "I swear people stare when I unload reusable shopping bags of groceries in my driveway." Carla laughed at this.

"Which house is yours?" she asked.

"Oh, we're in the little cape on the corner, my son, Ethan and I," she said, and Carla read through the subtext that it was just the two of them. Nancy was appearing to drift in their general direction, and Jen turned away from the crowd.

"Here she comes, scatter, scatter!" Carla laughed and peeled off from the food and headed back toward the bar. Her glass was empty, and she reached for the bottle, when she felt a hand on her upper arm. She turned to face her husband.

". . . the hell are you doing?"

"Getting a drink, thanks."

"Why would you leave me there, he's awful." Phil gestured with a head nod toward Gavin and Amanda.

"She's awful too."

"She was trying," Phil said with sigh. "More than I can say for the rest of the people here. You'd think we were carrying some pathogen." Carla drank deeply from her glass, thinking about Jen, and how somehow, she'd probably made her first friend here.

"Why were you so weird back there?" Carla asked pointedly.

"Weird about what?"

"Not having a job. You were very uncomfortable."

"I'm who you're mad at? That dude literally just asked if I was even looking. Like, of course I'm fucking looking for a job."

"How about you just own it. Is that so hard? How about you just own it, just be okay with it. Just be like, 'you know what? I haven't found one yet. I will soon, I went to fucking Princeton for christssakes.'"

"Are you drunk?" he whispered.

"I sure as shit wish I was," she said with a hiss, pulling another long sip from the glass.

"What are we even doing here?" Phil asked with exasperation.

"I'm trying to fit in. I have no idea what you're doing," Carla sniped. She felt bad, but at the same time, he was being over-the-top about not having a job. This wasn't a big thing; lots of people had been unemployed, she was sure even a few people here had to have been unemployed at one point in their lives. She felt like Phil's reticence and anxiety around talking about this was projecting into her and transforming into frustration.

"You really think we're going to fit in? Look around. Notice anything different about us—" He was interrupted as a group of children in bright bathing suits all jumped in splashy sloppy synchronization into the pool.

"You probably shouldn't be drinking, you know, in case, you're—"

"I'm not," she replied bitterly, cutting him off. "I took a test this morning," she said, pushing past him to the garden gate. She needed a minute, needed a second to be alone and not surrounded by all these sweaty white people. She herself was starting to sweat, her armpits were soaked. She looked at the black screen of her phone. Her makeup was holding back the shimmering. She'd be fine.

Outside the fence, alongside the side that faced the woods, she smelled something she didn't know she needed: cigarette smoke. Her head cocked immediately toward the smell. A teenager, tall with blonde hair, his hand in his khaki shorts pocket, stood by the side of the garage, beside the basement doors, smoking.

In late high school and undergrad, she picked up smoking from a friend, and had learned to use it to mitigate the stresses of her classes, her social schedule, her involvement. When she met Phil, the perpetual athlete, two years into undergrad, he insisted she stop, and so she did. She hadn't missed it as bad as she did back then after she'd first quit. Now, though, still, she missed that a wave of nicotine would wash over her, mixing with the cascade of serenity from the wine just on the edge of the horizon.

The kid, upon seeing her seized up and put his hand with the cigarette behind his back. She smiled a little at this and stepped toward him.

"Your folks in there?" she asked. He nodded. "Don't worry, I won't tell." He smiled at her weakly, and she smiled back.

"I'm Carla," she extended her hand.

"Kyle, Kyle Holbrooke," he took it. "I think I'm your neighbor."

"Are you? Good to meet you," she said, taking another sip of wine. "I used to smoke, a million years ago," Carla said, staring at her toes against the grass, undergrad feeling so very long ago. The kid looked out to the woods. "Oh, don't worry. I'm not about to lecture you. I miss it, actually."

"Smoking?"

"Yeah. There's nothing like a cigarette when you're stressed."

He laughed a cute laugh, she remembered when laughs like his would make her heart flutter, the raspiness of his deepening voice. Oh, to be seventeen again.

"I only smoke sometimes. Why'd you stop?"

"Health concerns. My husband hates it." He nodded, as if he understood, even though, at basically half her age, there was no way he could have.

"I gotta tell you though," she started, stepping closer. He didn't step away. "If I ever got a terminal diagnosis, you know, like I had six months to live, or whatever, I'd smoke like there's no tomorrow."

"Because there wouldn't be?" He brushed the bangs out of his eyes. She chuckled at this.

"Can I ask you something weird?" She noticed his eyes showed a flash of nervousness and he nodded.

"You don't mind if I stand here and smell it, do you? I just miss it so bad." He nodded and reached for his pocket.

"Here, have one," he said but she waved the carton off.

"No, no, I can't. I'll get hooked again. Smelling it's enough," she said taking another sip of wine and a long inhale of the nicotine tinged air.

Carla stood there, as the sun began to set golden beyond the trees, until Kyle finished his cigarette, and they returned to the party, pretending like they didn't know each other.

AMANDA

IN THE HOT AFTERNOON, Amanda, Gavin and Kyle made the same trek across the cul-de-sac to the Gornick's backyard. In the past few days, Gavin hadn't yielded on the allowance. She didn't ask again, in worry of offsetting the delicate peace that had resettled in the house since the fight.

Instead, for the first time in five or six years, she did not bring her famous punchbowl of mojitos. In shame, she purchased two cantaloupes at $1.49 each, and a pre-made container of a fruit-yogurt dip for two dollars. She actually had a ten-spot left over, which she decided she'd keep, slipping it into a battered white envelope in her dresser drawer. She'd used to do this all the time, but recently had cleaned it out in favor of buying Kyle birthday presents.

She sliced the melon almost aggressively, using an ill-suited serrated blade, hacking through the thick tortoise outer shell of the melon. There was a violence to it. She hacked and sawed the melon into roughshod

98

pieces, displaying them around the contained of dip in a halo of salmon colored chunks. She impaled each of them on a toothpick and declared it a poor substitute for her elaborate mojito recipe. She hoped—no, prayed—that nobody would take the lack of mojitos as a concern that they weren't doing as well financially. She'd voice that concern to her husband of course, but he'd claim he didn't care if the neighbors thought he was rich, a posturing which was full of shit, she noted as he revved the engine of his stupid Porsche every time he passed through the cul-de-sac.

She made Gavin carry the melon, and he did without resistance, a small comfort as they crossed the dry grass and the smooth macadam of the cul-de-sac. She pushed open the side door in the fence to the back yard and took in the party. Gavin swept around her, shouting for John, handing off the dish almost dismissively to Nancy and giving his friend a strong handshake. The yard looked good, Amanda thought. Their grass was moist—it'd had just been watered, she could tell, it shined in the sunlight. They'd also vacuumed the pool: the surface was spotless, compared to the leaves and detritus, that had gathered on the surface of their own. Five or six splashing elementary schoolers shrieked at each other, giggling. The Gornick pool was rectangular, though. Amanda much preferred the contours and curves of their kidney-shaped pool. Kyle splintered off once in the gate, the teenagers often gathered together at this thing, but Ethan Carlisle, his best friend, wasn't there. She wondered for a second where he was.

Nancy met her with a glass of white wine, and

briefly clinked glasses with her own. They drank and stepped back to look at the party.

"Good turnout this year," Amanda said, looking at the engaged people who laughed, the children splashing in the pool, the men gathering around the grill, grunting and pointing at the roasting wads of meat.

"I think so, and we've got some newcomers on the list this year," Nancy said, drinking from her glass.

"I see even Jen made it this year. That's good," Amanda said under her breath, spotting her neighbor, Jennifer across the space chatting with Kyle, she knew they saw each other at school every now and then.

"Overall good turnout, I think," she said.

"Did you invite my new neighbors?" Amanda asked, positively begging for more information, her thumb rubbing on the frosty outer lip of her glass, a rubbery squeak, the moisture almost refreshing on the hot afternoon.

"Of course I did. It's that nice young African-American couple," Nancy said, looking at the small crowd.

"There's a black couple in the neighborhood?" Amanda said in a bare whisper. She immediately scanned for Gavin; he'd hate that. He'd always expressed that he wasn't a racist, and maintained that when he was on the force, he'd never chosen who he was serving, regardless of their racial group. She thought this was a front. She noticed how he gawked whenever they adventured into New York around Christmastime or would drive through a tough part of New Haven. He did a slow sort of head shake, as if disappointed, like he would in looking at a grade on Kyle's report card. It was like he was let down.

The opposite gate opened, and in they came, the black couple. The woman peered nervously around the edge of the fence, her hands carrying a big glass punchbowl full of fruit. Was she being upstaged? Did this woman bring mojitos? That was her thing! As they entered, it looked more like it was a white sangria, there were chunks of apple and orange floating on the surface. She was relieved.

"Hang on, let me go say hello," Nancy said, pulling away from Amanda without looking. She flung her arms into the air and crossed the grass.

"I guess these are our new neighbors," Amanda said in a low voice to Gavin who'd since left John and approached her. She gestured with her wineglass.

"Huh." He rattled the ice in his glass. John had poured him a scotch. He leaned back and tossed the remainder of the glass back.

"Easy there, sailor," she said with a smile. He smirked at her.

"I hate this fucking thing so much, it's too hot." He was right, she thought, it was a dry heat, like being inside an oven. Even with the sun waning, the pool looked appetizing, but without a bathing suit, that wasn't likely to happen. She almost wished someone would push her in. Nancy returned.

"They're just lovely, such a pleasant addition to the neighborhood," she said. The couple began approaching, *Time to meet the neighbors*, Amanda thought. She moved to the side as they approached. As they neared, Amanda got a good look at them. The woman was beautiful, with big dark eyes, and full lips. Her hair was curly, and shiny, and done up in a bun at the back of her head. The man was tall and broad-chested, handsome, with soft gray eyes and a scruffy stubble. He wore a perfectly fitting gray polo, and a big shiny silver watch.

"Oh, where are my manners. Amanda, Gavin, this is Carla and Phil,"

"A pleasure," the woman named Carla said.

"They just moved here from St. Louis, wasn't it?" Nancy said.

"Chicago," the man called Phil said with a smile that made her smile back. "Close enough." Amanda outright laughed at this, and the man smiled again. She could watch that smile all day.

"They just moved here, as Carla is starting to teach law at Yale in the fall." Nancy began, and Amanda nodded along. "Oh Bill and Rhonda are here! I have to say hello! Welcome!" Nancy yelled, distracted and moved away.

"He's the lawyer, actually," Carla said, smiling at them warmly. "I'm a political scientist."

"Where do you practice?" Gavin said in an assertive tone, crossing his arms.

"Oh, uh, not, anywhere yet," Phil said quietly.

"What do you mean?" Amanda asked, curious. Maybe he'd just graduated. Maybe he was much younger than she was. She felt a burp bubble up inside of her, and she covered her mouth briefly.

"Well, we moved here for Carla's new job, and so I haven't found a new position for myself yet." Poor man, she thought. Who wouldn't hire him?

"Are you looking?" Gavin replied. She looked at him with a glare. What was he doing? Jesus! He was going to piss them off already!

"Yeah, uh of course," Phil said, in a quiet sort of voice. Gavin snorted. He was being ridiculous. She threw back the rest of her glass of wine.

"I mean, it's also probably been helpful to be able to get the house all unpacked and what not," she said, eager to diffuse the tension. Phil nodded, but Carla seemed distracted, she seemed elsewhere.

"I need a refill. Anyone else? Great," Carla said quickly and stepped away toward the bar.

"Sorry about that," Phil said, looking amicably at them, slipping his big hands into the pockets of his khakis. He briefly looked at Gavin, hoping, no doubt to give a *women are crazy* shrug. Gavin barely grunted in recognition. "The move's been kind of hard, this area is lovely, but so different from Illinois."

"I'd hope so," Gavin said, and Phil looked away. What was his problem? She was mortified.

John slid back to their group and stumbled a little bit, clinking glasses with Gavin, and went to do the same with Phil but he didn't have a drink in his hand. They both shrugged and took sips.

"Wait, so, did I tell you what I got for a quote for the area over the garage," John said only to Gavin, Amanda looked at Phil who gave her a weak smile.

"How much?" Gavin asked.

"Okay hear this, sixteen grand," John said.

"Are you fucking kidding me?"

"I almost threw him the fuck outta my house when he said it." She made eye contact with Phil and just delicately raised her eyebrows, and tilted her glass to her mouth. As she did so she executed a slow, brief roll of her eyes. She caught him smile out of the corner of his mouth at her, and then refocused his attention at the men.

"It needs like sheetrock and insulation, done," Gavin said, chopping outward with a flat hand.

"And carpet," John added.

"I could get a crew of illegal Mexicans to do it for like three thousand bucks, cash," Gavin said, and Amanda suddenly wished she was in a different place. She wished she was anywhere else but here, and judging by how Phil looked, he did too. First it looked like he was nodding along, happy to talk about home renovations, but then he seemed like he drifted away, his hands on his hips, his head turned toward the sky.

He looked around, spying his wife at the bar table uncorking wine, and turned his shoulders. She felt bad for him; he was kind of alone.

"Pardon me, I should go see what's up. So great to meet you, though," he said, shaking each of their hands and moving quickly across the grass.

AFTER THE SUN SET, AND SHE'D HAD ENOUGH WINE THAT

the flames from the tiki torches were blurring, Amanda, and Gavin left the garden party. Her wedge sandals were hurting her feet, and once out on the street in the hot night she stopped and leaned against her husband to undo them.

"One second."

He slipped his hand around her waist as she stopped in the moonlight. Louie Louie was playing from over the fence in the Gornick yard. They'd left as it started to get rowdy.

"You smell good," Gavin whispered.

"I think I smell like sweat," she said, removing her second shoe and wiggled out of his arm. He pitched as if he was going to fall over, but righted himself. He was wasted, she thought.

As she walked, she pulled the elastic out of her hair, her hair falling long, down around her shoulders. They keyed into the house with the security code and stepped into the arctic air of the air conditioning. They'd left it on during the party, and the house was refreshingly chilly. She yawned at the base of the stairs. From the living room, up over the banister, she could see the light on in Kyle's room.

"Mom?" He called, his head poking out the lit doorway in the dark.

"Yes honey?"

"I'm going to a movie with Ethan. Be back in a couple of hours."

"Okay," she said as she started up the stairs, Gavin just steps behind her. She walked past his room and a wave of body spray and toward her own. Why did boys always do that? They stank like chemicals. She entered and threw her shoes down by the dresser. She opened the bathroom door and started the shower. She could hear Gavin and Kyle next door.

"You're going to see a film?" Gavin said, slurring his words. She froze, her hand on the lid of the hamper, listening through the wall.

"Yeah."

"What're you gunna see?" He said slowly.

"The November Man, it has James Bond in it."

"Sweet dude," he said, and Amanda rolled her eyes. When Gavin was drunk, he'd often think that he knew how to be *hip* and speak the *lingo of the youth.*

"Well, here, pal." She heard him say as she flicked the lights on in her bathroom. "All I've got is sixty bucks but here, buy some snacks for your friends, be the generous guy." She froze as she reached into the shower to turn the knob on the faucet.

"Dad you don't have to do this. I have money."

"But I want to, kiddo. How many more times can I do this before you leave in the fall?" he said, his voice echoing from just down the hall. She shook her head. He was going to give Kyle sixty bucks to go to the fucking movies, but she couldn't have money to buy food for a party? She reached for the shower, letting the hush of the water silence further conversation she didn't want to hear.

She undressed in the hot fog from the shower and stepped in, the heat making her dizzy. She thought she might get sick. She'd had how much wine? She heard the door open and she looked through the fogged glass door to see a Gavin-sized shape enter. Sometimes he came in to pee while she showered. He crossed the tiled bathroom and began taking his clothes off. He slid the door open to the side and stepped in. She looked into his eyes; they were vacant. He was blitzed. He moved toward her and took her in his arms. For a moment she sighed, and closed her eyes, her head against his chest. It would be okay. They would be okay. He was drunk, he didn't know what he was doing. It was okay. He loved her, and she him. It would be fine. He leaned down and kissed her and she smiled. He kissed her again and carefully ran his thumb over her nipple. Nope, no, she didn't want that. She smiled but moved back a little.

"Not tonight honey, okay? I'm so tired, and so drunk."

"C'mon, we haven't since like last week," he groaned. They'd had sex Monday, she wanted to remind him. But instead, wanting to keep the tenuous peace between them, tried to change tact.

"No, no, come on now. When I'm done, I'll give you a nice long back rub," she said with a smile, reaching for the body wash and lathering her body.

"I don't want a back rub. I want to have sex, with you." She shook her head.

"C'mere," she said, reaching out for another hug. He rolled his eyes and moved toward her. She pulled him into a hug, squeezed tight. Could that be enough? He limply patted her back, his hands sliding down onto her soapy behind. She reached behind her and pushed his hands away.

"Not tonight, sweetie. Okay?" She felt dizzy, the contrast of the heat of the day, the chill of the house, and now the steam of the shower was too much. She wasn't taking some kind of stand, she thought, she just really didn't feel like it, she thought she might get sick.

She rinsed off and moved down the stall so he could get in the water, and slid past him and reached for her razor. She bent over to begin long even strokes of her shins, when he spoke again.

"Forget it," he said with a long sigh. "I don't want to fuck you anyway. Nobody does."

She stopped, her hand on the wall of the shower for stabilization. Bent over, she could feel acid swirling inside her folded stomach. How dare he. She didn't say anything, and glanced down, a thin line of blood ran from her leg and swirled into the drain, as if the very remark, with its harsh consonant sound had perforated the fibers of her skin. Who the fuck did he think he was? She began to feel dizzy and set her razor down. She moved back, slid open the door, and stepped on wobbly ankles out onto the bathmat.

"Oh, give me a break," he called from behind the glass. Her knees felt weak, and she staggered to the sink, unleashing a volley of sick. She felt weak and suddenly so tired, so wiped, just needed bed, just needed sleep.

"Whoa, are you okay?" he yelled now, sliding the door open, peering around. She wiped her face with trembling hands, rinsed the sink and left the bathroom, stepping back into the chill of her bedroom. She walked to the bed, still wet, feeling shivery, to her side, and climbed in. Gavin followed a minute later, and huffed while he rolled over. He whispered something, good-night or whatever—she couldn't really tell—and she rolled away from him, pulling up the cold sheets around her.

ETHAN

HE'D NEVER UNDERSTOOD smoking cigarettes. Middle school had gotten to him, back then he was a TADAA student—Teens Against Drugs and Alcohol—and somehow, despite his attitudes on drinking and smoking pot, cigarettes seemed positively repulsive. Even that hot night as they drove in Kyle's convertible to the house party, and Kyle blew his smoke out the open roof, it smelled disgusting. Ethan felt like sticking his head out over the door, letting the wind cleanse his lungs, blow through his hair like a dog.

The car took a turn quickly and the bottles in the backpack behind Ethan's seat rattled. Driving in the convertible was fun, and for the first time in days, Ethan felt a little back to normal, and he was thankful he wasn't driving. There was something about the way Kyle sighed as he climbed into the passenger seat of his old Volvo station wagon—the station *swag-on*, he tried, but he couldn't shake the feeling Kyle felt bad for him. Tonight, he felt relieved that Kyle was driving, and he could roll up to the party looking slick as hell in the convertible.

"Dude, stuff those under your seat so they don't rattle in case we get pulled over." Ethan reached back and pushed the black backpack deep under his seat. They wouldn't get pulled over, the party wasn't far, barely a mile and a half from Staniford. Jeff Polinsky was hosting, one of the Lacrosse players who lived just over on Deerfield. His folks were in Europe for the month, and so, his house was the destination for the evening.

Ethan had started drinking early.

The night had started over at the Gornick's garden party, at which, he was disappointed to learn Mackenzie wasn't home, and he missed the image of her in a white bikini, her tanned breasts emerging from the water in some fantasy, running her hands over her wet hair as she climbed the steps out of the pool. He and Kyle had stolen two open bottles of white wine and sat behind the fence where the end of the yard sloped down into the forest, and drank, each from a bottle. When they were done, they hurled the bottles down into the forest. Ethan was disappointed when his didn't hit a rock and smash like Kyle's did.

They pulled into the driveway behind a line of other cars. Red sedans and convertibles, and big hulking SUV's that glittered in the moonlight. The house was wide in the dark, a big colonial with bay windows on both floors. When the car silenced, they could hear music pulsing from within the house.

"How are they inside on a night like this?" Ethan

whispered as they retrieved the bag from under the seat and headed toward the open garage door.

"Air conditioning, bruh," Kyle said. Ethan forgot this was normal, since his house had none.

They stepped up and into the house and moved quietly into the kitchen. Ethan transferred the hard alcohol to the fridge, and then followed Kyle in. Kids from all over town were scattered around the living room, seated on furniture, some watching TV, others fiddling with the Bluetooth speaker. Several groups of girls in tank tops and jeans stood in packs around the periphery of the great room, and the door to the deck was open. Jeff rose from the couch to greet them.

"Boys, welcome!" he shouted, and the party turned to look at him. Some waved, some smiled, and Ethan gave a short wave. Jeff handed him a glass of what smelled like tequila and he tossed it back, wincing at the tang. For a minute he was reminded of Neil, sitting there beside the empty tequila bottle.

Across the party he noticed Mackenzie. She was facing away from him, chatting with a group of girls, her phone in her hand. He called her name and she waved to him, breaking from the girls to move toward him. He found himself drawn across the room to her.

"Ethan Carlisle, how are you!" she cried, pulling him into a hug in which he could feel her breasts squish up against him. She was tall and thin, with freckles across her sharp nose and her hard-edged cheekbones, and gently pouting lips. Her light brown hair was up in a high ponytail, and she wore thin, wide silver hoop earrings, so thin it was like they were barely there.

She released him quickly and walked him over to the kitchen table where bottles were displayed in an ersatz fashion.

"What are you drinking?" she said, grabbing the frosted bottle of Grey Goose and pouring a healthy measure into her pint glass.

"I think this was tequila," he said, setting his glass down on the table in the kitchen as she uncorked the bottle of Patrón with a glassy pop. She topped off his juice glass and stood there.

"Shit you got tall," she said standing back from him and looking up at him, her careful blue eyes scanning him. He shrugged. "And you're team manager for next year, I see. Great gig," she said halfheartedly. He knew she was lying and drank another long draw from his juice glass.

"I don't know. It's not what I wanted."

"Oh, come on, it's an important job," she said checking her phone and then promptly scanning the door for someone.

"You know it isn't."

"Oh, stop that," she said sipping from her glass and stifling a still audible shudder. He drank, too, taking caution to hide his own disappointment. It was getting easier to drink, he found, his sips were longer, more drawn out.

"Sorry, I'm just feeling kind of down about it. One bad game last season and . . ." She gave him a shove.

"Get out of your own way! It's okay! At least you'll still be near the team, you know? We can sit in the stands near each other," she said, still scanning the doorway and for a second, he wondered if she'd be like that too at the lacrosse games, distant, scanning the field, the scoreboard, instead of paying attention to him.

"I don't know," he said, his voice trickling off.

"I mean, we're running out of time, you know? Like, we only have a year left. This time next year we'll be gone. We'll all be all over the country and never seeing each other again. We need to make the most of this year, while we can. If there anything you want to do, just fucking do it, you know?" For a moment, he imagined leaning in close and kissing her. He felt himself start to lean forward, and then caught himself. Mackenzie hadn't noticed, she was looking at her phone.

The song changed in the background to one by Lana del Rey, a smoky, lounge singer voice, crooning over a warped auto-tuned sound.

"Hang on, I have to go see Laura, this is her song. Lor! Lor!" she yelled, bouncing on her heels and briefly put her hand on his arm, moving around him toward the living room. He'd felt like he'd been blown by, like a cyclone had swept around him, poured him a glass of tequila spoke for a minute and then whirled by, sweeping past him on the way. He followed her with his eyes, as the girls began singing along into their glasses. The door from the garage into the kitchen opened and a massive figure stepped in, Mike Powell, the captain of the lacrosse team.

"Captain on deck!" Mackenzie yelled, stopping her song, and Mike waved genially. The girls and lacrosse players whooped. She moved toward him and he scooped her up into a hug lifting her little figure off the ground into the air where she kicked her legs, her gold flip-flops slipping off her feet. Ethan felt angry, and quickly too; the anger welled up inside him fast, the reaction boiling over the beaker too quickly.

There was a soft touch on his arm. Chelsea was there, and he exhaled.

"You okay?" she asked softly, and it took a second for his fury to subside. He turned to look at her.

"I'm fine. Since when are you here?" She shrugged her little shoulders and tossed her dark bangs to the side.

"I slipped in the back door a little while ago."

"How are you feeling now?" she asked.

"Honestly," he said, looking to the small crowd fawning around Mike who still hadn't made it out of the doorway yet. "I don't even want to fucking be here."

"Let's take a walk," she said quietly as she grabbed him by the wrist. For a moment, he couldn't look away, and noticed he was being pulled, and went along with it.

Outside in the hot night, they walked to Kyle's convertible, found it unlocked and lowered the top with a mechanical groan. They climbed into the backseat. Even with the light from the house, the stars were beautiful, the sky a sweeping purple sheet.

"You know, especially in this dry spell, there's barely clouds, so the stars are so much more beautiful," she said sighing.

"Okay," he said barely paying attention.

"I could look at the stars constantly and never get bored. C'mon, look up." He leaned back and cocked his head up like hers. For a second, he felt like his eyeballs were swimming in the tequila, a filmy fuzziness came over them, and he had to push to focus on the pinpricks of light.

"There, see? Your problems don't seem so big now do they," Chelsea said quietly.

"Yeah, way to make me feel insignificant," he said with a snort, still without looking away.

"In a way, you should feel better about this. So you're not playing lacrosse next season, big deal."

"It's more than that though," he said quietly. "I'm definitely not going to get any scholarship money now."

"Your mom will figure that part out," she said softly still. "Some of the stars we're looking at don't even exist anymore, did you know that?"

"What are you talking about?" he asked, sitting up and sipping from his glass.

"Some of the stars are already burned out, but they're so many light-years away, that their light is still traveling all that distance so we can see it. But if we could fly to the star, it'd be gone by now, a black hole or a white dwarf or whatever, I read that this morning."

"Great," he said, now not only feeling insignificant, but stupid as well. He felt her fingers crawl over to his and grab them. He was feeling the booze now, and curious where this was headed. She put her head on his shoulder.

"Thanks for being my friend," she said softly.

"No problem. Thanks for reminding me I don't matter," he said with a chuckle.

"None of us do, if it makes you feel any better." She sighed again. He did too. He felt his eyes flutter closed, and then, softly, he felt something gentle and wet on his neck. She'd kissed him. He turned his head to look down at her and she pulled back, her eyes shining in the starlight.

". . . do you think we should?" she whispered. He shrugged and she reached for his face, and kissed him again, this time on his mouth and he felt goose bumps shoot down his arms. He reached around for her, and moved her on top of him. Her lips were warm, her breath smelled fresh, albeit a little boozy from whatever she'd been drinking. He felt her unbuckle his pants and he gasped as she reached into his pants. Her hands were cold, but he warmed quickly. *Was this really happening?* he wondered as her dark hair became a curtain around his face, her lips slowly moved on his, her hand on him. He pushed in to her movements and reached for her white shorts, popping the brass button and she slid them down to her ankles with her underwear.

"Wait, I don't have a condom," he whispered in between breaths, remembering briefly the parable of his cousin, pregnant at sixteen.

"It's okay, you can just pull out," she whispered back.

In the moment before, he imagined Mackenzie, her eyes closed, moving on top of him. When Chelsea slipped down onto him, an unbelievably new and stunning sensation, he closed his eyes and instead, he imagined it was Mackenzie with him in the car, and not a hundred feet away, inside, fawning over the varsity lacrosse captain.

CHAPTER 4

MONDAY, AUGUST 11

NEIL

9:09 PM

MONDAY NIGHT, Neil met Tony, his drug dealer, in the same place they always met: at the little diner by the highway on-ramp in New Haven after work. The diner was clean, hardly a railroad car; its previous incarnation was that of a Mexican restaurant, all adobe brown and brickwork around the edges of the roof. Now it was a diner, serving breakfast, lunch, and surprisingly, dinner. They had a neon sign in the window advertising that they were open late, and Neil imagined drunk Yale kids staggering in at three a.m., blitzed and ordering more food than they could ever eat, ignoring the waitress as she frowned at their six separated checks, all with credit cards.

As was usual, Neil waited in a booth, one of only two occupied tables in the whole restaurant, his hands and phone on the Formica table. The waitress, a young girl with a long dark ponytail and big, sharp eyebrows, stopped at his table.

"What can I get you?" she said with a tired enthusiasm.

"Coffee would be great," Neil said, looking up, smiling at her.

"Anything to eat?"

"Nah, I think I'm okay."

"I can like, even do like a side of fries or whatever," she said, obviously eager to increase the percentage of her tip.

"Sure, that's great."

"Sure, a coffee and a side of fries. Be right out." She moved away from the table, reaching into her apron for her phone.

The sky outside the window was shot with purple streaks, pink streamers. The sun set so late now; it was almost nine when it would finally go down. He pressed the single button on his phone and the screen lit up, a space-station photo of the earth, below thin white font reading 9:21 PM. Tony was late. It was no surprise, he usually was. But this time, he was really late.

The door tinkled and in he came. Tony was a big man, tall and wide, probably younger than he was, Neil reasoned, with sun-tanned skin and big sunglasses which he removed and clipped onto the collar of his shirt, a green V-neck. He was clean-shaven, a stark contrast to the last time they'd met, a just a few months ago.

In entering, he immediately removed his Yankees cap, revealing his shaved head and nodded with a smile at Neil. Neil rose and they shook hands and pulled in for a brief bro-hug; it was always amiable between them. Tony slid into the booth bench across from him.

"How's it been going man?" Tony asked, setting his hat down on the table beside the ketchup and napkin dispenser and tossing his iPhone onto the table. For a second, Neil thought it odd how it was that here was this drug dealer, respectfully removing his hat indoors.

"Good, it's been good. How've you been? You look sharp these days."

"You know, keeping up appearances, trying to elevate my social standing," Tony said with a bright white smile.

"Expanding into new segments, heading to into the white-collar prescription market?"

"Something like that," Tony laughed hoarsely that turned into a cough.

"Want anything?" Neil said as the waitress buffed a table two down from them.

"Nah man, I'm good. The question is," Tony began, "what is it you want?"

Neil shrugged.

"The usual is great," Neil said, looking around furtively. This part always made him nervous. The usual was just some pot, and maybe some coke, but that was it.

"Anything else, I know sometimes you want a little of another." Something else usually meant cocaine—something, this time, Neil didn't want. He shook his head. The waitress approached, bearing his coffee and an oval-shaped plate with a mound of fries. She slid the plate down along with two side plates and stack of napkins, with two utensil wrap-ups.

"Anything for you, sir?" she said to Tony, who looked up and smiled again, honest.

"No thanks, sweetheart, I'm just going to pick at these."

"Let me know what else you need," she said, returning the smile and turning away from the table. Neil pointed the round base of the ketchup bottle over the table, and Tony shook his head.

"You shouldn't be eating those," he said, looking at Neil's plate.

"So now you're a nutritionist too?"

Tony smiled at this and rubbed his mouth and neck —a reaction. Apparently he wanted some.

"Listen man, we're only as good as what we eat."

"What about the reason we're here. That isn't good for you."

Tony shrugged at this.

"That doesn't really matter as much as you'd think. That wears off. Eating bad food, no, that shit hangs on. Lot more insidious, you know?" To this, Neil shrugged and ate another fry. Tony's phone lit up from the table; upside down. He picked it up, and Neil could read the display of who was calling, just one word; *jackrabbit*.

"Does that say jackrabbit?" he asked, pointing toward the phone with a French fry. Tony chuckled again and pressed the button on the side, declining the call. "Is that a codename?"

"Everybody's got a spirit animal. It helps me keep everybody straight."

"I don't see how this makes it less complicated." Tony shrugged again.

"We get stuck in habits, you know? Doing the same things over and over again. After a while, it's second nature."

Neil didn't say anything to this but sipped from his coffee.

"Speaking of which, I got something new I wanted to see if you're interested in." Neil looked up, as now Tony looked around.

"It's called Fever, and it's nuts."

"What is it?" Neil asked, setting his porcelain coffee mug down on the table.

"It's a pill. People love it."

"Really addictive?"

Tony shrugged at this. "Not really. It's making the rounds on the recreation circuit, people are taking it and having orgies."

Neil's eyes widened. "What?"

"Yeah, you gotta try it."

"I don't know, man. I don't think I'm the right kind of guy for it."

"Trust me on this. Have I ever led you wrong?"

"Well, no, not really."

"Why's it called Fever?" Neil asked, acknowledging his curiosity.

"The only side effect it's like you run a fever while you're high. Not that you'd notice, what with it being a hundred fuckin' degrees out there anyway." Neil elected to not point out that wasn't how fevers worked.

"Just take some, see if you like it."

"Nah, just the pot is fine." Neil shook his head, quickly scanning with his eyes.

"Here, I can do business. I'll throw some in for you, think of it as a demo."

Neil rolled his eyes at this and nodded. "Fine, fine."

The waitress returned with the check, and Neil left the bills facedown under the stiff check on the table. He pushed a couple of bills across the table to Tony, who took them. They stood and walked out together to the parking lot. Neil unlocked his car remotely, and Tony reached for a handshake. Neil took his hand and felt a plastic bag in his grip. He moved swiftly from the hand-shake to his pocket.

"Thanks, sir," Neil said.

"No problem, my man." Tony turned to leave.

"Hey, what's my animal name?" Neil called after him. Tony smiled in the fading light, turning back to face him.

"You're a wombat."

"Really?" Neil called with a laugh.

"Get outta here," Tony called with a wave and a chuckle, unlocking a shiny red Ford F350, an absolute monster of a truck, a distance away.

In his car, using the light inside the glove box, he examined the second little bag containing four, shim-mery red capsules. They looked like acetaminophen gel caps; something marketed by Tylenol, taken for a headache, something extra strength. For a second, he wondered if he was being taken for a fool, but then remembered he didn't actually pay for it and slipped the packet of pills and the little bag of weed into his breast pocket.

AT HOME, FORTY MINUTES LATER, HE EXAMINED IT again under the banker's lamp on the desk he never used that had once been his father's. *If you could see me now, Dad*, he thought with a smirk as he held the pills up to the light. They were filled with some tiny liquid, the color unknown, shaded district-light-red, and he removed one capsule from the bag and set it down on his desk to study further. Next, he searched on his phone for Fever side effects. Seconds after the results loaded, he realized he needed to refine his search parameters, and added the word *drug*.

Surprisingly, there was an absolute lack of information about any drug called Fever. He even checked with the FDA webpage and police department pages. Nothing. This was strange; it must be completely new. He stared at the little red pill on the dark wood of his desk and asked aloud, "What are you?" before snatching up his phone again. He had a thought to text Tony and find out more about this drug, but that would seem strange and might scare him off for good. He briefly imagined the word wombat popping up on Tony's screen in the middle of another deal in some alley somewhere and deleted the half-composed message he'd written. Shrugging and figuring he had sick days to use if it backfired, he picked up the little red pill and carried it to the sink, filled a glass of water, and swallowed it. Now to wait.

First, he put the TV on, muted, catching the eleven

o'clock local news, but suddenly scrambled for the remote and hit mute again when he realized the newscaster was in front of Dorset Town Hall. She was cute, and he leaned in to see what she was reporting.

"Local animal control warns that this bear is very large, and very dangerous. If sighted, immediately call the police and secure your family inside your house." He shook his head as they changed topics to talk about a piece of state legislation and switched the TV off and stood up again.

Undoing his tie, he slid the door open to the pool deck, and the wave of heat crashed over him. It was another hot night; a low steam rose off his pool. For a second, he wanted to go for a swim in the blue light, but remembered he'd just taken an unknown drug and wasn't sure what the effects would be. He elected to sit in the warm summer night and stare at the stars.

The effect of the drug was anything but instantaneous. Fifteen minutes later, after checking his watch and wondering if he was being taken for a ride, he stretched his arms, pulling on the muscles out in front of him. When he relaxed, his forearms returning to the aluminum of the deck chair, goosebumps rippled up his calves. The chair arms had somehow turned to ice, chilly and cool. His pants felt tight; he had an erection like no other, and he could feel his pulse pounding in his ears. Suddenly, even the cold metal of the arms of the chair felt sexual, he felt himself shiver, felt his body tighten, felt sweat run down his neck. He pulled his shirt off over his head. His vision was slanting. Everything felt hot. Now he wanted to get in the pool, bad. He tore his shoes off and struggled out of his belt. Fuck it was hot, he thought angrily as he jumped out of his boxers, one leg at a time. His socks were soaked through, and he peeled them off quickly.

Into the pool he leapt, and the sensation was instant, causing him to yelp, the rippling tickles all over his body, over parts of himself he'd never thought of as sexual before: the underside of his buttocks, the wrinkled skin on the underside of his feet. He wanted to feel more. He swam a lap and his nerves shuddered as the water cascaded over him, brushing through every hair on his arms and legs, even the tiny hairs on his knuckles were rushed past. He felt a hunger inside him. He wanted to fuck the embracing water—no, no he wanted Sarah again, no Vanessa, no the hot black girl across the street. He wanted all of them, and for a moment he was taken away to an image of the three of them at once, trying to all lick him at once, their tongues touching each other. The image was so strong, he could smell the sweat and chlorine on their bodies, he wanted that sex smell, that brutal animal smell of aroused flesh. He climbed out of the pool like a zombie, the water felt like it was trying to pull him back within her folds, to soak him inside her. He stepped free using the side of the pool as a railing and stepped, dripping across the deck and pulled the slider open. The blast of cold air from the central air conditioning bombarded his nerves again in shuddering cascades of polar wind, electric charges over his skin. and he gasped and dropped to his knees on the soft carpet. The carpet was so soft and gentle, it felt like the underside of Vanessa's legs. He moaned as he rubbed against it, moaning loudly, loudly enough to be heard but he didn't notice or care. The carpet felt so good on his wet arms, his wet legs. He rolled over onto his back and immediately thought of Sarah the other night.

He grabbed himself, swollen, angry, and he believed it would tear free of the skin, like it could be longer, harder, taller if it wasn't being held back by the stupid membrane. He felt the wet fibers of the carpet rubbing back and forth across his shoulders and spine, tickling, electrifying. The images came fast now, a girl from the internet, Vanessa straddling him, his back against the cold headboard of their bed, Sarah's loud fake moan, Vanessa's nipples bumping his face as she moved on him. He felt higher then lower, higher then lower, like a roller coaster ride, the feeling of the back of his neck on the carpet, making each drop lower and lower. Finally, the sensation he sought arrived, crashing like a breaking wave, too great, too potent, too severe, and Neil lost consciousness.

CARLA

9:15 PM

SHE HAD no idea why the idea of taking a pregnancy test came over her during after-dinner drinks at the Gornick's house. Something about the way Phil slapped his bare knee fake laughing at a bad joke from John made her recall the sound of slapping flesh from the sex they'd had just yesterday. Still, the call of test nudged her, and Carla wondered briefly if this was the sign she'd been waiting for. She excused herself to the bathroom, which was sort of hard to find—Jen had been right—retrieving her purse from the dining chair on the way. She always carried a test with her for this very reason, in case her body sent her some sign the biological trap had snapped shut, starting the process for procreation.

She waited under the fluorescent light of the Gornick's downstairs bathroom, squeezing the little plastic wand. This had to be the time. It just had to be. She glanced at the little Zen garden on the wide vanity, the sinks' large brass bowls inset in the dark wood. She closed her eyes and remembered back to childhood, to church, to praying hard, to the dusty smell of incense and the ethereal whisper of the responsorial psalm. Carla begged for that peace again, for that calming wave of belief, a feeling from long ago, before she questioned everything, back before when she still felt wonder on Christmas mornings.

She opened her eyes and took one last pass through the little white tiled bathroom. She squeezed the stick again in her palm, once more for good luck and looked down.

Negative again. She sighed and sat down on the toilet seat, her head in her hands. Once again, a big fucking negative. She hurled the plastic test into the wicker trashcan. It hit the plastic liner and the can with a clatter. For a second, she stared in the mirror, daring herself not to cry. She stared herself down. She wished she could give herself a pep talk like she used to in college. She'd stare in the mirror and bark orders at herself. Now, she didn't have the energy to. She took a deep breath and shoved the echoing impulse to cry down deep, popped the door lock, and opened the door. She stepped into the hallway and directly into a pretty young girl with long light brown hair and Nancy's sharp nose.

"Ooop, I'm sorry," Carla said.

"No, no," she said quickly. "My fault, I didn't know anyone was in there."

"I'm Carla," she said, extending her hand.

"So nice to meet you, I'm Mackenzie," she said, extending her hand proudly. Carla shook it, and then stepped to the side. Carla was impressed; despite meeting this young girl in such awkward circumstances, she was friendly and bubbly and so confident. Carla immediately believed there was nowhere this girl couldn't go, or anything this girl couldn't do. For a second, she felt pleased for the next generation of women to have been born when they were.

"Pleasure," she said, as the girl stepped around her to the bathroom door. Carla heard the lock click after the door closed. For a moment, she held in the youth of the girl. She recalled the heat radiating off her own skin from her teenage years baking in the sun. She'd sneak Coronas with her friends and drink them in the park. She longed for that youth again.

In the living room tucked in among the suede sectional, Carla found her husband and the Gornick's.

"Was that your daughter?" Carla asked.

"Better be," John said with a laugh that sounded like a cough. "Or there's some other teenager wandering around our house." Nancy cackled at this, and Phil managed a chuckle, staring straight at Carla with a fixed expression that begged for her to rescue him from this conversation.

ON THE WALK HOME IN THE HOT NIGHT, CARLA thought about Mackenzie, how beautiful and polite she was, how proud and friendly, how quickly she'd thrust her hand out in friendship. For a moment as they walked down the burned grass to the hot pavement, she wished they would have a daughter like her, peppy, friendly, smart, confident.

As if reading her mind, Phil spoke.

"That Mackenzie is something, eh?"

"I was just thinking the same thing, what a great kid."

"John was telling me about her—captain of the field hockey team, honors student, running for student council president," Phil rattled off.

"I can't believe she came from Nancy and John," she said under her breath.

Phil laughed loudly and took her hand as they started up the steps to their driveway.

"We have to make better friends," he said as they keyed into the garage with the code and walked up into the frigidity of their house. She agreed. Inside the door, she leaned on the end table in the kitchen and unbuckled her wedges one at a time. Standing on the cold tile flat on her bare feet, she yawned.

"Don't get too sleepy," Phil said, scooping her up in his arms.

"Oh c'mon honey, not tonight, I'm not emotionally up for it." He tutted and pulled her in for a long hug, and she exhaled a breath into his shirt and could smell his sweat. "It's okay. I love you, okay?"

She nodded into him and felt the tears start. Before she knew it, her nose was running, and Phil had picked her up and carried her up to their bed. There, wrapped in the covers in the icy cold of the air conditioning, she told him about the test, about how she had a feeling, but it was all wrong.

"Well, damn," he said, and she looked up at him.

"Well, damn, what?" she replied, wiping her eyes again.

"I guess we'll just have to try some more. Like right now," he said, pushing her down against the pillows. She actually chuckled and sniffed.

"You're incorrigible." He smiled a goofy grin, and she laughed again. How she loved this man. "My make-up's all run. At least let me go wash my face," she said, sliding off the bed and moving toward their bathroom. Looking at herself in the mirror, she took a few deep breaths and washed her face. She gargled some Lister-ine, and the sting of the mint made her focus. She shook her shoulders to relax. *That worked*, she thought as she pulled her sundress up over her head and put her hands on her hips above her white panties, bright against her skin. She turned a little. She was still attractive, she thought, especially with some tears in her eyes. She clicked open the door and flicked off the light, stepping back into the bedroom, chuckling slightly as she spotted Phil, completely naked, leaning on one elbow on the bed, his eyebrows wiggling as he saw her.

"You're absolutely ridiculous, you know, right," she said as she climbed onto the bed.

"Sure do," he said, as she straddled him, sliding his hands over her underwear, pushing them down and running his smooth palms over her behind.

"Take it easy, I'm emotionally wounded," she said with a smile, and he smiled back.

"I'll be nice," he said, sitting up, tilting his chin up to her to kiss her slowly.

The sex was calm and measured, delicate as if either of them could be injured at any time, but still sweet. There was no raunchy dirty talk, just whispered declarations of love and reflections on her beauty. She got close to coming at one point, but Phil shifted his weight, and the progress was lost.

IN THE DARK, MANY HOURS LATER, CARLA COULDN'T fall asleep, as Phil snored, his big hairy arms wrapped around her. Sometimes, sex did that for her—charged her up where it wiped him out. He changed position and rolled away from her toward the window, his large shape like a mountain range, blocking the moonlight.

She slipped out of bed, and crept to the dresser, pulling out some spandex, socks, a sports bra, and a tank top. She carried her orange sneakers and snuck out the door and down the stairs. Out in front of the house, she slipped her sneakers on, and jogged off into the warm night.

She moved quickly, working her breaths in sync with her steps, jogging toward the cul-de-sac and down Staniford out to Cliff Road. From there she ran down the dark street by the woods and found an entrance to a trail. The sky was lighting off in the distance, and an early morning fog had settled over the woods. She took a left, then a right, banking into a trail overgrown with rocks and roots.

She pounded the earth, the leaf-strewn floor, running at full velocity, fiercely getting into the stride, unsure of where she was headed, and then slowed down in the foggy wood. She bent over briefly, breathing heavy, and looked down the path. The path banked sharply to the left from what looked like an overlook. She walked slowly towards it, her hands on her hips in the early morning light. The drop was fifty or sixty feet down to jagged rocks below, and she looked down and felt dizzy. She staggered backward and stood still for a second, closing her eyes.

Standing for just a moment at the precipice, taking in the view, she turned around, and ran back the way she'd come.

AMANDA

11:21 AM

ARRIVING HOME from the grocery store the earlier that day with eighty dollars left for the period, Amanda turned slowly into her driveway when she saw something she'd never seen before. In the yard next door, the black man, Phillip, she recalled, was doubled over the flower beds, a wheelbarrow full of dark healthy-looking mulch. He'd been out there a while it looked like, the sun was glistening on his shaved head and in big wet patches on his shirt around his neck. She parked her big white BMW SUV and popped the trunk.

"Well hello neighbor," she called, friendlier than she meant. But he turned around, noticing her and waved one dirty glove at her.

"Hello," he called serenely, sitting upright, and wiping his forehead on his arm.

"It's a lovely morning," she said, noticing that even drenched in sweat, he was handsome, and tall, too, broad shoulders, that bright smile in the dark stubble. She smiled back.

"It's a little hot," he called back.

"Well when you're done, feel free to pop over for a dip in the pool."

"I wouldn't want to impose," he called back.

"Nonsense! Come on over!"

"Are you sure?"

"Of course," she called. My God, how she wanted to see him without his shirt on. "And bring your wife too," she added, querying if she was around.

"Oh. She's at work," he said. "It's just me."

"Damn," she said loudly across the grass. "Well, still, come over anyway."

"Alright, let me just finish this bed," he said. "Thanks!"

Amanda struggled to repress a smile as she nodded her confirmation. She was having a handsome man over midday to swim in the pool. This would drive Gavin crazy if he'd found out, but somehow, that felt good. There was no harm in this, after all, she reasoned. Still, she'd have to freshen up and make some lemonade or something.

Inside the air-conditioned kitchen, she put the meager groceries away and stood on a stool to retrieve a glass pitcher from the cabinet over the refrigerator. Selecting one, she added some powdered iced-tea and several cups of water and ice, and stirred the mixture with a big wooden spoon, the wood clacking against the glass in the tempest. Using two hands, she picked up the pitcher and set it down on a flowered tray, blue and white hibiscus. She selected two glasses and filled an ice bucket. Carrying it with a slight sway in her step, she descended the steps and slid the tray onto the glass top table and briefly dusted her hands. She returned inside to touch up her makeup and adjust her hair.

Phil arrived about fifteen minutes later, in the same sweat-stained shirt and black swim trunks. She rose as he walked around the side of the house.

"Thanks so much for offering, I could really use a dip," he said quietly, reaching out his hand to her.

"Of course! We never get in enough. I swear we open it and it never gets used. It's a crime," she said, sitting back down. He reached down and flipped the shirt up over his head, discarding it to the concrete deck. His chest was well built and brown, glistening in the sun, and she felt herself shiver slightly despite the near-hundred-degree temperature. He kicked off his black sport sandals and dove in, headfirst, arms outstretched. She caught herself smiling as she watched him dive in. She shook it off by pouring two glasses of iced tea while he emerged from the surface of the water.

"The water is fantastic. Aren't you coming in?" he called, resting his arms on the deck. She shook her head and rose from the table with one glass and walked it over to him, placing it in his hand, and for a second, their fingers brushed, and she felt herself tense all over.

"Thanks so much, and thanks for breaking the rules for me."

She stepped back, confused. What was he saying?

"What rules?" she asked. How could he know that Gavin wouldn't be okay with him being here?

"Isn't there always a no-glass-on-the-pool-deck

rule?" he asked sipping from the glass and setting it gingerly down on the cement.

"Oh, that's just for the kids. Us adults can behave ourselves," she said, surprising even herself with her flirting. That wasn't like her at all. He pushed back from the wall with his strong legs and outstretched his arms, moving in slow circles, the water rolling off his muscles in his forearms.

"Do you guys have any kids?" she asked, suddenly realizing she didn't know.

"Oh, not yet," he said, swimming back to the side, and picking up his glass again.

"Not yet?" she pushed.

"Between you and me," he began, and propped himself up, and she leaned forward, despite the ten feet between them. "We're trying, especially now that we're settled."

She didn't know how to react to this, so she forced a smile and clapped her hands quickly and tightly, like a seal. "That's so exciting!" she cried without feeling it was.

"Yeah, we'll see."

"Well good luck. Dorset's a lovely place to raise kids," she said now refilling her empty glass. He smelled of chlorine.

"Now you guys have just Kyle, right?" he asked. She nodded. When did he meet Kyle? Impressive; he even could remember her son's name. Gavin, in contrast, she was sure, wouldn't even remember Phil's name.

"Remind me again, what does Gavin do for work?"

Phil asked offhandedly, tracing a line in the cement with a wet finger, droplets expanding on the deck and then shrinking in the sun. This question must've been hard for him, she realized, as he wasn't working.

"Security, he owns a security firm," she said without looking at the cameras mounted in the corners of the patio, a coping mechanism she'd developed, as if to pretend they weren't there. She didn't like the idea of robotic eyes seeing everything, even if they weren't recording all the time. For a moment, she felt nervous their eyes would spot her and Phil, but she remembered that they didn't activate until the house was armed. She opened her mouth to ask how he was doing on the job search when he spoke again.

"How does one get into security?"

"Oh, he was a cop for a zillion years," she said, brushing his question off with a wave of her hand. "Let me top you off," she rose with the pitcher and walked to the side of the pool and picked up his glass, refilling it.

THAT AFTERNOON, AFTER PHIL HAD TOWELED OFF, HE thanked her again. He invited her and Gavin over for dinner, a date she knew they'd never keep, and he returned home, mentioning how he needed to set up a couple more bathrooms. Later, she smelled the towel for a minute before tossing it into the washing machine.

She sat out on the pool deck in the sun, her eyes closed after he left, finishing the iced tea when she heard the side door slam and two teen voices bantering back and forth, making fun of each other.

"Ma?" Kyle called.

"Out here, honey," she called back. She heard the footsteps grow nearer and the sliding screen move and turned to see Kyle and Ethan stepping onto the deck.

"Ethan, sweetheart, how are you?" she said, smiling warmly and rising from the seat.

"Hi Mrs. Holbrooke," Ethan said and brushed his long dark bangs out of his blue eyes.

"The iced tea is gone?" Kyle said, picking up the pitcher with less than a milliliter left in it.

"I'll make some more, don't worry," she said, rising and collecting the tray and grabbing the pitcher from Kyle. "Do you guys want some lunch?"

"Sure," they both said.

"No problem."

"Why are there two glasses?" Kyle called after her. She felt her heart clench up.

"The neighbors came over for a minute," she said, starting to move toward the slider.

"Why aren't there three glasses, then?" Kyle asked with a laugh. Ethan moved away from them and removed his shirt, and she looked away.

"It was just the woman, the . . ." she lied, lowering her voice. "The black lady."

"Carla," Kyle said, correcting her.

"Yeah, she was home for a few hours and popped by to say hello."

"She's cool," Kyle said, kicking out of his shoes and pulling his shirt up over his long blonde hair. *When did he meet her?* She wondered. But at the risk of being caught in her lie further, she moved into the

143

house and heard splashes as the boys plunged into the pool.

In the kitchen, from the window over the sink that looked down toward the pool, she smiled and thought about how powerful and strong Phil was earlier, how at ease and relaxed he seemed, even in this foreign environment. For a moment, she was jealous of his marriage, of his life, of his educated earnestness. Watching the boys do laps, racing each other, she reached for the iced tea mix again, but stopped, her hand on the cabinet. She so wanted a drink. She cranked the window open and called out.

"Do either of you boys have to go anywhere this afternoon?" Ethan looked at Kyle, and Kyle looked up at her and shook his head.

"Nah, why?"

She declined to answer as she retrieved three cold bottles of beer from the fridge—Coronas—uncapped them with the head of the corkscrew and carried them out, wedged between her fingers.

She walked to the edge of the pool and reached out with one toward Ethan. He reached up, a smile growing across his face. Kyle was in shock, sitting astride a plastic pool noodle, he swam quickly over to the side.

"Seriously?" he asked, reaching up and taking it from her hand.

"As long as you aren't driving. I figure it's a hot day, and you boys are old enough."

"We're still four years away from drinking," Ethan said with a cautious smile, he still hadn't drunk from his yet.

"Well, in Europe the drinking age is eighteen, so let's go with that."

"Thanks Mom!" Kyle cried with a laugh as he sipped from the glass mouth. She turned back toward the house and stopped at the screen door.

"But if either of you breaks that glass on the pool deck, I swear I'll kill you both." They laughed together, that perfect youthful laugh, that summery sunny laugh that basks in the years ahead, so many more than behind.

From inside the house again, the window over the pool, their youth in the sun was still intoxicating. She missed being that young again, she missed being able to ogle at a beautiful boy like Ethan. For a moment, she felt jealous of Kyle, getting to spend all that time with him, with whatever it was they did when they hung out. Ethan slid off his pool float and into the water with a splash, and she remembered another hot summer years and years ago.

Kyle had to have been five or six and had been running a fever for almost two days. She'd began to worry. Her little boy, his cheeks rosy, dizzy, looking like he'd been flattened, and the heat that summer wasn't helping. She wanted his fever to wane so badly, she took him out to the pool in the middle of the night, just them in the muggy darkness. In the trees around their house, peepers clicked and croaked, and the hum of the pool filter churned somewhere in the dark. She held him on her hip like she'd used to when he was much littler, and slowly descended the steps into the pool with him, holding him in the cool water, hoping his temperature would start to fall. She remembered his eyes fluttering as she gently waved him through the water, immersing his legs, his torso, trying to cool down his sticky little frame. She remembered that helpless feeling—that there was nothing she could do to help him feel better, and she hoped the water could.

She missed a lot about that chapter in her life, when Kyle was young. She missed that feeling of being loved unconditionally, the way he'd jump into her arms when he leapt from the school bus every day. When was the last time she held him? Like, really held him? Had it been years? It had certainly at least been months. The distance between them now was normal, right? That was what happened with teenage boys and their moms naturally, she hoped. Still, she felt like holding her son was a commodity now, a rarity. She must at least squeeze a few more in before he left in the fall.

Amanda shook herself loose from her thoughts and took a sip from her beer. It was crisp and cold. She loved the bitterness. The boys were at opposite ends of the pool on lounges, floating slowly, holding their precious beers with both hands. She sighed loudly and went about fixing lunch for the three of them.

ETHAN

AROUND DINNER TIME, his hands and feet pruned, Ethan returned home. With just the hint of a buzz on from the beer, (Amanda only gave them each one) he found he had the audacity to text his mother about the lacrosse team. She reacted sympathetically over text, all apologies and promises of hugs. Still, he stalled as long as he could—talked to Kyle about anything he could. He debriefed the party the other night, omitting the part about having sex with Chelsea in the back of Kyle's car, and instead adding that he and Chelsea hooked up, nonspecific as to where. Since then, he'd been ignoring her.

In the day or so since they'd fucked, she'd reached out to him four times to chat, likely, he reasoned, to see where their relationship was now—questions he didn't feel like finding answers for. Rather, ones he didn't have.

Finally walking in the front door, he heard the buzz of the TV click off, and saw his mother rise from the couch. She looked tired, like she'd just woken from a nap; her hair was up in an unkempt short ponytail, and her gray eyes had bags under them. She rose silently and crossed the room to him, her arms outstretched. She took him in her arms, and while he hugged her, he realized how small she was now. When he was younger, she seemed so much bigger, so much taller and stronger, and now here she was, tiny.

"I'm sorry baby," she said quietly after a minute.

"I'm okay, Mom," he said, without meaning it. She released him and guided him toward the table. There was a salad there, and two plates, and two glasses of seltzer. He sat down and she reached with the scissor handled tongs and scooped some salad onto his plate and onto hers.

"I was so sorry to hear that today honey," his mother said quietly, the only sound her fork in the lettuce. "At least you're still involved with the team, and you can travel with them, and—"

"I'm not taking the manager job."

"Why not?"

"Because it's a fucking shitty position, and I'd rather not be on the team at all."

She sighed.

"Don't make any decisions now," she said quietly. "Sleep on it, make a decision in the morning." He remembered that he'd only told her today, instead of last week. This decision was a few days coming. "It's nice that they clearly still want you around, at least," she said, trying, and avoiding his eyes.

"Apparently not enough to put me on the fucking team."

"What do you think it really means?" she asked innocuously, looking away.

"What *what* means?"

"Your frustration about this. What do you think it means?"

"Please, Mom, don't be on the clock with me right now," he said, referring to his mother's job, a school psychologist in the school system.

"Well, I think you should dig a little deeper into your feelings and see what it means."

"It means I'm not fucking playing lacrosse in college, that's what it fucking means." He slammed his fork down.

"Ethan, calm down, please," she said, sitting upright, leaning away from the table.

"I'm going out for a bit. I have my phone," he said, standing up from the table quickly ignoring his full plate of salad.

"Where are you going?"

"Stop and Shop, or whatever. I'll be back later." He grabbed his keys from the hook by the door and walked past his mother's Prius, with the faded Obama 2008 stickers. He climbed into his old Volvo and started the rumbling motor. The old V6 revved and rumbled, and he lowered the windows and backed down the driveway to the cul-de-sac, where he backed out and to the left, and then out onto Cliff Road. He tore down the wooded road as the sun set beyond the trees on another sweltering day.

He wasn't about to tell his mother that this wasn't about the fucking position, he thought savagely, taking turns too quickly, the bald tires on the Volvo skipping up pebbles and sand in his wake. This wasn't just about losing the chance for lacrosse scholarships. This was about being excluded from this social circle for the entirety of his final year of high school. It was about burning all of his popularity off before college. It was about losing his sense of identity.

He turned left onto the main road that ran perpendicular to the coast. Maybe he'd go down to the water; it was only a half-hour away. He accelerated. A text tone plinked into his phone, but because of the massive crack, he couldn't tell who it was at a glance. He held it up in front of the steering wheel. It was Chelsea again, wanting to meet up.

The moment before the accident, he was looking at his phone, but looked up just in time to see the pair of headlights from the oncoming lane racing toward him. He pounded his brake pedal to the floor and pulled sharply to the right onto the shoulder. The car behind him wasn't so lucky. He watched in the rearview mirror as the car coming from the other direction, a big SUV, crossing the lanes of traffic collided head-on with the car behind him, some kind of sedan, and watched as the sedan crumpled and tumbled off the road and down into the woods. The SUV, still moving at unstoppable velocity flipped backward, screeching for a while skidding back down the road. The whole thing was over in seconds. Before he knew it, he was out of his car, had his phone in his hand and ran toward the accident.

Ten yards away, he stopped and took a deep breath. *Brace yourself*, he thought. *You're about to see a dead body.* There was an eerie silence, birds in the nearby trees chirped their nighttime songs, and the sun was nearly gone now, but the sky was still alight. He dialed 911 as fast as he could, the numbers not even feeling like he'd pressed them, his hands shaking, his fingers numb, not working correctly and waited while being connected. He gave directions and his approximate location, and then, he heard it, the loud pained shriek. Ethan dropped his phone and ran toward the SUV from where the scream issued. Another scream again, and he yelled back.

"I'm here, I'm here!"

Approaching the car, suspended upside down, trapped, was a woman, her long blonde hair hanging low around her face. He crouched down to see better in the dimming light.

"Get me out of here!" she shrieked, sobbing.

"I can't pull you out of there, in case you get hurt worse, okay? Listen, I already called 911, they're on their way, okay?" He recalled from TV, that passerby should never move an injured person; they had to wait for an ambulance. He suddenly padded his pockets for his phone, only to see he'd dropped it on the pavement a distance back.

"Please, please, oh my God, oh my God this hurts so bad," she sobbed.

"Listen, calm down, hey." He reached up, he could see one of her hands, wedged in the steering wheel, her fingers bloody. He reached up and in and gently touched her hand.

"Hey, hey, you feel that?"

"Yes, yes," she cried.

"Okay, it's going to be okay," he said loudly, cocking his head to get a better look at the other car, smoldering down in the woods a couple hundred feet away, harder and harder to see as the sun set.

"I'm going to die," she sobbed. "This hurts oh my God."

"It's okay," he said quietly and stroked her fingers with his thumb. "What's your name?"

"T-t-tracy," she stuttered. Her breathing was ragged.

"Hi Tracy, I'm Ethan, do me a favor, okay? Take a deep breath for me for a second." He heard her inhale and then yelp and exhale.

"It hurts to breathe deep, holy shit." He could see her struggle against her retracted seatbelt.

"Tracy, I need you to stay still, okay? I already called 911, they'll be here any minute."

"I think I dozed off, I think I fell asleep, I woke up right as I hit the other car, oh god, the other car, is the other person okay?"

"I haven't been to look, if I can let go of your hand, I'll go look," he said, starting to stand again.

"No, please don't go, please," she begged.

"Okay, okay, I'll stay right here." They stayed quiet there, a moment in the gathering darkness, a cool breeze settling over the accident, over the headlights, the scattered detritus over the road.

"I'm going to die, aren't I?" she said at last, her

voice now ragged and broken, he could hear her sniff. "I don't want to die. Oh my God, I don't want to die." He stopped for a second and whispered a harsh shh, and immediately regretted it when she sucked back in her tears.

"You hear that?" he whispered, lying.

"Hear what?" she sobbed.

"Listen close, you can hear the sirens," he lied again. She sniffed and held her breath. Just then on the periphery of his hearing he could suddenly hear them wailing.

"D'you hear them Tracy?" he whispered. "They're coming for you right now, just hang on, okay?"

Her breathing was labored, and she spoke. "I can, I can hear them." They sat in silence again as the sirens, now definitely nearby, grew louder and louder. Finally, at the curve at the end of the road two police cars, an ambulance and a fire truck came wailing around the corner, casting the scene of the accident in alternating red and blue light. The sound was piercing. Ethan briefly covered an ear with his free hand to stifle it, then used it to wave to them.

"See the lights, Tracy?" he shouted over the oncoming lights and sirens, tears in his own eyes now.

"Thank God, thank God," she began crying again. "Thank you, thank you so much, please, stay with me until they get here." He positioned himself on the ground, cross-legged, still reaching up into the hot wreckage of the car holding her sweaty and bloody fingers.

"I'm not going anywhere."

The paramedics moved quickly around him, talking her through every step of the process, telling him to let go of her hand as they cut into the vehicle and extracted the tiny woman from within, pulling her out and onto a stretcher, slipping an oxygen mask over her face. Ethan surged forward and grabbed her hand one last time and gave it a squeeze, and then shouted to the paramedics about the other car deep in the woods, its taillights still burning red against the darkness of the trees.

To the police, he explained he wasn't involved in the accident, declined a medical evaluation, despite their advocacy and climbed back into his car. The first batch of emergency responders quickly boarded their various vehicles and sped off, as a second ambulance and more police arrived. A second firetruck. Officers, firefighters, paramedics flitted about the scene, the police carrying clipboards, examining road damage, the damage to the trees and bushes along the side of the road. Ethan suddenly felt he was invisible behind his steering wheel, watching the gathering darkness, scattershot by blue police lights dancing on the trees and the road ahead.

CHAPTER 5

TUESDAY, AUGUST 12 — WEDNESDAY,
AUGUST 13

NEIL

TUESDAY, 7:41 AM

THE SUNLIGHT BURNED HIS EYES, and Neil rolled his elbow over his face, tearing his sweat-sticky torso off the carpet he had fused to sometime in the night. He was naked, and the blinds were open on the door to the patio, the bright morning sun streaming in. His head was pounding, and after looking around, he put his head down again and sighed. On the following inhale, he smelled something uric and tart. Urine. He'd pissed himself in the night. He sat upright, covering his eyes for a minute, blocking the harsh sunlight from the delicate ovals of his eye sockets. That drug, Fever, was something intense. He sat up slowly, carefully, waiting for the hangover headache, waiting for the pressure in his skull to burst, like a bumped end-table in the night, tearing open his skull with the crash of the shattered lamp the noise echoing everything, waking everyone up, but it didn't come.

He lifted his arms over his head, and pulled on his deltoids, pulling his fingers and leaning which way and then the other. His muscles felt sore, like he'd had a massage yesterday, or had participated in some strenuous exercise, and he smiled a little bit, immaturely. He doubted jacking-off counted.

As he rose from the carpet he saw the yellow stain, bright against the white, and cursed himself and that stupid drug. He couldn't believe he'd passed out so cold he'd pissed himself. What was he, four? Standing now, still no headache came, but he felt thirsty, but not in a cotton-mouth sensation, it was just as though he'd been in the sun, and he could feel his lips chapped and dry. He walked to the kitchen, snatched a forgotten glass on the island counter, and pushed in on the refrigerator door filling it and drank it down fully before refilling it again. The webbing between his fingers was still stiff and sticky, and he realized he needed a shower. More importantly, it was seven forty-five, and he was supposed to be in work for eight. Locating his nearly dead phone on the island counter, Neil emailed his boss that he felt sick and would be staying home. He finished the email with the line *see you tomorrow*, and upon hitting send realized the tacit acceptance that this was a fake sick day. If he was really sick, how would he know he'd be better tomorrow? He cursed his unplanned email and headed upstairs to shower. *Fuck them*, he thought bitterly. His father had just died. They owed him to not ask questions.

On his way up the stairs, he turned the thermostat down to sixty-four degrees, and he could hear the vents kick in the central air conditioning. He showered, pissed again, and googled a carpet cleaning company on his laptop from bed. He called, explaining his girlfriend had just brought her dog over, and the animal had pissed on the carpet and he needed it cleaned pronto. The man understood and told him he'd be over by three o'clock.

Emerging from the shower now with a free and sunny day before him, Neil faced the dilemma of what to do. For a while, he thought about reaching out to one of the women from the adulterer's site, but for some reason, he wasn't hungry for it. For the first time in a long time, he wasn't hungering for sex, for the sweaty carnality of it. It was like he'd just woken up; the thought of sleeping more seemed unnecessary, redundant. Despite the earliness of the day, what he wanted, more than ever, was a beer. A cold one. Checking both doors to the refrigerator, his searching coming up empty, Neil determined a trip to the supermarket was in order.

He dressed casually and left the house via the garage door. It was a hot day again, but not overbearingly, and Neil pleasantly popped his sunglasses on as he backed out of the driveway and turned down Staniford. He was in an impeccable mood. He hadn't been this happy in weeks, at least not before his father's passing. Even the pall of that memory didn't dampen his spirits. He drove the scenic route, down by the river, the branches and leaves swaying in the warm wind, the sun dappling on the water. What was in that pill? He wondered if it was cut with some kind of drug with mood-boosting attributes. He shrugged and almost didn't want to know. He wanted more, though. That was crazy good, and how rested he felt, despite having slept on the floor, was almost worth the carpet marks on his back, and however much the carpet cleaning service would cost.

The road segued out onto the connector, and he drove south toward town, stopping at the light. He flicked on the radio and heard some upbeat teenage singer and he found himself drumming along to it on his wheel. A car pulled up beside him, in the left turn lane, and he promptly stopped, his arms suddenly locked. The light changed, and he turned right and headed into downtown Dorset, the strip of main street proceeding between the little shops and the narrow spit of town green. He cruised past the iconic pillared Dorset Library and the white Congregational Church on the green, and, deciding he wanted a coffee, found a parking space in front of the little coffee shop. He happily bleeped his horn again as the car locked and he headed into the store, through the jangling-belled door.

Returning mere moments later with a cold brew, he slid the cup into his cupholder and started his car.

Through the glass, he noticed something he didn't see on his way in. At the Italian deli beside the coffee shop, at one of the outdoor tables, was the young black couple who'd moved in across the street. He watched as the woman rose from the table, crossed to her husband, kissed his smooth head, picked up her purse and her sunglasses from the table, and dug around in her purse for her keys. She unlocked her silver Audi, three cars down from his, and slid in behind the wheel. She was beautiful, he thought, with her dark eyes, her hair today in a bun on top of her head, she retouched her lipstick in the visor mirror before backing out of her space quickly and heading off down the street.

The husband remained seated, scrolling through his phone. Neil suddenly noticed the contrast. The husband was in gym shorts and a T-shirt, while his wife had been dressed as if for work. The husband gestured for the waitress, a summer high school student in a little black apron who dug a slip of paper out of a pocket on the front. He smiled as he received it. Realizing how creepy it would be if the husband had noticed him, Neil backed his car out, much slower than the woman and headed to the supermarket for the beer he decided he wanted.

AT HIS POOL LATER ON THAT MORNING, TWO CORONAS in, the wooden door in the fence swung open and Ethan stepped through.

"Is this a bad time?" he asked, already through the door. Neil shrugged. The boy looked taller than he had when last he saw him, and he'd looked tired, his eyes baggy and ringed.

"Not at all," Neil said as he cracked a third Corona and handed it out to him. Ethan brightened slightly at the prospect. For a moment, before the teen crossed the yard and took the glass bottle from him, Neil thought about how tall he'd grown since they met years ago.

As part of his community service requirement for graduating from Dorset High, Neil had been required to perform a certain number of hours of community service, including participating in a mentorship program with kids from the town's elementary school. He signed up begrudgingly, after determining that the biweekly meetings for a semester should satiate the requisite hours on time for graduation.

He'd attended that first meeting as nervously as the mentees seemed to be, they all clung to each other on the soccer field of the elementary school, fearful of being singled out. The woman, the organizer, a well-meaning middle-aged facilitator from Dorset Youth and Family Services, began calling out pairings of mentors and mentees.

Neil thought then, as she ran down the list, that he'd need to charm her to make sure she would vouch for the correct number of hours of service. She handed out some of those Velcro ball-and-catch mitt things, so they could get to know each other. When she called Ethan's name, Neil was surprised at how like him this kid was, brooding and sour, even in third grade. They retreated to a corner of the field and Neil shrunk to his knees to shake his hand. Ethan wasn't timid like the others: he shook his hand and looked him square in the eye. Throwing the Velcro covered ball, Neil was surprised with the ease with which Ethan caught it on his opposite covered plate, moving with the caught ball to reduce its momentum. It was like he knew intuitively. Upon chatting with the boy, he'd been surprised to learn he was bright too. He wondered why he was even in the mentoring program.

Two meetings and two craft-and-outdoors activities later, Ethan opened up. His father wasn't in the picture, his mom, a middle school psychiatrist, was raising him alone, and before Neil suddenly a painting emerged: a tired single mom, believing in her town's system, seeing this program advertised and then emailing to sign her son up, figuring he could use a male role model. The kid also lived next door, he found out one day, in the one little house on the cul-de-sac near the end of Staniford Drive.

That was the end of the deep conversation, though. Neil figured it was best to keep their relationship topical, as he tried his best to remain disconnected, showing up for only the hours he needed, being available the minimum he had to be. He and Ethan lost touch after Neil graduated from high school, and then near the end of senior year of college, Ethan added him on Facebook, and Neil, surprised to see this kid, now in eighth grade, almost ready for high school, accepted the request. The first private message came two years later. Ethan had been almost ghosting him on Facebook, liking the occasional post, always writing him a terse birthday message, but never commenting. When he messaged, it came through simply with a plink on Neil's phone. The message was simple; *hey, do you have any beer you'd be willing to sell?* Surprised when he received it, thinking of what that middle-aged mentorship facilitator would think if she knew, he smiled at himself. Perhaps, this was just the next phase of his mentorship. He replied to come over later after work. Ethan emerged from the door-in-the-fence then too.

Now as Ethan's fingers closed around the bottle and Neil released it, he slid over and plopped down next to him on the other aluminum chair by the pool.

"Thanks man," Ethan said.

"Good timing," Neil replied.

"Sorry about the other night, you definitely didn't need to give that to me for free. I brought cash if you want . . ." Ethan began.

"What?"

"When you gave me all the booze in there? You were pretty hammered." *The mystery of the missing bottles had been solved*, Neil thought.

"Of course not, no, no, it's all good," he said with a forced smile.

They sat there in silence for a little while.

"So what can I help you with today?" Neil asked after a moment.

"Maybe some pot?" Ethan asked, and then smiled. "That'd I'd pay you for." He pulled a wallet out of his front pocket. Neil rose.

"No problem." He went upstairs to his sock drawer where he retrieved one of the little bags from Tony. For a moment, he stopped at the remaining three caplets of Fever in the little baggy. He had to get more of those. He dumped two out and left them precariously on his dresser, settled on a tissue. He brought the bag with the one pill too.

"Here you go," he said and handed the bag to him, and then showed him the other bag. "Also, take this, but be careful, it's really intense." Ethan smiled and shelled out some bills—it didn't matter to Neil what—handed them to Neil, who slipped them into his own pocket.

"What is it?" he asked, looking over the little red caplet, holding the bag up to the sun.

"It's called Fever. It's really intense. It's like a

sensory stimulant. It's great before sex," Neil advised without having had experience. Ethan nodded and put it in his pocket quickly. "You know, if you can handle it," he said with a chuckle.

Ethan smirked, drained his beer, and rose. "Thanks, I'll catch you later." He headed toward the door in the fence and disappeared.

Neil sat and finished two more beers as the sun began to move westward across the sky, casting the yard in a content, warm afternoon light.

CARLA

AS SHE DROVE HOME in the gathering darkness, Carla recalled how almost worried she felt about Phil after she left him at the little café downtown. Maybe it was the way he'd looked at her so sadly, as if he wished he was going with her, like a child or a puppy, upset to see her leave. She hoped he'd made progress today on the job search. Without a job, Phil seemed so rudderless and lost, and part of this, she determined was her fault. As if she'd created the breeding ground for his loneliness and sadness. She'd had to though, of course. This opportunity was too incredible, and too rare. She couldn't've passed it up. It would have been irresponsible to herself and to everything she'd worked for to decline. If the situation was reversed, she wondered, would Phil feel the same way she did? Would she feel the same way he did now? She shook her head. She was doing good work, important work, and she had to focus. Phil's pieces would settle into place. They had to.

She thought about her day. She had curriculum planning meetings all morning at Yale, and then had to meet a colleague for coffee, as well as to do some research on voter demographics on Connecticut for a first week's lesson plan. She'd felt good. She was hitting the ground running for her Political Parties and Elections class she'd be teaching in the fall, and the retrieved statistics from the Secretary of State's office would be a perfect first-lesson plan. She'd been buried all afternoon, barely looking up from her computer until the sun slid down, exhausted in the sky, and she realized she'd better head home.

As she came down Cliff Road, she suddenly noticed red and blue dancing lights on the trees. She turned slowly onto Staniford and stopped. A circle of police vehicles was in the cul-de-sac, their lights on, but no sirens. She pulled off to the side of the street, in front of the small house on the corner. She climbed out and quickly approached the crowd that had formed around the police cars. As she drew close, some of the police moved, and she suddenly saw in the red and blue lights a heaping mass at least three feet high and four feet wide of dark hair on the pavement. Nearby a police officer stood with his hand on his gun, another talking with him, and two more keeping people back. It was an animal of some kind, a huge one, thick black fur matted with something shimmering in the lights. It was a bear. It looked like it had been shot on the street. Across the crowd, she could see John and Nancy Gornick, and Amanda and Gavin Holbrooke, and another man, one she didn't know, tall with thick stubble, and a kid, with dark hair, all bathed in police light. No Phil, though.

One officer put his hands up to the gathered crowd and began speaking in a rehearsed clear, loud voice.

"Folks, we're just waiting for animal control to come collect the carcass, nothing else to see here, go on back to your homes." People started to move. Carla saw John and Nancy turn back toward their house. She turned and went back to the car on the curb, starting it up. She just needed to get into the driveway. She slowly approached the crowd, lowered her window, and called for the police officer—a white man, of course—making sure to keep both of her hands visible on the wheel. She got his attention and asked if he'd mind if she could pull in her driveway, and he nodded and turned to move people and officers away, so she could move tight to the curb into her driveway. She waved thanks and pulled slowly into the driveway toward the garage and breathed a sigh of relief.

She suddenly paid notice to her nagging hunger, having skipped lunch earlier. The exterior lights on their house were off, and for a moment, she wondered if Phil wasn't home. His SUV was parked there, though. She opened the garage door and rolled in, shutting the car off, the sudden darkness that swallowed her up when her headlights clicked off. She climbed out and made for the light switch. She unlocked the door and went up through the door and up four steps to the main level. The house was dark. What the hell was going on? She called her husband's name up into the darkness as she used the railing to guide herself up and over the threshold. She heard movement. A cough.

"Honey?"

Suddenly, with the bright dazzling flash of a star going nova, the lights came on to the kitchen and living space, the recessed lighting blinding for a moment before, squinting she saw Phil yawn across the room.

"What time is it?"

"Seven-thirty," she said, quickly glancing at her watch and blinking.

"Yikes, I shouldn't've slept this long. Hey," he said as he crossed to her and took her in his arms. He yawned again, and she smiled slightly as she embraced her husband. Her stomach rumbled.

"Did you sleep through all that?" she asked, releasing from the embrace.

"All what?" he asked with a yawn.

"Look outside. The police shot a bear in the middle of the street," she said, taking off one shoe, the cold wood floor on her foot. Phil moved quickly and drew the curtains and for a minute the red and blue danced across the kitchen.

"Jesus Christ. This really is the sticks, isn't it?"

"It was enormous, I saw it," she said as he closed the curtains.

"What do you think they'll do with it?" he asked, standing at the sink, yawning again.

"The cops out there said they were waiting for animal control."

"Right, but like what will animal control do?"

"A bear autopsy?" Her stomach rumbled again.

"Maybe, to see if it has rabies," he said, his head cocked sideways.

"Speaking of which," she said, "I'm as hungry as a bear. What's for dinner?" She asked, hanging her purse on the railing post on the stairs up from the garage.

"Oh, shit, I didn't do dinner, I'm sorry, I'll figure something out," he said, immediately moving toward the fridge. She metered her response, modulated; it wasn't an expectation that he'd have dinner ready, but what else did he do all day?

"No worries, I'm not that hungry," she said aloud, directly contradicting herself. She began ascending the stairs. "I'm going to hop in the shower," she said, to give him some time.

Rising with each stair, she proceeded to their bathroom and nearly tripped over the boxes still littered about the bedroom floor. He hadn't gotten to this yet? She took her shirt off and tossed it onto the unmade bed. He hadn't even made the bed? What was the point of being home all day if he didn't even finish up the unpacking and the maintenance of the house? If the situation were reversed, she'd have made unpacking the house a project. Even if the job prospects were slim, she'd focus on delivering success in the form of a fully unpacked home—tidy, clean—and dinner ready when he got home.

She undressed and stepped into the hush of the shower and took a deep breath in the steam. Goose-bumps raised on her skin from the clash of the air conditioning and the heat of the water. It wasn't his fault, she thought. He must be hating himself, unable to find a job, and here she was, being angry that he hadn't done more work today. Maybe he'd been applying to jobs all day today. Maybe he'd had a phone interview. Maybe he'd read a book to distract himself. The sudden image of Phil laying outside on the chaise lounge reading a thriller made her sad—the idea that his world was so terrible, that he'd need to escape. She rubbed the purple loofa over her skin. She shaved her legs. She peed, spent as much time as she could, and when she opened the bathroom door, she could smell cooking happening. *Thank God*, she thought mercilessly. She pulled on a pair of sweatpants and a t-shirt and padded down the stairs in her bare feet.

Phil was cooking breaded chicken breasts with spinach and, what smelled like plenty of garlic.

"That smells incredible. Any update on outside?" she said as she went to the window and pulled the curtain back.

"Oh, I didn't look," he said, following her. The bear was gone, the last two police cars turned off their lights and drove away off the street.

"Looks like the party's over," she said, sitting down at the island counter across from him. He returned to the stove and smiled at her.

"So, what went on today?" she asked, deciding she wanted wine and rose from the stool to the fridge door, opening it and finding the chilled bottle of chardonnay. She found two white-wine glasses in the cabinet, pleased to discover they'd been unpacked, and poured two glasses.

"Oh, I wasn't sure I wanted . . ." he started, but she smiled and set his glass down next to him.

"Sure you did," she said with a wink. "So, what went on today," she said again, delicate with her phrasing, being sure she didn't say *what did you do all day.*

"Well, after breakfast, I found this civil rights law firm in Bridgeport," he started, picking at the wilted spinach.

"Did they have anything?" she asked hopefully.

"I couldn't tell. I put a call in today."

He turned with the pan in his hand and used a white spatula to dish the chicken and spinach onto two plates. He handed it over the faucet to her, and she took utensils out of a drawer. They stood at the counter and ate. She wolfed the food down, cursing herself for not eating lunch.

"Hey, that's something!" she said with a smile between forkfuls.

"I mean it's not a job," Phil said bitterly.

She didn't know what to say. He spoke first.

"We'll have to see. I blindly applied to a few others today as well, just saw openings and tossed my hat in. A few of them might be a little bit less salary than we'd had back home."

That stung slightly. Was this not really home yet?

"Well, that's to be expected, I mean, we're out in the 'burbs. We knew that would happen, that's why we planned for this."

He nodded, but looked as though he'd been looking

somewhere else, or was nodding to a beat in a song she couldn't hear. Like he was listening to a different conversation—one she wasn't a part of. He waved his hand as he ate to move the conversation away from this.

"Yeah, so what did you do today?"

"Nothing. Just meetings and stuff. What did you do after you called the firm?"

"I unpacked a few boxes in here and took a nap."

"If it's what your body needs, you have to do it," she said, perhaps too enthusiastically, nodding while chewing.

"Can you just stop?" he said angrily. "Don't pretend like you didn't have an important day while I put fucking champagne flutes away and fell asleep."

"I wasn't, honey," she said, the last word with a hard edge.

"Like don't try and conflate our days as equals." He stood up and shoved his plate into the sink. "I'm going to bed."

"Didn't you just wake up?"

He didn't answer this and instead turned up the stairs, and she heard the door upstairs close with a decisive snap. She finished her wine, knowing better than to try and make him feel better when he was like this.

She finished his dinner and tried to do a little work on her laptop in the study, but she wasn't feeling it. She'd have killed for a cigarette, she thought as she closed her laptop lid, clicking the lights to her study off as she ascended the stairs.

As she slowly opened the door, she could hear his breathing, but she knew he was faking asleep; his rhythm was all off, she'd knew his pattern, and he'd slept all afternoon. She climbed into bed beside him, and tried to fall asleep, as her eyes felt hot with tears. Soon after, in the darkness, her husband lying awake beside her, she too laid awake, worrying about this man she loved, pretending she too was asleep.

AMANDA

SHE SLEPT late and awoke to the sound of the land-scapers arriving, the big rumble of the mowers and the calls to each other in Spanish. She lay there a while, the hush of the central air around her in the chilly bedroom. The boys must've gotten up and been out before her. This wasn't like her, she thought, sitting up in bed, looking around at her room. Gavin must've dressed in a hurry. Clothes were discarded throughout their room, hanging out of the dresser as if the armoire itself had gotten sick and vomited the contents of its stomach all over. Amanda rose slowly and proceeded to the bath-room to ready for her day.

In the driveway, she put the windows of her SUV down. The clean-cut smell of the grass, intermingled with the scent of the burning gas from the mowers filled the car. She paused for a moment before her back tires dropped onto the cul-de-sac and closed her eyes. She loved the smell of gasoline. Even while being cut, the grass was brown and burned, yellowing and gross. The drought was bad, she'd heard on the local news, post-shower. The local farms were struggling, and certain districts had minor water rationing, watering lawns had been banned in Glastonbury. They needed a rainstorm. The whole area just looked depressing.

Even at the grocery store, the normally big display of local produce looked wilted. She picked up one ear of local corn and held it in her hand, maybe something as "meat and potatoes" as corn would appease Gavin. The corn seemed spotty and brown; the green husks dented in places. It was a sad crop indeed. The writing on the chalkboard sign even looked neglected: *Organic Corn, Dudley Farm, Durham, CT*. She thought twice and put the corn back, opting for the shinier, non-local corn two bins over. This bin had no charming, folksy chalkboard sign informing consumers where it was from. Likely, she reasoned, from Mexico.

As she bagged four ears and dropped them into the child-seat area of her basket, she looked across the produce section to see a familiar face pushing a cart around the corner. It was Phil. She raised her hand to wave, but he was already around the corner. She thought about calling out to him, but he was too far away unless she'd shouted. She pushed her cart down past the produce cooler cases and around the corner, but he was gone. Where the hell did he go? She thought, wondering if she'd really seen him at all, looking to the left down an aisle with cereal and coffee. No luck, she rolled to the next one, crackers and oils, and spotted his gray t-shirt moving around the corner at the end of the aisle. She proceeded to the next one, determined to catch him.

She barreled down the aisle and heard a cart approaching. She turned away quickly and busied herself looking on a lower shelf.

"Amanda?" She looked up.

"Well hello there," she said with a smile and rose with a bottle of something in her hand.

"I thought that was you," he said, and she felt herself smile. Had he noticed her earlier in produce when she saw him? "What are you making that has fish sauce?" She looked up at the aisle header on the shelf above her, bearing the name Vietnam, after Mexico and Thailand.

"Oh, just for a stir-fry," she lied, suddenly staggering, her confidence erased away. She set the bottle in her cart, beside the corn. "You know, fish sauce and corn." He chuckled at this combination, and she chuckled too.

"I can't stop thinking about your pool. It was so great the other day," he said beaming. "I even said something to Carla about getting one." She waved him off.

"It's just a money and time-suck. I'm glad somebody at least used it. You should come by this afternoon, it's so hot out there."

"That would be great," he said, smiling again, and she found herself smiling back. Damn, he was good looking, his smile made her all warm inside. "What time?"

She looked at her phone in her hand.

"How about one?"

"Sounds great."

"Well, good luck with the stir-fry," he said, maneuvering his cart around hers.

"See you later," she said turning away from him and back to the shelves looking serious and listening as the wheels of his cart, and the squeak of his sneakers rounded the corner and out of earshot. She returned the bottle of fish sauce back to the shelf and headed down the aisle toward the front of the store and returned to the produce section to get a bulb of garlic.

At check-out, as she handed one of the few remaining tens she had left for the eight-dollar total. While the girl made change, Amanda looked down the store. Two check-out lanes down was another mother, another woman like her, yammering away on her cell phone while the two teenagers in bright store-colored collared shirts scanned and bleeped what looked like thousands of items: hundreds of liters of soda, bags of chips, bulk packages of paper towels and toilet paper. She heard the girl at the end trying to get the woman's attention, still engrossed in her phone call.

"Ma'am, it's two-twenty-three eighty. Ma'am?" The woman finally looked over and nodded, then fished in her big designer purse for a shiny visa—or at least, it looked shiny—which she swiped quickly, and turned away to resume her call.

"One-sixty-four is your change. Have a great day," the girl at her register said to her, holding out a receipt with a dollar, two quarters, a dime and four pennies on it to her. Amanda smiled at her briefly.

"Thanks, sweetie, you too," she said, tucking her

change in her purse and pushing her cart with one plastic bag in it out of the check-out lane.

At home, at twelve-forty-five, she blended a half bottle of tequila and the can of mix in the blender, putting two cocktail glasses on the plastic tray with the blue hibiscus flowers on it, again. She slid the tray into the increasingly empty refrigerator and took a magazine down to the pool to wait.

Sure enough at 1:02, the door in her gate opened, and Phil entered, this time wearing a red and white checked dress shirt over his black bathing suit. He'd changed since the store. *Was he cleaning up for me?* She wondered with a brief rush of excitement. He crossed the pool deck to her and handed her a bottle of white wine.

"Thanks so much for having me over, it's so hot," he said, briefly, but respectfully embracing her with one arm.

"Not at all, it gets so boring here some days," she said, setting the wine down and moving to the glass door.

"That needs a chill, but I figured since we've got no plans, we'd have a glass or two," he said with a smile. She laughed a little.

"I had the same idea. Go on, jump in, I'll be right back," she said, turning away through the sliding glass door and dashing to the kitchen window so she could catch a glimpse of him removing his shirt before diving headfirst into the pool. No such luck. Halfway to the kitchen she heard a splash. She moved to the fridge and slid the wine in, and removed the tray, returning to the patio.

"Frozen margaritas?" he called from the water. "This *is* a party!" She turned away and repressed a smile. She poured two of them and wedged a sliced lime wedge on the rim of the glasses. She walked one over to the pool and set it by the side. Again, his dripping arm reached out, but their fingers didn't connect this time. "What service," he said. "Thanks." She retreated to the chair by the table and sat down. She raised her glass.

"To the perks of being stay-at-home spouses," she said, moving the glass to her lips. For a second, she saw his smile falter, and but he drank anyway, and she realized what she'd said. The margaritas were sweet and tangy with the bite of the tequila.

"I'm sorry, I didn't mean to be insensitive," she said quietly. "I know you don't want to be at home all day."

"Oh no, I don't mind it. I just don't think I'm good at it. You should see me at the supermarket. There's no strategy, I wander for hours."

"You just need a list," she said, setting her glass down.

"Carla puts it in order according to aisle, so we go in a geographic pattern." Amanda smiled at this, wondering why she didn't do the same.

"So how goes the job hunt?" she said, extending her legs in the sun, leaning back.

"Honestly," he said, lifting himself out of the pool with his strong arms and sitting on the deck, dripping, lifting his glass and sipping from it. "Honestly, terrible. I can't seem to get any hits."

"I can't believe that," she said leaning forward slightly.

"Believe it. I have no idea why I'm having such a hard time."

She listened for a while as he went on about the places he'd applied, even some financial firms, with nothing. They drank, she'd refilled both glasses, and she lamented how long she'd been out of the job market, how if he was having a hard time, she'd have an even harder time. He seemed to agree. Suddenly seeming like he'd said too much, he suddenly sat up rigid in the chair and reached for the pitcher, now empty. Her face was feeling warm, and she rose to retrieve the bottle of wine from the fridge. Rising to her feet, the world was at an angle, and slightly fuzzy around the edges. She found the bottle, and uncorked it, bringing it down to where Phil sat, now wearing his shirt again. She reached for his glass and suddenly noticed it was a martini glass.

"Oh, I'm so dumb," she said, suddenly looking back into the house. "I forgot wineglasses." He laughed for a second and waved her away.

"This is great." She poured the pinot grigio into the two martini glasses. She saw him chuckle a little before lifting the glass to his lips.

"What?" she said with a smile too, repressing a giggle.

"People here are so weird about glassware," he said sipping from his. "Carla gave me shit for serving red in a white wine glass the other night." Hearing him swear felt so strange hearing his usually excellent diction revert to profanity and so forbidden and she giggled at it for a second.

"It is really stupid," she said, leaning back, drinking from her own. "Like who gives a shit about which glass a beverage is served in," she said, unintentionally mirroring his word choice. It doesn't make sense that that's part of the whole recipe."

"Right?" He said, laughing too. His laughter trailed off, and he looked out past the yard, up into the sky. Dark clouds gathered there, rolling in, big and purple.

"Looks like rain," he said.

"Good, we need it."

"Hey, what time ya got?" He asked, suddenly, and she realized his slang must've been alcohol-induced. She reached for her phone on the glass table between them and pressed the home button. The screen lit up briefly.

"Four-oh-eight."

"Yikes, I've got to get going, I need to make dinner with a buzz on," he said rising, slipping his feet back into his sandals. She suddenly felt a panic, she needed to get started on dinner herself. She rose, still feeling woozy, and moved toward the grill, cranking the dials and hitting the starter a few times before it finally caught with a little poof.

"Hey, thanks for being a friend," he said, turning to her, her hand raised. What was he doing, she wondered through the lens of her booze. Oh, shit, she thought too slowly, he was going for a high five. She reached her arm up, and he slapped her palm. "Here's to day-drinking."

"Thanks for coming by," she said, watching him nod and turn, dashing around the pool, and through the door in the fence, clipping the edge of the fence with his shoulder as he ran, with a force that shook the fence. She heard a muffled "fuck," from the other side.

"Y'okay?" she shouted over the fence, watching the sky.

"I'm good, we're good!" he called back. She turned inside to get the corn while the grill came to temperature.

ETHAN

THE STORM NEVER CAME. The clouds rolled over, dry, and pulled the sunset with it. Ethan watched from his bedroom window above the window-unit fan that hummed into the dimness of his room. He dressed slowly, pulling on shorts, a graphic T-shirt, and ran his fingers through his hair. He was still thinking about the accident from the other night, how desperate Tracy had been. He'd never found out what happened to her. He answered questions from the police for fifteen minutes after the accident, and then, he was left to furiously google for *fatality, route eighty, Tracy,* etc. No hits led him to believe she'd died. No news was good news, he reasoned. He checked his phone. He needed to get going.

That early evening, Ethan headed to the mentoring program summer barbecue, organized by the town youth and family services. When he was younger, he was in the program as a mentee at his mother's behest, it was how he'd met Neil. He smiled a little thinking about the nature of their relationship now. His current kid, Danny, was the socially awkward type Ethan would've been when he was in sixth grade if he hadn't played sports; much more interested in playing video games than making friends with the other mentor/mentee pairings. Mackenzie Gornick was a mentor as well, her mentee was a kid with ADHD named Caleb who could never sit still, firing from one activity to the next. He knew she'd be at this event, a mid-summer barbecue at the nearby state park to keep everyone in touch between the end and the start of the school year when they'd resume meetings with weekly regularity.

He composed a text to Mackenzie and waited.

What time are you leaving? He saw the three dots appear, her response in progress, and then her reply plinked into his phone.

Should be at 7PM on the dot. Want to pick me up? He felt his heart quicken. Of course he did.

Sure, be there in 10. That okay?

Yep.

He slipped his phone into his pocket and pounded down the stairs. His mother was on the couch, watching cable news. Wolf Blitzer was on showing the results of some primary election. Whatever it was, it was *breaking news*. Everything was breaking news, though. Nothing on cable news wasn't breaking constantly. He expected the banner across the bottom of the screen to read *Breaking news, Cialis commercial coming up next.*

"Heading out?" she asked over the couch.

"Yeah it's just the mentoring barbecue at Braywood, I'm picking up Mackenzie."

"Alrighty, have fun," she said, turning back to the news. He grabbed his keys from the hook and proceeded out to the Volvo. He took a second before starting it, gathering up the trash from under the seats, from the doors, and threw it loose in the trash bin beside the garage. He started the old car up, backed it slowly out onto the cul-de-sac, and drove it around to the Gornick's house. He texted her a subtle *here* from the curb, and moments later, the garage door opened, and she came out with a wave. She opened the door and sat down beside him.

"Thanks for driving, I just didn't feel like it tonight," she said, clicking her sunglasses down as he drove around the cul-de-sac again and out onto the main road. He, of course, wasn't sure why she'd rather ride in his banged-up ancient Volvo than her shiny brand new white Jeep Cherokee.

"Of course." They chatted briefly about the program, about the mentees, and pulled in to the state park and followed the balloons to the open area with picnic tables where several grills were lit, and a fire crackled. They walked to the middle-aged woman, Deb, the program director, and checked in.

"Thanks for coming guys," she said warmly, and they joined the other few mentors by the fire. "Okay, so you guys are on fire duty, the mentees and parents should be here soon. Don't let anyone touch the fire," she said seriously. Ethan tried not to laugh.

"No third-degree burns. You got that, Kenz?" he said at Mackenzie, and she rolled her eyes. The director walked away to give further instructions to others.

"Was that because my kid's a lunatic?" she said as she moved to one of the lawn chairs beside the fire. Ethan chose one beside her. "We should have brought a flask," she said quietly to him as the first few cars arrived, parents gingerly following their children toward the clearing. The kids all ran and intermixed, hugging and chasing one another, and the parents followed, slowly, looking around. Mackenzie's mentee ran right at her, she jumped clear from the chair moments before he ran over it.

"Careful around the fire, Caleb. How's your summer been?" she asked as a haggard-looking mother approached her. Ethan scanned the group. Danny, his mentee was nowhere to be found. Finally, a beat-up Honda pulled in, and he saw Danny and his mother emerge. The boy was overweight and wore glasses, looking around anxiously, and his mother, a tall, thin woman with gray hair followed him, nudging him briefly to keep walking.

"Watch the fire for a second," he said to Mackenzie, who nodded, not before Caleb tore off past her into the woods, his mother suddenly giving chase.

"No running into the woods alone, honey!" she yelled after him. Ethan moved through the group to the periphery where Danny and his mother stood. He stopped a few feet away and waved. The mother waved back, and he advanced, reaching his hand out to Danny, their customary, formal greeting, who gave his hand one shake.

"How's your summer been, sir?" he asked, slipping his hands into his pockets.

"Okay, I guess."

"Danny just got back from a week with his Dad in New Hampshire," his mother prompted.

"Oh, how was it?" he said, feeling a sudden rush of affection for the boy, mixed with mild jealousy that the kid had had a relationship with his father, where he never did and probably never would.

"Good," Danny said quietly.

"Cool," Ethan responded. "Want to roast a marshmallow? Go see Mackenzie over there." He pointed at Mackenzie over by the fire, who'd just yanked a stick out of Caleb's hand which was being used to whack another kid. Danny nodded and walked slowly toward the fire pit.

"Thanks for coming tonight, he's the greatest," Ethan said to the mother as they stood there.

"Of course. He just adores you," she said. He didn't believe her, but he waved his hand.

"He's the best."

"He really loves coming to these things," she said, something Ethan didn't believe either.

"Well, we love having him."

The program director approached for a word with Danny's mother, and Ethan stepped away, returning to Mackenzie's side to assist with the marshmallows.

"Where did you go," she hissed in a moment of quiet. "I'm dying over here."

"Don't touch the fire, Mackenzie," he said, smiling as Danny stood next to him, hanging his marshmallow over the fire as if fishing.

"I'm about to throw Caleb in," she whispered.

"That's definitely against the mentor handbook."

"That'd burn too," she hissed as Caleb returned.

"Mackenzie! Mackenzie! I need, like, four more marshmallows." She looked at his mother, who, seated at another chair, looked at her phone and threw an *I don't care* shrug.

"Maybe we start with one," she said, snatching the bag from the fireside before Caleb could grab it.

The event was only an hour, as the sun set, most of the parents and mentees had left. Soon just the mentor group and the director were left. They scooped up the trash, the smashed marshmallows in the pine needles, and popped the balloons. Ethan volunteered to stay behind and make sure the fire was out, and Mackenzie sat beside it too as he pushed the embers around, pouring water on it, waiting for the embers to cool. Her phone lit her face in the gathering darkness.

"Mike is being such a dick," she muttered under her breath. His ears perked up.

"What?"

"He's the worst. We're supposed to go to this party together later on, and he's not telling me if he'll pick me up or not." He felt himself gulp. They were going to a party together? There was a party he didn't know about? His exile had already begun.

"That sucks," he said, pouring some more water on the embers, still glowing orange as his own frustration began to heat up.

"It's just like, I don't know if he fucking likes me or not," she said jamming her phone back into her pocket angrily and pulling her hair back into a ponytail.

"Has he said he does?" Ethan asked.

"No, not yet, but we made out a few weeks ago, and I thought that meant he at least had a passing interest. I feel stupid."

"Yeah," Ethan said. *I know how you feel*, he thought. She sighed loudly.

"At least I have you to talk to. You're such a good listener," she said, putting her hand on his knee and patting briefly, just enough to establish friendliness. He felt himself go hard in his khaki shorts. He poured the last of the water to a stream of smoke and rose, dusting off his hands on his bare calves. She stood up too.

"Hey, do you want to give me a lift to Laura's house for the party?"

He couldn't say no. Secretly, he hoped for an added invitation to that party that never came, even up until she popped the door in front of a colonial across town and thanked him before he drove off.

Driving maybe too quickly, Ethan could barely contain his frustration as he pulled away from the curb and headed back toward Staniford Drive and home. As he turned back onto the main road, he felt his eyes grow hot. Here he had just dropped off the girl he'd been dreaming of for ages at a party with the rest of her popular friends, while he headed home alone, to do what? Fuck around on Xbox for five hours until he fell asleep? For a second, he felt pitiful; a societal reject. He slammed his fist down on the car door lip beside the window, and he heard the plastic inside crack.

Great. Fucking great.

CHAPTER 6

THURSDAY, AUGUST 14

NEIL
7:02 AM

HE'D DREAMT about the ocean again.

The first time, weeks ago, he'd dreamed about it, he didn't remember how it had begun. All he knew he was in the ocean, a vast, blue ocean, and the water was warm. It was a bright day, too, so sunny, and the waves were gentle and small. He was naked and couldn't see the shore, but he didn't mind. He wasn't nervous. There was a cascade of relief over him. He was completely alone, swimming without getting tired. The sun was so hot, and the water warm. Deeper, where only his toes could reach, was cooler, fresher water. He hadn't been to the ocean in years. He could taste the salt off his skin, and floated on his back, buoyed only by the waves.

He'd been having that dream more and more often lately. Even if it wasn't the same, the ocean remained. It was a perpetual constant. The night before last, he dreamt he'd lost Vanessa on a long, dotted coastline. He wandered along that same ocean; how did he know it was the same? He just knew. He didn't know where she was, but he worried she was in danger. He ran along the coastline, calling her name, feeling anxious. He even waded into the warm surf looking for her. He needed to get altitude to see where she was. He hopped out of the water and found himself floating, and he flew high above the beach, the clear water over the crests and troughs of the sand. From that height, he realized, the sand looked pinkish, an almost peach, and he coasted low over the surf, seeking her.

There was a house at the end of the point, a big contemporary structure, and he flew to it, touching down in the dry sand. He scaled the outer wall, that sloped down to the sand. She was in that house, he realized, that was where she was. He climbed up the smooth rock and his fingers closed around the edge of the deck and a breeze began. Suddenly his fingers felt fuzzy, like they were out of focus, like he couldn't grip. He felt himself being yanked away, his heart leaping as the wind whisked him into the sky, blowing him out to sea. Suddenly he couldn't fly anymore. He was thrown clear of the shore, to where he fell down into the pounding waves. The falling took forever.

He eased back into consciousness, propped up on his headboard, as his eyes slowly adjusted to the light. He felt like he fell for ages, and even in his pre-awake state, he thought the blankets felt like water, their messy curls and whorls the waves. He struggled to free his legs. He sighed heavily, rubbing his eyes and checking his phone. It was six. He yawned and slowly pulled himself free from the blankets and stepped onto the carpet. His head felt like he was still falling, this empty feeling, this delicately nervous inverted tumble from the sky. He drew in deep breaths and the sensation quieted. The dream was coming more and more frequently now, that ocean always seeming to be just below his consciousness, in the darkness, waiting for him. He realized now maybe what he'd dreamt last night was the first part of the dream, that he was whisked away by the wind and thrown far out to sea, plunging down with a splash, and that's where he started: in that warm ocean, swimming for miles without getting tired, not knowing whether he was swimming further out to sea or shore, and not caring.

He scrolled Facebook on his phone, barely taking in any of the images or the blocks of text, when he saw her.

They certainly weren't Facebook friends anymore, but a handful of friends they shared remained. One of them, a girl they'd went to college with had posted a selfie, and there, right in the center was Vanessa.

She looked radiant, her dark hair was long, and she was in a white gown, a veil blowing in the light breeze. People were all packed in around her face, but she gave that roguish smile he knew so well. He clicked on the picture to magnify. It was indeed her wedding. This mutual friend had posted a selfie, congratulating the beautiful Mrs. Larson—a new last name for a new life. The hashtag, #VanessaSaysYessa was so obnoxious and never the sort of thing she would invent, but obviously from a wedding party participant.

For a minute, he closed his eyes and remembered one of the last really good times with her, he thought back to a vacation they'd taken together some years ago. They went to the Bahamas and stayed at a big resort. One afternoon, Vanessa insisted they leave the confines of the hotel, and insisted they find a way to immerse themselves in the raw of the Caribbean. They walked down the beach, beyond the vendors selling beaded wares, past the signs and ropes marking the end of one resort and the beginning of another. They walked past lounges and chairs, rounding a corner and finding a seemingly untouched section of beach. Neil didn't want to tell her he could see a spire of a different hotel over the palm tree line off in the distance. Vanessa seemed satisfied. They waded into the sea slowly. The water was warm, just like in his dream. Maybe that's where the ocean from his dream originated.

They swam out from the beach just before sunset so they could take in the entire coastline. The sky was orange and pink in the glow as the sun slipped behind the resorts along the shore. Alone, out where it was deep, they treaded water, the gentle lapping the only sound. He remembered looking over at her, her hair tied in a loose bun at the back of her head. She was so beautiful then, her little upturned nose, her sharp-lined eyebrows. Looking at her was a sharp, pained feeling, the kind where he'd look at her and know it would one day be over. He knew he'd never keep her. This moment couldn't be sustained. He knew he'd do something one day that'd drive her away. Still, in that moment, he hadn't fucked up. Not yet. He opened his mouth to say something, and she turned and looked at him.

"Don't. Just don't say anything."

He closed his mouth like a gasping fish. He wondered what she was thinking, floating there, her arms outstretched on either side of her, her head pitching slowly to the right or the left as she moved with the waves. He missed that kind of raw sexuality, that breathless excitement, that delicate nervousness that any wrong move or line could end the passion forever. It did, of course.

Six months after the vacation in the Caribbean, it ended with her hurling a plate across the kitchen at him, and him standing there, feeling numb as she slammed the door and left.

The end had begun when she uncovered that he was a member on a few dating sites under another name. He'd thought he was clever, using a different name and a distant photo, but one of her single friends had matched with him when they both happened to be in New York for a weekend. He'd just never disconnected his accounts, he explained when she confronted him, and privately, he'd like the flirting. He met up with one girl from California once, when Vanessa was away. The girl, Kara, was her name, happened to be in New Haven for a weekend and they'd matched on some dating app hours earlier. They had fast, bad oral sex in her hotel room before she'd booted him out when her husband called.

Vanessa took all of his friends, too. That was his mistake, he'd realized. He should never have integrated their friendships like that. Like roots that had over-grown, they'd grown seamlessly into one another, their external relationships contingent on their relationship.

She'd moved quick, then, spreading the word of his indiscretion. It was the most expansive PR operation he'd ever seen. Even close childhood friends he'd run into felt weird about seeing him. Conversations were strained, distant. He'd text people, inviting them over, or suggesting to meet them at a bar, and they'd answer with things like *I don't know man* or *I don't really feel like going out* which after three or four of these replies from several people, he'd realized that they probably didn't want to know him anymore. He'd never make the mistake of sharing a friend group again, he vowed. If he ever found someone he wanted to be with for eternity, he'd never let them bond with his friend group. He deserved to own his own.

HE SLID OUT OF BED AND WIPED HIS EYES. HE stretched, feeling his head, curling his fingers around the back of his skull, pushing on his temples with the meat of his palms. It was rare he didn't wake up with a headache these days, but apparently, he hadn't drunk as much as he thought he did the night before. He was pleasantly surprised. He rose and bent over once, stretched his shoulders, his arms, and went to the shower to ready for work.

CARLA

12:32 PM

SHE CHECKED HER WATCH. She'd been waiting at the aluminum and glass computer store in New Haven for fifteen minutes. When she'd arrived at noon, she figured she could pop in, get someone to look at her laptop and head back to her office for her 1:30. It was 12:35 now, and she was beginning to worry if she'd get seen at all. When she arrived, she was greeted by a friendly teen in a blue T-shirt, the eponymous store logo the only thing embellishing the shirt, holding a tablet. He welcomed her pleasantly, she explained she was a walk-in to see one of their experts to look at her computer. The teen smiled warmly and added her name to a list on his tablet, and then waved his arm in a cavalier loop, telling her to feel free to look around while she waited. There were three other customers ahead of her. There was no discernible line, she reasoned, looking around. Maybe there was a vast, invisible line snaking its way through the store, corralled by the keepers, young people, smiling, shiny fixed smiles in their bright blue shirts, little pops of color against all the chrome and glass and blonde wood.

When she'd left for work that morning, Phil was still sleeping. He'd slept in every morning that week. It wasn't like him. He used to rise with her, get up, make breakfast. She'd read New York Times online, he'd have skimmed the headlines already, his knowledge of the current events of the day at that time a mile wide, and an inch deep. By dinner, somehow, even when he was working, he'd have read everything, ready to discuss Mohammed Karzai, or new sanctions on Russian trade. Not so much anymore, she thought.

Still, every morning for the last few, he'd slept in, and it wasn't like she was getting up at the crack of dawn either, her appointments in New Haven were after eleven usually, she shot to be at her office by 10:30ish, so these mornings were supposed to be leisurely. It wouldn't be like this once the school year was in session, she reminded herself. She imagined them making a big breakfast, western omelets, and drinking their coffee together, maybe sneaking back to bed for an hour for a quick fuck before heading out for the day.

Maybe it was the heat, she reasoned, it was tiring him out, and he needed more time to recharge. Even she knew that wasn't an explanation. She knew what it was, he was depressed, and in some small part of herself, she thought it was her fault. If only she hadn't taken this job in Connecticut. They could have stayed in Chicago, and none of this would be happening. Then again, she reminded herself, she'd still be lecturing full time at Loyola, zipping uptown and downtown between extra adjunct classes at DePaul on her lunch hours. It was exhausting, and this position at Yale was a dream, she still couldn't believe she'd gotten the job.

"CARLA B?" SHE HEARD HER NAME CALLED, AND SHE looked around for a moment, foolishly, as if there was a different Carla B. in this store in New Haven. She moved toward the polished blonde wood counter.

"What seems to be the problem, Carla?" The using of her first name constantly was weird, she decided, as she explained what her computer was doing, the eager expert plugging her computer in, hammering on keys and leaned on the counter with one elbow. He decided that it would have to be restored and reset and left over night.

"Overnight, like, I have to come back?" she asked incredulously.

"Yeah, as it turns out, we'll need to do some hardware replacements."

"I need my computer."

"I know, Carla," he began, and she struggled to not roll her eyes. "We should have it done tomorrow, but in some cases, it can take a few days." Even his language was delicate, designed not to upset her delicate consumer sensibilities.

"Great," she said angrily, providing her contact information and then all-but stomping out across the store in her heels. She'd come back Monday, she decided as she plopped down in the car seat and began the drive home. Along the way up the quiet silent highway, she thought of Phil home alone all day, and she worried about him. Never before in all their time together had he seemed so, well, lost.

Back at Princeton in undergrad, he was young and vibrant, his life was a never-ending series of social events, people clamored to hang out with him, the young valedictorian, she was shocked one night at a frat party that he actually wanted to talk to her. She was bookish but did okay. She had her share of suitors, too, she remembered, but nobody like Phil. The room was hot, and she was sure she was sweating. It was early sophomore year, a hot September, and the apartment was thick with pot smoke as she moved through the space and felt someone touch her arm.

"I've been looking for you all night," he said, opening with a wide, perfect smile.

"Like hell you were. You don't even know my name," she said, playing hard to get, but sure that her eyes were giving her away.

"Sure I do. You're Carla Woods, I was in your building last year."

"You were?" she asked, already knowing this to be true.

"Yeah, you lived on three-south," he said, correctly recalling her freshman year room.

"Good memory," she said.

"Do you remember where I lived?"

"I didn't even remember you were in the building," she lied, knowing full well he was on the other tower of the dorm, four-north.

"I'm Phil . . . Bishop," he said pausing between the

words, trying to extend his hand, but the crowd of people around them pressed in on them. He tucked his arm close to his Clinton '96 T-shirt and extended his hand toward her. She had to switch her beer to the other hand to shake it.

"I like that shirt," she said.

"I like the President," Phil said.

A year later, when that very president experienced the blistering heat of national shame for definitely having sexual relations with that woman, Phil shook his head at the CNN newscasters.

"Nobody's going to remember the budget surplus or any of the other good shit he did now," he said, scoffing and leaning back in his desk chair, and bending over the LSAT book again. Carla, feet away on her bed, her own book open, shook her head.

Returning to the car, Carla exited the highway and paused at the end of the exit ramp. She felt bad for being snarky, however light it might have been last night over dinner. She turned left, heading for their favorite pizzeria. She'd manage dinner tonight. She pulled into the parking lot as the sun started its downward slide into dusk and walked to the counter, ordering whatever large pizza they had that was hot and ready, and walked out with something called a verdura, something she'd later discover was covered in vegetables. She stopped at the package store beside the pizzeria too, and picked out a malbec, returning to her car with the pizza and wine. She drove home, wholly pleased with herself.

As she approached from the road, she could see lights on in the house, and she parked and walked up the path, and let herself in the front door, swinging the pizza box through the door as an unwieldy tray, the wine pinched under her arm.

"Phillip!" She called playfully into the house. A smell reached her nose; pasta and sauce. He stepped out from the counter, a dishcloth over his shoulder. He smiled when he saw her.

"I brought home dinner," she said smiling, and he beamed back too.

"That's funny because I've just finished making meatballs and sauce. I felt bad about last night," he said quietly moving across the wood to grab the box from her.

"*I* felt bad about last night," she said back as she handed him the greasy white cardboard and kissed his scruffy cheek. She did like that, she realized, his unshaven face, maybe this unemployment thing isn't that bad, she thought, and then, mortified at her thoughts, stifled that one away. Together they moved into the kitchen, and she removed the bottle from her armpit, and set it on the stone of the kitchen island with a clink.

"This smells good, and shit, it's hot," he said dropping the edge of crust he'd just lifted from the open box, propped open, the lid leaning on the faucet.

"Oh don't bother eating that," she said tutting and moving over to the pot of meatballs and sauce and breathing in the smell of the tomato and oregano.

"I can freeze the sauce. This pizza's hot and looks good."

"Let's have both."

They stood there, at the island counter for a few minutes, quietly eating without plates, smiling at each other's earnestness. After a while she opened the wine, and they drank it, they moved to the pot and picked at the meatballs in the sauce with forks, like an Italian fondue. Maybe it was the red wine, but she was feeling flushed with affection for him, and he seemed like he was thawing a little. He'd chuckled a little at her story about the computer store, about the weirdness of someone who uses the other's first name constantly.

"I just felt like I was at a twelve step-meeting, you know? Everyone kept smiling at me and saying 'hey Carla B.' Like, I don't know you!" He smiled and drank from his glass.

"I'd never noticed it before," he said. "And I've been in those stores dozens of times."

"It's weird, it's like some cult behavior," she said setting her empty glass down, and reaching for the bottle, strangely light. She held it up to the recessed fixture, and looked inside, it was gone. Phil yawned and moved to start cleaning up, he dug Tupperware out of a box on the counter and she watched him move. How she loved every inch of him, every flex of his arms, his fingers, and now, flush with malbec and worry about him, she was glad to just even spend time in his company.

"I'm going to take a shower," she said slowly. "Why don't you join me?"

He smirked, his hands in the sink full of soapy water.

"I'm going to clean up down here, then I'll be up,

I'm pooped," he said as she turned away and started up the stairs to the master bath. She got the shower good and steamy, a contrast to the polar chill of the air conditioning, and stepped in, relaxing between the wine and the hot water.

When she exited the shower to the chill of her bedroom, Phil was there, yawning and pulling a shirt on, before moving toward the bed. She stopped and re-tucked her towel. Her eyes fell as he put a shirt on. She was crestfallen. She wanted to put her affection to use with him.

"PJ's? C'mon. You don't want to fool around?" she said, crossing the space and sitting down on the bed. He laid back and lifted his legs onto the bed.

"C'mhere," he said quietly, and she moved across the bed to him. He closed his eyes and wrapped his arms around her, breathing one heavy breath.

"I love you," he whispered. She smiled and kissed his shirt.

"Love you too," she whispered back. She closed her eyes for a moment and felt his muscles relax around her, and soon, he was breathing rhythmically, steadily, slowly. Soon his arms released, and he rolled away from her, asleep.

AMANDA

8:25 AM

EARLIER IN THE DAY, as Amanda used a spatula to scoop eggs onto Kyle's plate at the island counter, her son, ignoring anything that wasn't on his phone, Gavin descended to the kitchen with a wide smile.

"It's a beautiful morning," he sang and reached over her head and opened a cabinet. She felt his arm snake around her waist as he did so, and he kissed her wet hair behind her ear.

"Well, you're happy this morning," she said, enjoying this moment of affection. Things hadn't been great lately—she'd be the first to admit it. But seeing Gavin in such a good mood was already improving hers. For a minute she closed her eyes, relishing in this moment. Everyone was home, everyone was happy, everything was in balance.

"I am happy this morning, correctamundo baby," he said, pouring coffee into his mug.

"Clue us in, what's the good news?" she asked,

looking to Kyle who was scarfing his food down now, still his eyes fixed on his phone.

"A hotel owner would like to meet with me at his resort in the Dominican Republic next week!"

"Holy cow!" she said aloud and embracing him, and he hugged back. "When should we leave?" He released her and looked elsewhere in the kitchen.

"Uh, well, sweetie, I don't think you should go on this business trip," he said quietly, grabbing his coffee cup, sipping from it and putting his meaty hand down on the counter. What was he talking about?

"What do you mean?" she asked, now turning to face him. Kyle rose from the other side of the island and picked up his satchel from beside his stool.

"Thanks for breakfast Ma," he said, still glancing at his phone.

"Hold on there, buddy," Gavin said, looking away from her. "Any chance you'd want to come to Punta Cana with me next week and stay at a fancy resort?"

"Sure. Can I bring a friend?" Kyle said flatly, looking up at his father, then his mother. She busied herself, reaching forward and taking his plate and sliding it into the dishwasher. Gavin shrugged.

"Yeah so long as you don't mind sharing a room with him, I don't feel like paying for two rooms."

"Great, I'll talk to some people. Thanks, Pop," he said, still monotone and looking back at his phone again. He turned the corner, around to the stairs down to the garage, and called back up. "See you tonight."

Amanda waited until she heard the door to the garage close, and the garage bay doors roll open.

"Are you kidding me?" she said turning to face him, trying hard to mitigate her anger raging inside. In just seconds, the delicate balance in the house had been upset. "I can't go with you, but he can?"

"C'mon sweetie, he's been working so hard all summer at his internship, he deserves a treat. Plus, what would you do all day while I was in meetings?" Gavin said, now looking at his phone.

"I'd go to the spa, or read, or occupy myself. I can entertain myself without you, you know."

"Yeah, so can Kyle, and probably less expensively than you can."

"You literally are paying for a second room you don't have to," she said, her pulse rising. This was ridiculous. Gavin set his coffee down, shrugged and moved to the doorway.

"I don't know what you want from me here," he said, as he moved to cross through the door. She couldn't hold it in any longer.

"Gee, I don't know, Einstein, maybe to go on your fucking trip to a resort with you. Not sure where I got that idea." He stopped in the doorway and turned slowly.

"What did you just say to me?" His eyes had narrowed to slits and she could see the vein in his temple pulsing, even across the kitchen, but she wasn't turning back now.

"You just asked what I wanted from you, I want to go," she said defiantly, putting her hand on the counter. He began breathing hard and took a step through the doorway, shoulders first. She stepped back toward the dishwasher. He was trembling and breathing hard between words.

"Don't you . .. ever . . . fucking speak to me that way again, or I will shut you the hell up. You hear me?" He pointed at her across the kitchen. She didn't respond but glared at his shoes.

"I ASKED," he bellowed. "IF YOU HEAR ME?" She suddenly felt a flash of panic. That was loud enough the neighbors could hear.

"Yes," she said, feeling herself shrink, feeling herself constricting, feeling her muscles folding in on themselves, her bones telescoping, making her smaller.

"Fan-fucking-tastic," he said and spun out the door, pounded down the stairs and slammed the door to the garage. For a minute, she waited, her hand on the counter, frozen as she heard his car start, and then back out, and drive down the driveway, waiting until she couldn't hear him anymore. When she couldn't hear him, she slowly let herself move again, putting the pan into the sink, shaking. This wasn't the first time he'd shouted at her, but it never got easier, she realized. It never didn't hurt, she never didn't panic, and she never didn't wish she could transform into a mouse and scuttle into a hole in the cabinet.

THAT AFTERNOON, AT PHIL'S HOUSE, SHE STOOD AT THE island counter and drank white wine while he made meatballs. It was another hot day, and her phone told her it was 105 degrees. Phil stood beside the counter with a big glass bowl of mixed meat and seasonings. He would pick up wads of it and throw it, cupped from hand to hand with a *whap, whap, whap*, as the ball took shape. Once he was satisfied, he'd set it gingerly down on a big white serving plate. He was wearing a blue polo today, that fit tight across his chest. He looked good, she thought objectively, as he wiped his hands on a towel over his shoulder.

"How many pounds does this recipe make?" she asked after a long period of silence followed by the *whap, whap, whap* of his throwing the beat between his hands.

"Well, I used four pounds of meat."

"Jesus, you'll be eating meatballs for a decade."

"I usually freeze some."

"Want a hand?"

"Sure," he said with a smile. She rose, pulling her sleeves up, and moving to the sink, briefly washing her hands, shaking them off over the sink, and then stepping to the side of him.

"So, like pinch off a decent amount," he said, reaching into the bowl, and pulling a clump off, setting it in his hand, fingers spread wide to show her. She spotted his gold wedding band. "Then," he said, squishing it, before whipping it into his other hand, "you need to throw it between your hands, so it cups, like a snowball."

"Like a snowball of meat," she said under her breath, but Phil was standing close enough that he heard it and chuckled.

"Yes, like a snowball of meat." She smiled too.

They stood there a while together in silence, just

forming meatballs and dropping them on the plate. She pretended she didn't notice how after she'd put one down, Phil would pinch off a little extra meat from the bowl and added it to her meatballs.

"So, Gavin and Kyle are going to the D.R. next week," she said quietly, to break up the silence.

"What for?"

"Gavin's meeting with a potential customer, and he figured Kyle could use a quick trip."

"Why aren't you going?" He asked, taking a step back.

"Oh, I don't know, it seems like a boys bonding thing," she lied.

"We'll have to have you over for dinner or something that weekend then!" Phil said almost too excitedly as he placed the last meatball on the plate, now a pyramid of spheres of raw meat.

"Yeah, maybe," she said, holding her hands up so not as to touch anything as Phil moved the now empty bowl into the sink.

"I am planning on enjoying some alone time without the two of them at home," she said, and he nodded with a smile.

"I feel like I don't get enough time with Carla with her being gone all day."

He gestured with his head toward the bathroom, wiping his nose on his upper arm sleeve. She moved across the smooth wood floor and entered the bathroom, rinsing the fat and greasiness off her hands, using some hand soap, and finishing up with a lavender lotion on the counter. She was almost surprised to remember that a woman lived here too with him.

She returned to the kitchen where he was stirring a pot with olive oil in the base. She returned to her wine glass and drained it, as he began dropping some meat-balls in the pot with a sizzle as they landed. As she watched him push them around in the oil, occasionally recoiling his hands and fingers from the jumping spits of oil, she thought how odd it was that his wife would be eating meatballs made by her, a stranger's hands.

"Maybe dinner is a good idea next week," she thought aloud. "I'd love the chance to really meet Carla, I feel like we didn't get a chance to talk a few weeks ago at the garden party."

"You'd love her," he said over his shoulder, with a spoon, pushing the meat around, not taking his eyes off the pot. "She's so snarky, you'd get a kick out of her."

"I bet I would." She moved across the kitchen and set her wineglass in the sink.

"Done so early?" he asked, now looking at her. She nodded and put her hand on his upper arm affection-ately, and patted. The muscles under his t-shirt were strong and solid, like wood.

"I should get on home, I need to figure out dinner for the beasts, and I have not been making meatballs all afternoon," she said with a faint smile, struggling to show her dread at returning to the house.

"See you later?" he said to her with a smile as she walked to the back slider and pulled it open, hitting a wall of heat as she did so.

"Of course. I'll see you next week." She tried to turn

her grin away from him as she moved through the slider, out across their patio in the glaring sunlight, and through the door in the fence.

AT HOME, LATER, AFTER SHE'D GRILLED CHICKEN breast, spending as little time in the heat as she could, she heard Gavin's car pull into the garage. She tensed up as she heard his heavy footfalls on the stairs and put the island counter between herself and the doorway before he appeared. When he did, he was carrying a large bouquet of flowers wrapped in clear plastic.

"Hi," he said slowly, his frame filling most of the doorway. His gray eyes looked tired, sad.

"Hi, what's this?" she asked, moving around the island counter against her will, finding herself almost pulled toward him with the sad eyes.

"I felt bad about this morning's unpleasantness. Here," he said, pushing the bouquet into her hands. She closed her eyes and smelled them. They smelled fresh, but she spotted a supermarket sticker tucked low on the plastic. She pretended she didn't see it.

"Oh sweetie," she said and moved in for a hug that almost lifted her off the ground. "It's fine, it's fine, I've completely forgotten it," she lied, and he held her close, and she felt him kiss her cheek.

"What's for dinner? I could eat a horse!"

ETHAN

11:04 AM

His mood was actually improving, he noted, as he and Mackenzie stepped out from the dusty Dorset Youth and Family Services building, an old white colonial house, on the green downtown. It was sunny, and for the first time in a few days, the heat was letting up a little. They'd been discussing plans for how to move ahead for the mentoring program for the fall, a group of teenagers scattered around the floor, couches in Deb's office, a dusty room with framed posters celebrating Toni Morrison, Gloria Steinem, and Maya Angelou.

"I could really go for a coffee," he said to Mackenzie, pointing at a Starbucks, the only restaurant chain in Dorset that had to get special zoning dispensation to be built, he recalled from his mother who went to the town council meetings. It was down the street past the green.

"Sure, why not," she said, sliding her phone out of her purse. She looked pretty today, he thought, as they walked in the crosswalks, past the banks, the library, the

CVS, the gas station, the little independent bookstore. They chatted about the kids in the mentoring program, about Caleb, about Danny.

They got in line in the counter, and in a wave of generosity, Ethan sprung for her Frappuccino.

"Oh you're just the best," she said, putting her hand on his arm, and then dug through her purse looking for a lipstick. They retrieved their coffees and sat down in the overstuffed squashy armchairs in the corner by the logo-light in the window.

"I've got to keep an eye on the time," she said casually glancing down at her phone. "I want to pop by the lacrosse practice this afternoon before I go home. Are you going?"

"No," he confessed, and admitted he declined the manager's position, without digging into his reasons. He found his mood deflating.

"No of course, well, honestly, you don't want to be connected with them, they're not doing so great in practice. Next year is going to be a gamble," she said, looking down to her phone again. "If I wasn't hooking up with Mike, I probably wouldn't be following them, honestly," she said coldly, her lips catching the green straw between her teeth and pulling. For a moment, he was fixated on her lips, and he tried not to imagine what they'd done to Mike.

"Yeah, no I gotcha," he said.

"They need to be faster, maybe? I don't know," she said shaking her head now. "Something's gotta give or we're not bringing home the state championship again this year."

"That'd be the second time since, since when?"

"At least ten or fifteen years," she said.

"Yikes," he said.

"Well, it'll be this year if we don't." She stood up.

"I should roll, I gotta get up to the field in North Dorset. Catch you next week for the meeting?"

"Yeah, sounds great," he said, thinking hard. If the team wasn't doing well, he wondered, should he want to even be associated with them? "Hey," he called as he caught her, her hands on the door.

"Yeah?"

"What field are they playing on?"

"Overlook Road," she said. He nodded. "Thanks for the coffee," she called, and she left.

GIVING HER AMPLE TIME TO LEAVE AHEAD OF HIM, HE slowly walked back to his car, started it up and made for the field at Overlook Road, driving slowly so he could slip by unnoticed. He drove slowly through the wooded roads, past houses and mailboxes, and pulling over to the shoulder and looking out the window below to the field. He could see his old teammates, and Mike, the tallest one, his shaggy hair sticking out from under his helmet. They seemed slower, seemed weaker, they missed throws and goals. Sure, he reasoned, watching from the safe distance, they were out of shape, it was summer, but still, in his years of playing he'd never seen them move so slow. On one hand, he felt vindicated, proud, pleased that without him they were suffering. *Serves them right*, he thought savagely. *Cut me and see what happened? You're slow. You're weak.*

He felt his shoulders and neck pull forward, a wave of sadness so strong he couldn't see straight for a minute. On great days and shitty days, he'd been there when the team had been struggling. He'd been a part of them. Their victories were theirs together. Their defeat was theirs together too. Even when they stalked off the field, cursing and swearing, he wasn't alone, he was among them, one of them, not off in the distance, watching from afar through the scratched windshield of his car.

He drove home and pulled into the driveway behind his mother's car, and took his phone out. He thought of Mackenzie again, and for a minute behind the wheel, he closed his eyes and allowed himself a fantasy. He grew hard. He texted Chelsea, instead.

Hey, do you want to hang out?

He walked inside, waved a hello to his mother and continued up the stairs to his dusty bedroom where the fan blew hot air in off the roof. Her response plinked into his phone. He opened the message.

Hey, Ethan! Good to hear from you! He smiled. He wrote back with a smirk, a hint of flirtiness.

No problem! I've missed you. He saw the typing icon and waited for her reply.

Of course. Can you do me a quick favor?

He was briefly wondered what was up, but wrote back quickly. *Sure, what's up?*

Her response fired back like a bullet. *Can you never fucking talk to me again? Can you do that Ethan?*

He felt his intestines freeze. What was that about? He recalled the sex they'd had, but he did remember distinctly ignoring her messages to clarify what it meant.

What are you talking about? he replied. She was typing again, and it appeared a second later.

You're already not doing what I asked you to. Each following word arrived as its own message, its own gray bubble.

Don't.

Fucking.

Talk.

To.

Me.

Again.

Jesus, he thought. She was angry. He wrote again.

No problem. Bye. The message wouldn't send, however. A red exclamation point appeared beside it. *Message Unsent*, it read. She'd blocked his number. Fantastic. He composed a new text to Kyle.

You around?

Yeah, just in the pool. Come over.

He quickly changed into a bathing suit and pounded out down the stairs, snatching his sunglasses from Target off the hutch by the door. He thought about Kyle's Ray Bans, and how his own sunglasses, while polarized and a similar wayfarer shape, weren't big enough to pass as the real thing. In a way, he felt like he understood them. He deserved knockoff sunglasses.

"Where are you off to, didn't you just get home?" his mom called from the couch.

"Just going to Kyles, back for dinner."

"Good, have fun." She returned to her book. He headed out the door and crossed the pavement. Waves of heat blistered off the cul-de-sac, and he ran through them, immediately regretting it. It was like a hot bath, and on a triple digit temperature day, it was a bath he didn't feel like bathing in. He entered the Holbrooke house, and was greeted by an arctic chill, a freezing ache that immediately went to his extremities. It had to have been forty-degrees in the house, but he loved how it felt. He walked through the house, and out the back door to the pool. Kyle was there on a brown wood chaise lounge.

"'Sup," Kyle said lazily, and lifted a Corona to sip from it, from the side of the lounge.

"Hey," Ethan replied, finding the other lounge near Kyle and taking his shirt off. He laid down and closed his eyes to feel the sun. "You got another one of those?"

Kyle pointed without opening his eyes toward the house. "Mini-fridge in the garage."

Ethan jumped back up and headed back in, retrieved two, and pulled the bottle opener magnet off the side of the fridge door to take with him. Outside he opened it and drank from it, it was cold and damned refreshing.

"What's going on?"

"Living life. You know," Kyle said.

"Chelsea's blocked my number," Ethan said, now eager to confess to someone.

"Cuz you boned and then friendzoned?" Kyle said without looking up. Ethan tried not to chuckle.

"Yeah, exactly that."

"I coulda told you that was gunna happen. What'd you reach out for a booty call and get yelled at?"

"Yep," Ethan said with a smile.

"Yeah, that's how it goes with the females. You gotta pretend you're interested after you bone if you want to again."

"I'm not like new at this," he lied. "I know that," he lied again.

"Well, I've got something that'll take your mind off it."

"A single, moderately attractive cousin?" Kyle laughed at this.

"I'd hit that first," he said.

"A cousin?"

"Depends on how hot she is," he laughed again, and Ethan laughed too.

"No but what I was going to say was, if you want, you can come to the Dominican Republic with me and my dad next weekend, if you don't have anything going on."

Ethan was floored. What was this? "What, why, yeah, of course! But why?"

"My dad has a business trip and he has to stay in this dude's hotel to check out what his security camera situation is, so he's bringing me along and suggested I bring a drinking buddy."

"Are you kidding? Of course I'll go!" Ethan exclaimed, now excited.

"Sweet. I'll tell Dad."

"Thanks man," he said laying back down. "Probably be able to do better than a cousin in Punta Cana."

"If not, I'm in sad shape," Kyle said, raising his bottle. "Cheers."

The boys clinked bottles together and Ethan relaxed. He drank deeply from his bottle and closed his eyes, lifting his sunglasses off his head, and reclining.

"This is the fucking life," Kyle said quietly, taking another sip.

"Yeah, Holbrooke, it is," Ethan replied.

Laying there, drinking, enjoying the heat in the only way it was possible to, he thought about the team, and how much he'd be missing out on. Already parties were happening he wasn't invited to. What if, he wondered, under that bright, blinding sun, what if he could find a way to become invaluable to the team? What if he could find some way to stay a part of the social scene, hell, make himself critical? He thought about the Fever, the little red caplet in his desk drawer in a plastic bag and wondered if he should take it with him.

The idea clarified almost suddenly, distilled and pure, and for a minute, he wondered if the beer was helping him think more clearly. What if he could get Molly, or as he remembered it was known in his TADAA classes, Ecstasy? What if he could be the guy who literally brought the party? He suddenly shivered in the sun at the thought of everyone at a rave, like something he'd seen on HBO in the dark, lasers and lights darting about the dark space, Mackenzie, and he, tripping, but so ready, their lips connecting in the dark. He could do this. Hell, Neil could probably help.

Above him, a fluffy cloud parted, the swirls separating and spreading out across the sky, and despite Chelsea ignoring him, despite Mackenzie not knowing how he felt, despite his rejection from the team, and all the other pressures, Ethan at that moment felt at peace.

CHAPTER 7

THURSDAY, AUGUST 14 — MONDAY,
AUGUST 18

NEIL

THE DAY before Neil tried Fever with Sarah, Ethan visited him again. He'd texted and popped through the door in the fence. Neil was waiting, sitting on the side of the pool, his legs drifting with a nonexistent current. Ethan staggered a little as he climbed up the hill to the house barefoot.

"Y'okay buddy?" Neil called, lifting his glass of scotch.

"Yeah, I'm good. I'm a little buzzed though," Ethan said, careening down and landing in the soft grass beside the pool, and sitting there for a moment as if almost surprised at how he'd gotten there.

"You wanna take a dip?" Neil asked, noting his bathing suit.

"Nah, I've been day drinking at the pool all day at Holbrooke's. That's where I did the drinking," he said, looking suddenly up at the starry sky as if he hadn't noticed it was there before.

"So how can I help you," Neil said, eager to move this along.

"Can you acquire . . ." He looked around suspiciously, and Neil moved his head backward. "Ecstasy? Like a lot of it?" Ethan whispered.

Neil was wondering if he was being pranked and laughed.

"I'm serious," Ethan continued.

"I believe you, but I probably can't get that for you. Coke, though, if you're interested."

"Nah," Ethan said rising, suddenly, his eyes upturned to the stars. He turned back towards the fence. "I should go."

"Okay," Neil said, surprised at this state of his former mentee. "Be careful on the way out," he called after the boy who staggered down the hill and gave a little half salute before disappearing through the door in the gate. For a moment, he sat there wondering, who did the kid think he was? An all-purpose drug-store? Of course he couldn't get his hands on MDMA, and in mass quantity either. He shook his head and climbed out of the pool.

THE NEXT DAY, FRIDAY NIGHT, HE OPENED THE DOOR TO his house to a wave of heat. The blistering solar radiation wasn't giving up; the temperature was a firewall even this late at night that cascaded over him as he greeted Sarah at the front door. She was wearing a tank top and a tight pair of dark jeans. Her red hair was down and long.

"Good evening," she said as she stepped over the threshold and he pushed the door shut behind her.

"Hi," he said, awkwardly extending a hand.

"I think we can at least hug, right?" she said, reaching out and he gave her a brief embrace. "Of course, of course." They walked through the well-lit foyer to the kitchen.

"So, where's the wife tonight?" she asked, looking around slowly, as if expecting an angry middle-aged woman to emerge from somewhere screaming.

"Utah."

"Utah?"

"They have an annual retreat in Park City every year."

"Oh, okay." He'd practiced his alibi tonight beforehand. She seemed to buy it, even though in his opinion, he'd delivered it a little fast, and moved in through the house.

"So, what did you want to try with me?"

"Wait right there," he said, rising and dashing quickly up the stairs, and retrieving the Fever capsules from the little bag. He had two left. He carried them down and handed her one. She held it up to the light.

"What is this?"

"Fever," he said, filling a glass with water, and walking over to her.

"Take it. I'll take mine." She looked at him mischievously, and he swallowed the caplet with his water first, and then, she, watching him carefully, swallowed hers drinking from the same glass, her lipstick leaving a mark.

"Now what?" she asked, putting her hands on the counter. He took the glass from her and dumped it out in the sink, leaving the glass face up.

"Now we wait a few minutes. Let me make you a drink." As he moved toward the bar in the living room, he was flushed with a brief panic. Could he drink and take Fever? He realized he couldn't worry about this then, he thought as he poured light rum into a shaker and lime juice, and a dash of simple syrup.

"What are you making?"

"This," he said, as he shook the silver bullet ferociously, the clattering of the ice loud and cracking against the walls. "This is a real daiquiri," he said, remembering it was one of his father's favorite cocktails. "Not like one of those gross strawberry slushies, of course." She smiled at him knowingly.

"I'm excited to try one."

"They're delicious, unlike those disgusting things. Like what is this, a fucking Carnival Cruise?" He thought back to the last time he watched his father make a daiquiri, in Florida some years back. He squeezed the lime in between his aged palm, measured careful pours of rum and syrup.

Her eyebrow raised slightly. "I'm going on a Carnival Cruise in the winter," she said, taking the glass from him. He immediately recoiled. He felt his lips pull back, and his eyes withdraw into an apology. For a second, he wished she was Vanessa, who would have relished in the brutality of this humor. He shook his head.

"Smooth," she said, smiling again, and reaching out with her other hand and rubbing his arm, a subtle sign he took as that this was okay. They moved to the glass door, standing by it, looking out to the pool, green from the light, completely flat. The filter was off, the surface an even sheet. He stood there a minute as he drained his glass and turned back to face her.

"Wanna sit outside while we wait for this to kick in?"

She nodded, and he slid the slider open, carrying the shaker and glasses outside to the deck. They sat and drank, draining both glasses. It was a hot night, and when she gestured for a refill, he reached for the shaker on the table between them, the sudden cold of the metal surprising him. He felt goosebumps ripple up his arm. That cold was so crisp, so clear. So clean. Suddenly his vision seemed to be comprised of smoke—everything was melting around him.

"Here," he whispered, handing the shaker to her. "Feel this." She reached out her hand slowly, and he watched her eyes flutter closed as she relished in the sensation of the cold. She slid her hand down to the bottom of the shaker and gently curled her fingers around its base. He felt himself grow hard. She withdrew her hand and stood up. He stood up too. This action, standing up, was so erotic, the air rushed past his ears as he stood, every step felt like foreplay. He felt like he'd been teased for hours.

"Let's go," she said, moving toward the slider door. Inside, the air conditioning rippled across their sweaty skin, and he felt himself shudder. Sarah pulled her tank top up over her head and unclasped her bra. He almost gasped as he pulled her onto the couch.

In the unfolding hours, they had sex in all manner of positions, barely communicating, their bodies seeming to know exactly what they wanted. She bit his wrist and his ears, and from his lips, she drew blood. They fucked on every surface imaginable; the hardwood floor of the foyer, the cold granite of the countertops, the tile of the downstairs bathroom wall, the carpet in the living room, each new texture an added sensation to their pleasure.

In the morning, when they finally collapsed on the floor in the living room, a winter quilt dragged out and over them, he lay awake, watching the sun come up over the hills in the distance. The Fever wore off some-where around six or seven, while Sarah slept. Finally, when his caffeine headache beat a drumbeat against his head, he slipped out from under the blanket and rose to make coffee.

On his way over to the island counter, he took in the damage; they'd knocked over a table lamp and flipped an end table on its side. They'd shoved mail; magazines and envelopes off the island with a ferocity, the paper strewn about the kitchen, the fan spreading the detritus, and he cursed the drug while he chased business reply mail envelopes from the Jimmy Fund down the hallway, blown across the smooth wood by the air.

When the coffee maker beeped, Sarah startled on the floor and rose, wrapping herself in the blanket and crossing to him.

"What the fuck was that," she said, her tone exasperated and fascinated. "It's incredible."

"It's called Fever. I'd been meaning to try it with someone else."

"It's so crazy. What is it, some kind of Ecstasy?"

He furrowed his brow and poured her a mug of coffee. What was Fever? Maybe it was a kind of Ecstasy, some kind of club drug. That was the problem with the black market, he reasoned. None of these drugs came with nutrition facts. He briefly imagined himself consulting what looked like a can of red beans, but what was really Fever pills in an aisle at the grocery store, checking the back of the can with the white and black rubric, nodding to himself. *Oh, it has Ecstasy, Coke, and Speed. Interesting. But do they have the gluten-free one?* He smiled at himself.

"Where can I get more of this?" she asked, leaning forward and sliding up onto the stool at the counter. "Would my pot guy have it?"

He shook his head. "It's really hard to come by."

"It needs better market penetration," she said with a smile and reached for the mug. "Can I get some water, too?" As he filled a glass, he thought about this; if someone could introduce Fever to the local population, there would be money to be made. His brain was racing; this could be the new Vicodin, the new Oxy, and he could get a cut of it each time it was sold. He chuckled a little at himself, at business-optimizing a drug. But Sarah was right: it needed market penetration.

She rose from the stool.

"Now where did I leave my bag? I want to check my phone." She peered around before standing upright and dropping the quilt. "But first, I need to pee." She stepped quickly to the bathroom door and closed it. He heard her phone buzz from the foyer and found her black purse dangling from the banister.

He wasn't sure what compelled him to twist the clasp and open the purse, sliding her phone out carefully. On the home screen was a handsome man in his thirties crouched down with two kids, one little girl with blonde hair and a boy with red hair. They had a basket of apples in front of them, a red barn and hay-bales the backdrop behind them. The Carnival Cruise comment suddenly made sense.

Overlaid was an icon for a new text message from someone named Jack with a heart beside his name. For a moment, he felt disgusted at having participated in her cheating, at her betrayal of all this. He felt dirty. He felt vulgar. She had to go.

He heard the toilet flush and he slipped the phone back into the purse and redid the clasp. He carried the purse out and set it on the island counter. When Sarah emerged a second later, he pointed to it on the counter.

"Found your purse. It was on the banister."

"Thanks," she said, digging her phone back out again, and reading the text. He turned back to the counter, back to his own phone. How to make her leave, he wondered, how would one make someone having to go home? He had an idea.

"Yikes," he said, looking at his phone, at the ESPN app.

"What is it?" she said, looking up with concern.

"Vanessa is back early, she just landed at Bradley. You've got to go," he lied.

Even as she rushed to dress, he didn't believe she believed him.

CARLA

THAT NIGHT CARLA and Phillip drove into New Haven for dinner. Phil drove the Audi, her car, top down in the hot night. She unstuck her thighs from the leather seat and reached for the air conditioning.

"Don't do that," Phil admonished.

"Why not?"

"Because we have the top down," he said, gesturing to the air rushing around the vehicle as they skimmed down the highway.

"It's really hot," she said and reached for it first.

"It's just blowing out the open roof," he said, exasperated. She angled the vents and leaned back, closing her eyes and pretending she was actually feeling it. He was right, of course. Phil tutted and moved over a lane.

"My wife, the climate change denier," he said with a chuckle.

"My eyes are rolling." She turned to look out over the car door as they exited the highway and rolled to a stop at a light at the end of the highway off-ramp in the

236

periphery of the city. A nearby diner's neon sign flickered, and a group of children shouted from behind her. She smiled and turned around.

It was five or six kids, beautiful brown kids, two on bicycles, about half boys and half girls, all around twelve. They had big loud laughs, and for a moment, she imagined their child among them. The kids turned left at the light without looking, and for a moment, Carla found herself briefing looking for oncoming traffic and seeing none. At the light, away from her, the kids turned down a street towards a residential street lined with trees and stoops, where other people, other brown people, people like her sat out to escape the heat. A woman carrying a pizza box out to the curb waved at the kids who, in turn, waved as they passed. For a moment, Carla missed living in a place with diversity, and thinking about Staniford drive, made her feel very alone.

The glimpse was brief though, as Phil turned right at the light, and took them down a street lined with commercial buildings, and then around to Yale. She avoided glancing at her office window, even though she knew where it was, as if avoiding a former lover at a cocktail party.

He pulled into a garage and parked, putting the top back up, and clipping the ticket behind the visor. She checked her makeup in the visor mirror, kissing her lips together for a moment. She gathered her purse and the light sweater she carried from the harsh air conditioning, foolish now she realized, and left it on the passenger seat. Her heels clacked across the cement parking garage. She and Phil crossed to the elevator and waited for it. Phil checked his phone, and she dug in her purse for hers. There was a New York Times news alert; protests were continuing in Missouri for that boy killed by the police a few weeks ago. She closed her eyes briefly as they stepped into the elevator and wished a silent prayer of protection on the protestors.

She felt the elevators whisk them upward, like being sucked up a great straw to the nineteenth floor, where the elevator dinged, and she opened her eyes, and once again, they were returned to the whiteness. A white maître greeted them just off the elevator.

"Good evening," he said somberly. Carla couldn't find herself to respond. She tightened her smile, and Phil responded, picking up their reservation, and following the man to a table for two by the window, New Haven spread out below her. How isolated it felt to be up here, in this ivory tower of whiteness, surrounded by other white people, the brown people confined to the ground below. This restaurant almost seemed like it couldn't bear to be in such a diverse city as New Haven. Instead, it needed to be above it, quite literally, to tower over it, to remind everyone that they were better. This restaurant would have fit in well on Staniford Drive, she thought. Her stomach rumbled as the maître pulled her chair out for her, and she briefly wondered if she might be pregnant. She felt her stomach and wondered what a daughter of hers would be like having grown up on Staniford Drive.

She'd probably have only white friends. She'd play lacrosse and field hockey. She'd be popular and beautiful, tall like her father, proud and unashamed in her blackness. She'd wear her hair in long, beautiful braids. She'd likely be valedictorian, and teachers and the principal would love her. But in a way, she'd be lonely too; lonely like Carla was. Surrounded by all this swollen whiteness, she'd have to deal with kids in history class swiveling to look at her as the teacher moved on to teach about the antebellum south, or the Civil Rights Era, or the election of Barack Obama. She'd become the mascot for brown people everywhere. She'd be asked, under the misguided guise of seeking her perspective, by teachers *And what do you think about John Lewis' transition from activist to Congressman, Ms. Bishop?* as if she was the local expert on blackness, as if she needed to be responsible for black people everywhere. Girls would touch her hair without asking, and she'd grin and bear it, pretending she wasn't uncomfortable, pretending she believed they actually thought it was so pretty. By the time she'd get to senior year of high school, it would drag on her like a dent on the hull of a boat, slowing her down, the weight of representation, the constant spotlight, ruining her aerodynamics, like a bent wing, the constant attention for being the different one. She could feel it pulling back on her as she tried to move forward in that school system. She'd be exhausted carrying the mantle, in addition to all the other pressures; juggling boys, and schoolwork, and managing friends. She'd cry at home, late at night, and Carla would listen, knowing she couldn't go to her, because she'd lived it too. She knew. Phil would be passive about it, too passive, proud of his girl, but feel out of his depth, slightly awkward about parenting a girl, deferring to her judgment.

For a minute, she actually wondered if they should even have a baby.

"You see that?" Phil asked. Carla suddenly realized there was an open menu in her hands.

"What?" she said, coming back to the restaurant.

"They have a steelhead trout on a bed of lima beans. That sounds like you."

"Oh, where is it?" she asked, just now actually reading the menu despite having stared at it for God knows how long.

"Entrees. You okay hon?" he asked, leaning over his menu slightly. He reached his hand around the wall-like menu, and she reached out and squeezed it briefly before returning to the menu.

"I just keep thinking about Mike Brown," she said quietly. He nodded.

"Me too."

"I can't imagine being his folks," she said quietly, feeling her eyes grow hot.

"I know," he said quietly. A waiter suddenly appeared beside them.

"Have we taken a look at the wine list?" he asked. Carla held the tears back and looked up at Phil.

"Oh shoot, no we haven't. What are you in the mood for?" He looked shaken seeing her glassy eyes and put his menu down, taking the propped-up wine list from the center of the table.

"I don't know, hon, what do you want?"

"I'll give you a minute," the waiter said, stepping

back. Carla sniffed, dabbed at the corner of one of her eyes with her napkin and then straightened her posture. *Okay not now*, she thought. She had to be okay, had to be fine. Not here. She couldn't not be not fine here.

"I think I'm having steak," Phil said, scanning the reds.

"I'll just have the trout," she replied. The waiter returned and they ordered by the glass, a red for Phil and a light sauvignon white for Carla and were left alone with the menu again.

"So, Amanda Holbrooke wants to have lunch with us on Monday. You're just doing a half-day right?" He asked, still perusing the menu. She thought for a second.

"Yeah, I think I have an eleven AM meeting, but I'll head on out after it's over."

"Good. I want you to meet her, I think you two will really hit it off."

"Sure," she said, wondering what this was all about. "What are you making?" she said, closing her menu and setting it down in front of her.

"Haven't decided yet. Thanks for being around, by the way," he added sheepishly.

"Of course. What's her deal?" Phil put his menu down now too.

"Well . . ." He looked around the restaurant suspiciously. "She's in this bad marriage;" he said, his voice low. "He controls basically everything she does. She gets given an allowance every couple of weeks, and like, he's really serious about enforcing it. I worry about her."

"You got all this from seeing her at the supermarket?" Carla asked incredulously.

"I mean, I see her a fair bit, because we're both home, uh, all day." He looked sheepish, but she felt bad for pressing.

"Is he dangerous?" she asked in barely a whisper.

"I don't know if overtly, but I think it's really skewing toward the abuse line. I've been kind of trying to nudge her toward making some moves, but she doesn't seem to be responding. She's told me all this offhand."

Carla nodded.

The waiter returned.

"Have we made some decisions?"

AMANDA

THE DAY GAVIN and Kyle left for the Dominican Republic, Amanda waited in line at the American Financial bank branch wedged in the corner of the supermarket. It looked odd there, jammed into a section of the wall like a pharmacy or a display of *Nature's Vow*—the chain's attempt at an organic health-food brand. She stood at the sticky plastic counter, with a pen chained there. The slick-haired kid behind the desk—probably only five or six years older than Kyle—waited on the customer in front of her, an old woman with veiny hands and saggy skin who produced a stack of bills from her brown wallet in a little white envelope.

Amanda felt jittery, nervous, like she was doing something illegal, and she avoided looking around the space, worried about looking shifty. She hoped her anxiety wouldn't draw attention. She resisted the urge to swivel her head and look up and behind her, to spot the black bubble of the camera in the corner of the ceiling.

The kid—his name-tag bore the name Brett—called,

"Next." She advanced to his window, and just now noticed how his tie clashed with his shirt; the shirt a mint green, and the tie, a bright blue. She felt endeared to him, this kid who likely didn't have anyone to cross-check his wardrobe, and she wondered and hoped he was just working for the summer, to return to school in the fall, not to waste a life here in a grocery-store bank branch.

She stepped up to the counter and looked around again.

"Hi," she said quietly.

"How can I help you?" the kid said.

"I'd like to open a credit card."

"Sure. I'm sure we can help you with that. Swipe your debit card, and we'll get started. She suddenly found herself feeling stupid; of course they wouldn't just give her a credit card, she needed an account with American Financial.

"Oh, I don't have an account open with you folks."

"Would you like to open one?"

She squeezed her purse tighter against her hip. Gavin had just left her an envelope. She had the full hundred and fifty in it. Why not? She was already here, standing at the counter trying to get a Visa. Why couldn't she just open her own account anyway? It was what Phil had suggested a few days ago when last they spent time together. She reached into her purse and withdrew the white envelope. It felt final. There was no going back.

"Yeah, absolutely. Here," she said, sliding the envelope across the counter to him.

"Hold up, let me get some more information from you. Your name please?" She provided her name, her date of birth, her social security number. All the while, that white envelope sat between them, bulged slightly. Brett plugged away at a clunky keyboard. It was beige, like the computers she'd used in the computer laboratory at UCONN.

When he asked for her address, she began to panic that the bank materials would be shipped to her house. Her mind raced. Where could she send these things? Suddenly the answer fell in her lap. Phil's house. Anything that arrived for her, he'd bring over under the probably believing it to be some error. She provided his address.

"Ah, good news, you're pre-approved for a line of credit for three thousand."

"I am?" she said in shock, almost so in awe she didn't notice that he'd taken the envelope from the counter. She was surprised. She hadn't had her own banking information since before they were married, before Kyle was born. So what, eighteen years?

"Yep, and I'm opening a checking account for you as well, with an opening balance of one-hundred and fifty." She listened as the counting machine whirred.

"Do you want paper checks?"

"No, no thank you."

"Perfect, we'll send your cards to you in about three weeks. Welcome to American Financial." He handed her a fat folder with information in it. The kid reached his hand over the counter, and she shook it.

"Thank you, thank you," she said quietly.

"There are some temporary checks in there. You can use them as you would normally," he said as she nodded and stepped away from the counter. She rifled in the folder briefly, removed the five checks, numbered 001 through 005. Those she put in her wallet and then struggled to stuff half of the folder in her purse.

Across the supermarket, she shopped in an almost haze. What had happened? Did she really just open her own checking account, and get her own credit card? The shopping cart felt heavy, and when she reached the checkout counter, she paid with one of the temporary checks. The concept of check writing felt so foreign, so unnatural, that she needed to feel the physical cash in her hand to know it was real, that she still had it. So she wrote the check for an amount higher than her actual total and waited while the machine processed and the cashier handed her the remaining one-hundred and twenty. She slid the cash back into her purse, removing the green American Financial folder. On her way out of the store, she discarded the whole thing with a crash into a trash can.

THAT AFTERNOON, AMANDA CROSSED THE STEAMING pavement to Carla and Phil's house with a chilled bottle of white wine, condensation beading down the sides of the glass. It was brutally hot, and the sun beat down in waves. A breeze was nonexistent. The air was heavy, stagnant. She briefly wondered how weird she'd look if she approached the house holding the cold glass to her wrists. She walked up the stone path inlaid in the burned-out grass and knocked politely at the front door, even though Phil had often invited her up through the garage door. Phil answered it with a grin.

"Thanks for coming over," he said, reaching for a brief hug, and for a second, she could feel his tight muscles contract around her upper arms, and she tried to resist the temptation to let her legs give way, and have his strong forearms hold her up.

"Thanks for having me," she said moving inward to the house, refreshingly cool—not arctic like her own house. Phil took the wine from her, and she crossed the space with an ease she was uncomfortable with. She felt strange meeting Carla like this when she'd spent so much time with Phil alone.

"Where's Carla?" she asked, looking around. Phil placed the wine in the fridge door and removed a large green salad.

"On her way, I think," he said setting the salad bowl down and pressing the button on his phone. "Let's find out." He tapped and slid and peered down.

"Yep, she's on 95 now near the exit. She'll be here soon," he said, clicking the lock button on the side of his phone and turning to the cabinet.

"You can track her location?" Amanda said, her eyes locked on the black screen of his phone. He retrieved three plates and forks from the cabinet.

"We can track each other. It's a thing we set up. It eliminates unnecessary texting, like 'did you leave work yet, etc.' Instead, I can just click her name and see when she leaves work, and she can do the same with me," he said. "Except all she'll see me do is go to the super-market and be here."

"No news on that firm in Danbury?" she asked softly as he placed everything on a big tray, three white wine glasses.

"They had a strong internal candidate; it's okay. I'll figure the next one out." For a moment she felt a pang of sympathy for him, swept away momentarily by panic that Gavin could be tracking her movements in a similar way.

"That's so neat though," she said, changing topic, nodding at his phone again. "What's the app?"

He gave the name, and she burned it into memory so she could search her phone for it.

"The only way it works," Phil said, almost presciently, "is if you both have it installed, so you can track each other," he said, slowly, annunciating every word.

"Good to know," she said, and meant it, digging her phone out of her pocket, and searching her device for the application name. The search turned up nothing, and she breathed a sigh of relief. She heard a car in the garage, and moments later the door opened, and Carla burst into the kitchen.

"Sorry I'm late," she said moving in, standing on her toes to briefly kiss Phil on the cheek "I was chatting with Jen, she was outside." Amanda nodded.

"Oh, I love her, she's such a sweetheart, and so funny," Amanda said, as Carla rounded the island counter to Amanda.

For a moment, as she approached, Amanda took in her whole appearance. She was beautiful, she now realized. Stunning in fact. She had dark eyes, and full, plump lips. Her hair was in a ponytail that slung over one shoulder, and as Carla moved towards her, she too looked her over, almost as if she was studying her. Amanda had to disarm her; in an instant she opened her arms and Carla looked surprised, but moved in, wrapping her arms around her gently for a minute patting her shoulders.

"Oh, it's so good to finally spend some time with you," Amanda heard herself saying, although she felt discordant, disconnected from her body in the presence of such a beautiful woman.

"Of course," Carla said pulling back quickly.

"Thank you so much for keeping my husband such good company," she said, and Amanda imagined detecting a slight emphasis on the word *my*. Her relationship with Phil had validity too, she thought.

"I should thank you for having married such a welcoming guy. He's been such a good friend to me these past few weeks." Carla was moving now around the counter, rubbing Phil's arm in a gesture of apparent affection, a gesture she read as a warning.

"He is such a good guy," she said, looking up at her husband sweetly.

"Don't stop, ladies," Phil said, retrieving the corkscrew from a drawer in the island.

"There's that ego," Carla said opening the fridge door and retrieving a water bottle. "Water?" she asked, offering one to Amanda, who shook her head.

"Honey grab that nice white in the door. Amanda just brought it for lunch,"

"My kind of woman," Carla said. Amanda reasoned, apparently deciding Carla had already intimidated her enough, she eager to now be friendly again. The bottle clanged on the plastic edge of the fridge door on its way out.

"I'm all about the liquid lunch. We can just pretend we work at Sterling Cooper," Amanda tried as Phil lifted the tray, loaded for lunch, and made for the doorway. Carla chuckled.

"Well, if it was Sterling Cooper, I couldn't be there. At least not until last season anyway," Carla joked, opening the slider for her husband to pass through. Amanda felt her stomach go squeamish; she hadn't meant to make a racial joke. Carla laughed, and Amanda felt the laugh echo up from inside her as they moved to the patio. Carla had understood her joke; she evidently was a fan of the show as well.

Maybe we aren't so different, Amanda thought as they sat down for lunch.

ETHAN

SUNDAY, 11: 29 AM

HE FORMED the plan the day before they left.

Neil probably couldn't help him, he determined. But in the Dominican Republic, someone definitely could. Googling from the desk in his bedroom, a piece of furniture barely used in the summer, dusty, he conducted research on message boards, and posts all over the internet. MDMA, as it was known everywhere, wasn't too hard to come by. He just needed to be careful in asking the right people. He could do this.

Buying it wouldn't be a problem. But if he could find some way to smuggle it back, he could pull it out at a party and become a hero, and, he reasoned, get laid.

He decided against telling Kyle. He didn't even like the lacrosse team, he wouldn't understand. Instead, he built this plan in his head alone. When he was done, he cleared his browser history, erased his cookies, and even uninstalled and trashed his browser, and went to retrieve his passport from the desk drawer.

. . .

AT THE AIRPORT, COMING TO GRIPS WITH REALITY, Ethan realized his Spanish was embarrassingly poor, but it didn't matter. At the resort, El Paradiso, Gavin explained, the staff all should speak English. He pushed this belief harshly, unflinchingly, as if it was a matter of political pride. For a minute, Ethan thought of his mother, intensely liberal, scoffing at people who said things like; *this is America, speak English,* or labeling places like Nebraska and Iowa as *Real America.* Gavin was one of these people, Ethan determined. Not only did he insist everyone spoke English in America, now he was pushing his view on foreign countries as well.

To rebuff the ignorance, Ethan thought about downloading one of those refresher-course apps on Spanish, to re-learn conjugations and whatnot, but realized he probably wouldn't able to renew his proficiency in the time it would take to fly from Bradley to Punta Cana. He shoved his phone back into his pocket, the thought of practicing quickly dispersing.

Gavin wandered off to find some a magazine and Kyle leaned over the plastic leather seating to talk to him.

"You know the drinking age is eighteen in the Dominican Republic, right?"

"Of course," Ethan said, knowing he was only seventeen. "You don't think they'll card, do you?"

"Nah, not at a resort like this," Kyle said, leaning back upright.

Gavin returned some minutes later and offered a waved Playboy at them.

"You want one?"

"Dad, Jesus, no," Kyle said, disgusted.

"What? Oh what, you boys get all your shit from the internet, of course."

"Really not super interested in talking about porn with my father," Kyle snapped, and Ethan held down a chuckle. It was interesting watching Kyle and Gavin interact. They had a strange relationship. In some ways, Ethan knew, Kyle wanted to be just like his father: wealthy, commanding, even big, jammed between the fixed armrest seating of the waiting area. Not having a father of his own, Ethan was unsure if he'd want to discuss porn with his, but he imagined talking about the values of printed porn versus the internet with his mother, and he shifted uncomfortably in his seat.

"The problem is," Gavin went on, ignoring Kyle's covered eyes. "Is it gives you everything. It's called the paradox of choice. The choices are overwhelming. But this, this is professionally done, someone spent time and picked the images, it really ups the quality," Gavin said, flipping quickly through. "It's like it's been sort of hand-picked."

"Curated?" Ethan offered with a smirk, to which Kyle shook his head and stood up.

"Exactly! Curated! Like a museum."

"I'm going to find a soda," Kyle said, turning away. Ethan pivoted to Gavin, hoping to get a smile from busting Kyle's chops, but Gavin looked consternated and flipped open his magazine.

"He's such a pussy sometimes," Gavin said quietly. Ethan looked away.

. . .

AT EL PARADISO SOME HOURS LATER, KYLE AND ETHAN stretched out on lounge chairs beside a massive pool flanked by palm trees. It was hot here too, but not like at home, Ethan decided. The sky was perpetually sunny, and the grass was lush and spiky, he'd noticed it along the edge of the path from the pool to their ground floor hotel room. It was a thicker cut of grass than the burned variety across Staniford Drive. His house, on the corner of Staniford and Cliff never had the same almost-hand manicured grass the other houses did, something about having the oldest and smallest house, his mother didn't feel like they needed a professional landscaper. It still made him uncomfortable; it was just one more thing he didn't have in common with kids like Kyle.

Here in Punta Cana, though, on Gavin's ticket, he could be anyone. Nobody here would know he didn't make the cut for the varsity lacrosse team; nobody here would know he barely had the grades for Central Connecticut State let alone a private university. Nobody here would know he'd only had sex with one girl, who ordered him to never speak to her again. He suddenly had an idea.

"Hey, do you think we should come up with like a story?"

"What are you talking about?" Kyle said quickly with a sigh.

"Like, in case we meet older girls, you know?"

"Uh sure. It can be whatever you want."

Ethan suddenly felt stupid.

"I don't mean like write a fucking cover story. I just

meant, be consistent, like we're sophomores at UCONN or something."

"Technically, I'm an incoming freshman at UMASS."

"How's being an incoming freshman going to help you with girls? That screams 'hey, I'm just a notch over seventeen!'"

"We are seventeen, Carlisle."

"No, but you know what I mean."

"Okay, so we're sophomores at UCONN. What happens if we meet someone who goes to UCONN?"

"We pick a different school, but okay cool," Ethan said, rolling away from him, trying as hard as he could to move away from the conversation he'd started.

THAT AFTERNOON, AFTER THEY'D MET UP WITH GAVIN for lunch, who spent the whole meal on his phone, tapping out emails, and trying to recall numbers and models with his eyes closed.

"It's going okay, though, Dad?" Kyle said across hamburgers on a patio by the beach.

"There's a fuckton of money to be made, bud. A *fuckton*."

Kyle nodded like there was a depth to these words, like they were some kind of pearl of wisdom. Ethan briefly pictured Yoda in the swamp; *a fuckton of money to be made there is*. He avoided a laugh by eating another French fry.

· · ·

AFTER LUNCH, HE DECIDED, WAS AS GOOD A TIME AS any to take the first steps in the plan. He shook Kyle off by saying he wanted to wander around and find something to read. He headed to the open-air bar at the far end of the resort. The bartender, a kid himself almost probably his own age was unloading glassware from the dishwasher. At this time in the afternoon, the bar was deserted. He approached and smiled at the bartender, who smiled back. He ordered a beer, Presidente, with it's almost Miller-High-Life flavor and waited. The bartender was friendly, and they chatted briefly, the bartender in broken English, Ethan, pretending he hadn't had as much Spanish practice as he did. When the conversation lulled down, he leaned forward.

"Can I ask you a question?"

The bartender smiled.

"What's up my man," he asked.

"Do you know anywhere where I can get some," he paused before he said the word: "Ecstasy?"

The bartender looked around furtively.

"I mean, I don't want to get you in trouble," Ethan said quickly. The bartender nodded.

"I call my friend, and I tell you, okay?" the bartender said quietly. Ethan nodded. The bartender slid down the empty bar and pulled a flip-top phone from his apron. Ethan could see him texting out a message and snapping it shut. He looked away.

A few minutes later, the bartender returned after disappearing into the door beside the bar.

"My friend he says he can help you, but it's eighty dollars."

Ethan nodded, wondering briefly if he should nego-tiate, and cursed his thinking. Of course he wasn't going to negotiate. He nodded.

"Great, that's fine," he said, realizing he only had a hundred dollars he'd brought on the trip.

"I go on break, and you meet me back here at four?" Ethan nodded.

"Thanks, man," he said. The bartender put his fist out, and they bumped knuckles.

AT FOUR O'CLOCK SHARP, ETHAN RETURNED TO THE bar, cash in the pocket of his swimsuit. His bartender friend was there, but there were a handful of patrons waiting. The bartender signaled he'd be a minute, and Ethan nodded, sitting down as if he'd order a beer. His neck felt stiff, and his spine felt like a steel rod had been run the length of it. Here we go, he thought, this was the moment. The bartender sidled down to him.

"My friend, I found your phone," he said quietly. Ethan was confused. His phone? How did he find his phone? His phone was in his pocket right that minute. He suddenly realized and nodded. The bartender waved to the back room, and Ethan, feeling really like he shouldn't have been there, stepped around the bar and into the tight back room.

The walls were lined with shelves of bottles, mostly rum, some tequila, and he found himself looking around, before he realized the bartender was standing in front of him, holding out his hand, a baggy with at least two dozen tablets in it.

There it was, the Ecstasy. Right in front of him. He reached into his pocket and handed the man four twenties, and said a silent prayer of gratitude for the power of the US Dollar. The man put his fist out for a bump again, and Ethan bumped once more.

For a minute, on his brisk walk back to the room, he wondered if he should have stayed and had a drink, to add more reality to his cover, but he was already away, up the elevator and in the corridor toward the door to his and Kyle's room.

He slid the key in the lock, praying Kyle was still out.

The room was empty, and the beds were still unmade. Housekeeping must not have come yet. He turned into the bathroom where he'd left a small bottle of Tylenol that he'd bought at the resort gift shop earlier for this very purpose. He needed to transfer the tablets to the bottle, then, dispose of all the Tylenol somehow. He got an idea and flung back the toilet seat. His hands were shaking as he unscrewed the cap of the Tylenol, and peeled back the foil seal, and then, dumped the whole bottle into the toilet. The caplets shook and rattled against the plastic like a maraca and landed with plops in the toilet water. When he'd emptied the bottle into a floating island in the toilet, he flushed, listening to the rattle as they were sucked down the pipe. He felt briefly dangerous, like he was some head of a drug cartel, flushing white powder and baggies before the feds kicked down the door. Thinking of the door, he realized, he left the bathroom for a second and put the do-not-disturb sign on the handle and pulled the dead-bolt over.

He then returned to the brightly lit bathroom, and opened the little clear baggy, how stereotypical it looked, and poured its contents into the Tylenol bottle with a renewed comfort. For a second while the toilet refilled and his cache of evidence was destroyed he felt bad for the in-house plumber, but he figured he and Kyle were leaving soon anyway. The plastic baggy, he realized he couldn't flush, so after taking the bottle of Tylenol and stuffing it inside a sock, and inside another sock in his suitcase, he stretched and tore the bag up into little plastic pieces. He put the pieces in the little trashcan by the desk in the hotel room with plenty of toilet paper to conceal it, and removed the bag from the trash can and proceeded out into the hall.

He took the elevator up six floors, and exited, looking around for a housekeeping cart. He spotted one a dozen doors away. He moved swiftly down the carpeted hallway, stopping at the cart briefly, the door to a room was open and two women were inside, speaking rapid-fire Spanish. He slipped by quietly and set the bag gently in the trash receptacle hung in the center of the cart, without being seen. He went down the hallway and took the elevators down, pushing the buttons for three different floors first instead of ground, just to "throw them off." He rolled his eyes at his own paranoia and returned to his room to change back into his bathing suit.

That night at one of the bars at the resort, an open air bar by the water with white leather furniture, they did meet some girls, three juniors from Villanova, but they seemed much older and much more mature and not interested in talking to Ethan. He almost understood. He was immediately intimidated and didn't feel like trying to pitch himself. His plot was weighing heavily on him.

"Dude, have another drink," Kyle egged, from beside his new best friend Brittney or Jamie, or whatever. Ethan shook his head.

"Nah man, I'm wiped," he said and rose from the stool. "I'll catch you back at the room later."

He walked back through the quiet hotel, the music from the bars along the beach pulsing along beyond the walls. He began to round the corner toward their room when he heard a familiar voice talking to someone else.

"Easy there." It was Gavin. Ethan, still around the corner, froze.

"Are you gonna let me in?" a woman's voice asked. Ethan dared to peer around the corner and spotted Gavin framed in the doorway, his back against the door, almost pinned by a tiny woman with long shiny brown hair and matchstick-thin high heels. Ethan withdrew and waited.

"Only if you're a good girl," Gavin mumbled.

"Oh, I can't say I'll be that," she said theatrically, and Ethan, still openmouthed tried to slow down his pounding heart in his ears so he could hear more clearly. He heard the familiar welcome *bleep* of the card key and the door latch buzz. He heard it lock behind them. Looking around once more, Ethan crept around the corner and padded silently past Gavin's room, outside which, he heard nothing, and then continued two doors to his own.

In his room, he laid awake a while, remembering the Ecstasy in his suitcase, trying to forget what he'd just seen and heard. Kyle and one of the girls opened the door an hour later, casting a blast of light into the room with whispered shushing. Ethan pretended he was already asleep, his back to Kyle's bed. He tried not to listen to what was happening in the next bed, wishing he was anywhere but paradise.

CHAPTER 8

FRIDAY, AUGUST 22 - SATURDAY,
AUGUST 23

NEIL

FRIDAY, 5:09 PM

ABOUT A WEEK after Sarah and he took Fever and fucked, Neil stood in his kitchen, thinking about what she'd said, about how Fever could be a thing in the suburbs. Almost instantly, he started thinking about its marketing potential.

It would need to be kept out of the hands of poor people, he determined, and such, it should be priced out of the range. He found himself sketching idly on a yellow legal pad he had in a desk he never used. They'd have to set a high price tag, and figure out how to spread the word, he would need to talk to his neighbors, figure out how to penetrate the social periphery of neighborhoods like Staniford Drive, start going to cocktail parties, produce the little red pills at the end of the night, when everybody was already wasted, offer it as casually as one would a joint. The only catch was, he realized, Neil didn't know his neighbors anymore.

He stood up and walked to the edge of the sliding

glass door. In the years since his parents turned the house over to him, his neighbors all had turned over, new people—people only a few years older than him—had moved in, settled down their debris and remodeled the houses. The only person he could honestly say he knew was Ethan, and even that was a different dynamic. With the others, he needed an in. For a minute, he wished Vanessa hadn't taken all his friends in the breakup, as if he actually knew his neighbors or had friends, it would have helped getting started with fever. She was, of course, the victim, he'd blatantly betrayed her—and for what, a blowjob in a Marriott in New Haven? Had it been worth it? Somehow, even with so many years between now and then, he knew it hadn't been.

He shook his head to shake the image of her, looking so happy in the selfie, beautiful, content, perhaps a little drunk, celebrating her marriage. Had she even thought about him once? And had it really been long enough for her to find someone else, date for a time, move in together, get engaged, and then married? The picture seemed like some evangelical Christian bullshit, he decided. Although, the relaxed look of her eyes only ever existed after she'd had a few cocktails. Maybe it wasn't so picture-perfect after all, if she still needed alcohol to look that happy. He returned to the kitchen island.

Looking up now, he'd realized he'd taken almost a page of notes about how to make Fever popular, and what revenue could be gained by expanding it. There was more information he'd need, he realized. He made a second page listing the information he needed; risks, side effects, and how much the caplets actually cost, as Tony had given it to him as a sampler. Tony would want a cut, of course, and so he'd need to figure out how to hide how much the revenue was so he could undercut him and increase his own return.

He found himself putting his business bachelor's degree to use as he developed excel tables and threw together a quick five-slide PowerPoint about the market and where Fever could fit in. He found himself laughing slightly as he tracked down the white plastic adapter in a drawer of his unused desk to connect his laptop to the TV. He dug the phone out of his pocket and composed a text to Tony, smiling, thinking about how it might display the word *wombat* on Tony's phone.

Yo, I have a business proposition for you. Any interest in coming over here to discuss?

Immediately the three dots indicating typing began, and Neil felt excited and nervous, as if he was texting his high-school crush. He breathed out. He needed a drink. The message plinked in.

Sure. I can do 7PM. Where do you live?

Neil tapped back a reply, and Tony replied with an *okay*.

He tried to contain his excitement. This could be big money. He could really use it. He thought about texting Sarah to celebrate, but he'd just seen her, and had booted her under the premise that his wife was home from her trip. That was the downside to sites like this; he couldn't just maintain a regular relationship with anyone. He had to pretend to be doing this covertly. He couldn't admit to feelings; he couldn't ask to see her with any sign of interest. He had to focus wholly on the sex.

AT SEVEN O'CLOCK PROMPTLY, THE DOORBELL RANG, and Neil crossed the foyer to it, pulling it open. Tony stood on the doorstep, wearing a dark polo and a pair of dark jeans with boots, his red truck parked behind him in the driveway. He fit right in with the neighborhood —which was surprising, given that Tony was his dealer.

"Nice neighborhood," Tony said as he crossed the threshold, looking around quickly as he entered, closing the door behind him.

"Can I get you a drink?" Neil asked as he led him into the living room, stopping at the bar cart, tossing ice from a bucket into a shaker with a clatter and adding rum and unsweetened lime juice.

"Nah, I don't drink," Tony said, looking around the place. "Nice house. Are we, uh, alone?" he said quietly, peering around the archway to the dining room.

"Yeah, of course."

"Cool," Tony said, pulling his phone out, and Neil watched as he held the power button down, waiting for the red *power down* text to appear. He shut his phone completely off.

"Are you really not expecting anybody to contact you?" Neil said, shaking the shaker, the clattering too loud for Tony to talk over.

"I don't need to be tracked," he said, as Neil

finished, pouring one drink and carrying it over to the living room.

"Who's tracking you?" Neil asked with a faint smile.

"Anybody can if you carry one of these around, dude. Anybody can track you. They could be tracking you right now."

"I've got some tin foil in a drawer over there if you're looking for a new hat," Neil said, pointing across the kitchen, Tony smiled painfully, unamused.

"So, what did you want to talk about?"

"Well, I have a proposition for you." Neil crossed the room to the armchair by the TV and tapped twice on the laptop's trackpad. The PowerPoint slides he'd made appeared on the TV screen. Tony sat down across from him, and leaned on his haunches, forward, as if interested.

"I'd like to talk to you about taking Fever mainstream." So, he began, clicking the pad bringing up the first slide. He began his remarks, he addressed the market niche Fever would fit into, it could be the new OxyContin or the new Klonopin. He explained his price points, reduced from than he would actually offer people, to minimize Tony's return. He explained his projections for demand. Tony watched intently. When he clicked past slide five, and the screen went dark, he stood up and stopped himself before he took a bow. Tony stood up immediately, and Neil wasn't sure how to read his body language.

"That's a bad fuckin' idea, man," Tony said, shaking his head, and looking around.

"What is, the penetration?"

"No, keeping all this shit on your computer. You know how easily the cops could hack you, and arrest you? You'd have all the fucking evidence they'd need."

"That's what you have a problem with?" Neil said, unable to believe what he was hearing.

"Yeah, and that this plan is a pretty great way to get arrested," Tony said, shaking his head. "They're watching you, dude. They're watching all of us, and now you want to roll out some campaign to get rich people to try Fever?"

"It could work. Look, I worked out all the numbers," Neil said desperately, clicking back two slides to a table where he'd forecasted social events per month, and projected sales.

"If we just charge people forty-five dollars per pill, we can turn a profit of—"

"Dude, seriously, this is a terrible idea. And you gotta delete those files, stat. Is my name anywhere in there?" Tony asked, his eyes now registering concern.

"What? No, of course not. You're 'supplier.'"

"Jesus Christ man, this is the worst idea." He began pacing towards the door.

"Where are you going?!" Neil called after him.

"That is not cool, man. They're watching fuckin' everything, man. I gotta get out of here." He put his hand on the door handle. Was this really happening? Neil followed him into the foyer. Something was amiss. He wasn't acting his normal self.

"Wait," he called, figuring he'd ask at least for a second while Tony was still standing in his foyer.

"What," Tony said, his hand on the door handle.

"Can you get some Ecstasy for me?" The second the words left his mouth, Neil knew he'd made a mistake. Tony shook his head.

"You gotta learn how to read a room, man." And turned out the door, and down the driveway to his truck.

CARLA

FRIDAY, 7:31 PM

ON HER WAY home from work that same day that Tony left in a huff, Carla noticed a collection of cars parked outside on the street and in the driveway of the Gornick house. She could see the paper lanterns strung up in the backyard from the garden party lit. As she approached, she turned down the volume on the public radio she was listening to and lowered the windows.

The sounds of voices and music playing wafted temptingly over the high-walled garden. It sounded like a party. She slowed down in front of the house, and she could hear the sounds of glassware clinking and laughter. There was definitely a party happening. She briefly wondered if she'd been invited and forgot. No, that wasn't the case; she'd remembered if she'd been invited over the Gornick's for a party. She circled the cul-de-sac and pulled in the driveway, putting her windows up as she parked. Something was up, that was for sure. Maybe Phil was invited by Amanda and didn't tell her, she thought darkly. No, that wouldn't do. It had to be that they just weren't invited, a concept which gave her only brief pause, more favorable than the other, she determined.

Thinking of Amanda, lunch with her had been nice. She'd grown tired of hearing about their near-daily conversations, about how Phil was worried, about how he was concerned that she was in danger. In meeting her, and eating with her, she found she didn't seem rampantly uncomfortable at home. In fact, she seemed rather comfortable in Phil's presence, and Carla wondered how much time they actually *were* spending together. The woman seemed to adore him, you could see it in how she looked at him, and Carla felt the need to claim ownership, felt the need to be touchier, more public with her affections than she'd been in the past. She kissed him in front of her, she leaned on him when she rose to get a drink. She playfully slapped his cheeks when he swore, trying to make clear her role as his wife.

On that front—mating—there was no progress. Her period two weeks prior was late a day, leading to a hopeful pregnancy test that came back negative. For a brief few hours when she thought her period wasn't coming, she was overjoyed. But, sure as ever, the test read negative, and she threw it in the plastic bin in disgust.

She walked into the house at a clip and opened the door. She could hear the TV on in the other room. It was cable news, and the host, whoever it was, was howling about something, some grave injustice. Phil was in the fridge, and he popped his head around the door cheerfully when he heard her approach.

"Hey," he said with a smile, setting a bag of asparagus on the counter beside the sink.

"Hey," she said quickly, setting her purse on the ground beside the bar stools. "Did you get invited to a party over at Gornick's?"

His brow furrowed. "I don't think so. When is it?"

"Now. Tonight. Right now," she said, pointing exasperatedly toward their house.

"Definitely not," he said, and he looked down at the asparagus he was now washing in the sink, removing the rubber band with an audible snap.

"Wait, Amanda said something the other day," he said looking up. "We were talking about Nancy, and she said we'd get clarity by tonight, and I didn't think about it."

"You didn't think to dig a little deeper on that?" Carla barked, annoyed that somehow they'd had a conversation without her yesterday.

"No, sweetheart I didn't. I can't cross-examine every person in every conversation," he said, shaking the asparagus over the sink and then pulling out a length of paper towel from the cylindrical holder on the counter.

"She was obviously referencing this party," Carla said, lifting one calf to remove her heel.

"I'm sorry I didn't pick up on it," he said coldly, and rolled the asparagus out on the paper towel, dabbing it dry.

"You could do a little more to keep us in the social scene, you know," Carla said, turning away from it hoping it would be the last word. She could go upstairs, shower, reset herself, and then come back and have dinner, and all would be waived.

"And you could do a little more participating in the social scene." Phil cut back as she placed her hand on the banister to go upstairs.

"What's that supposed to mean?" she said pivoting on the first step and calling back to him.

"I mean you obviously have disdain for these people, I had to basically twist your arm to have lunch with Amanda," he said calmly.

"You just said *these people,* so I'll let you determine who has more disdain," Carla said coldly and started up the stairs. He didn't retort. For a moment, as she ascended, she missed Chicago; the privacy of it. At least in Illinois, her friends lived all over the city, and nothing went unplanned, or uninvited. In the various buildings they'd lived in over the years, they'd always heard other activity, other people singing, partying, fucking, but never so out in the open, and so exclusively as here, she realized. The openness mandated a friendliness, a relationship, in a way, while everyone had their own full houses, there was a lot less privacy than in a high rise in Lakeview.

And why couldn't she fit in here, she thought savagely as she removed her earrings in front of her mirror. She had a white collar-job for chrissakes. She had a Ph.D. from an Ivy League. Where did the rest of these people go to school? The local state University system? Under her initial layer of thoughts was a darker current, something she thought but didn't want to accept. Was this really because they were black? Was it because Phil was unemployed, and she was the bread-winner? In this community, it seemed, both were equally transgressive. For a moment from her bedroom window she could see over the fence across the street to a cake with candles on the glass-topped patio table. It must've been John's birthday, and there were at least a dozen people there. She wondered if Amanda was there, if Gavin was there, or if he was back after all.

A moment of comfort came over her; if Amanda was invited, or if Amanda actually was going, she'd have made sure Phil knew about it, and she took comfort in this strange woman's obsession with her husband—at least it would get them into the social sphere. Once they were in, though, it was on them to become loved.

For a moment, she pulled open the closet doors to find a summer dress, something she could wear to the party. She thought of dressing in it and crashing the party, slipping through the side-door and showing up with a couple of bottles of wine, pretending she was invited and just late. She'd have to get drunk first maybe, to try and eschew some of the embarrassment she'd feel invariably when she arrived.

No, she reasoned coldly, *no that wouldn't do*. She didn't want to make any discomfort about her, perceived or otherwise magnified. She snatched up her phone and started a new text message to Jen, she'd gotten her number when she saw her outside the other day. For a moment, as her fingers hovered over the software keyboard, she was struck with a pang of nervousness. Did Jen really want to hear from her? Had she given her the number obligatorily? The conversation was light enough from through the car window, across the seat between them, Jen had moved closer to the car to talk to her, away from her lawnmower. Carla had offered a glass of wine and, ah, yes, there it was, Jen offered her number first. *Well*, Carla thought, *here goes nothing.*

Any chance you're around for a glass of wine?

She set the phone down, she wouldn't stand there waiting. She moved into the bathroom and turned the shower on, heat rushing, when she heard the plink sound of a text message arrive. She felt the water with her hand, turned it down, and wiped her hand dry on a towel and picked her phone back up off the bed.

Are you kidding? Hell yes.

Carla felt a rush of relief. Here was someone who actually liked her, really was interested in hanging out with her.

Perfect. My house in say, half an hour? She replied, and Jen replied almost instantly with the thumbs-up emoji. She smiled as she set the phone down. This felt good, building a new friendship. Engaging just with Phil couldn't be everything, she thought as she showered, dressed in a light red cotton maxi dress and descended the stairs.

She caught Phil's eye in the kitchen as she passed him toward the patio.

"You can't be serious, Carla," he said, suddenly freezing behind the kitchen island. "You can't go over there. Seriously. I'm not kidding." She held in a chuckle, but it found its way past her teeth, out over her tongue.

"Would you relax. I'm having Jen over, the woman

in the little house at the corner over for a glass of wine." She watched him exhale.

"Jesus. I thought you were going to go crash that party," he said, shaking his head.

"No. I mean, I'm annoyed we didn't get invited, but I'm really not looking for *more* time with Nancy and John." He nodded to this, and the doorbell rang, and they both froze in place. She still wasn't used to what that sounded like. She turned from the patio door and crossed the kitchen again, toward the foyer.

"Just chill out," she hissed as she passed him.

She opened the door to Jen standing, looking around at the yard, a bottle of pink wine in each hand.

"I didn't know if you preferred red or white, so I brought two rosés," she said, holding them both out for a hug. Carla moved in for the hug and briefly felt the woman's sweaty arms on hers, before they released.

"Well come in, come in," she said, standing aside to let her in.

Jen was awed in all the right ways at the cavernous foyer, was appropriately smiley at Phil, the handsome, charming husband, a role he was so good at playing. He left them alone to drink on the back patio.

"So, he's pretty upset," Jen said, setting her glass down, and Carla nodded, listening to this mom share her struggles with her son. "And the worst part is, I don't know what to tell him, like, he's a good kid, but I only ever was the lacrosse mom because it was like the only thing he was interested in. I'm worried he thinks he's let me down."

"What do you mean?" she asked, eager to glean any parenting tips, hoping and praying she'd one day have a chance to use them.

"Like, if he were more into school, I'd have something in common with him, but now without lacrosse scholarships, his grades aren't good enough to get like really good financial aid." For a minute, Carla felt for her, for this boy she hadn't met or even seen.

"So, it's what, student loans?" Carla asked, reaching for the bottle and filling both glasses.

"Yeah, but at fifty thousand a year, times four, he's starting adulthood with a mortgage and no house." She shrugged, and for a minute, Carla pitied her, in this tough spot, but she had Phil had done the student loans thing too, but they were pretty much paid off.

A glass smashed across the street, and there was a smattering of laughter.

"Ugh, boy, would I rather be here than there," Jen said and raised her glass, and Carla cheersed and felt her affection warming her from inside.

"I think my invite got lost in the mail," she said, looking down into her glass, and then back up at her. She wondered for a minute if could Jen handle what she suspected had unfolded with the invitation. She decided to take a risk and raise her eyebrows ever so slightly as she made eye contact.

"You have got to be kidding me," Jen said, setting her glass down on the table. "They didn't invite you?"

Carla shook her head.

"Sometimes she really disgusts me, because that is repugnant. Everybody was invited, even I was, but I pretended I had some things going on. They didn't want me there anyway. I'd rather be here with you and Phil any day."

Somehow, despite the warmth she felt at this swelling friendship, Carla felt worse than she did before.

AMANDA

FRIDAY, 9:31 PM

FOR THOSE BRIEF days Gavin and Kyle were in the Dominican Republic, Amanda found herself relaxing in a way she never had before. She'd enjoyed lunch with Carla and Phil, drank white wine on her patio, and even allowed herself a chance to skinny dip in the fluorescent pool after dark. She flipped the light off, though, using the firm switch beside the pump, just in case anybody could see. She knew that was silly, the high wooden fence topped with lattice sealed the yard. With the exception of Phil's door (that was what she was calling it now), nobody could enter.

She briefly imagined Phil sneaking in for a swim and catching her naked, falling for her. That was how the well-worn harlequin romance books on her night-stands always began; a woman, bathing, surprised by a burly and unruly man, handsome and rugged, though none of those adjectives could be applied to Phil. He was refined and careful, deliberative, he was smart and methodical, cultured and sophisticated. In her fantasy, he wasn't. In her fantasy, he'd skip shaving, wear an open tattered white dress shirt like the models on the covers of the paperbacks she'd read in her twenties. He'd emerge through the fence, bursting, she'd modified, instead of caught in an illicit swim, telling her he was leaving Carla for her, and she was all he wanted.

Not that she didn't like Carla, of course. They'd had a good lunch the other day. Carla was kind, and listened to her, and was obviously very smart. Amanda briefly wished she didn't feel so compelled to prove it, though. Every topic Amanda would bring up, it seemed like Carla had read something, or heard something on the radio about it. She seemed to speak at ease on any topic, something that lessened the load of conversation, if not wholly tipping the scales lopsided to away from her. She was fine, she decided, but not likely someone she'd be friends with if they didn't have Phil in common. In her fantasy now, Carla decided to pursue a job across the country, and Phil couldn't stand to leave Connecticut, a revised less tragic ending for her, she'd decided.

She was shaken from her reverie standing beside the pool. She let her bathrobe fall away ,and she stepped slowly into the warm, black water, gasping slightly as she immersed her hips, her stomach, and eventually her breasts. The water was warm and wrapped around her whole body, slipping in. Once she'd adjusted to the temperature of the hot night and the warm water, with only the stars as the light, she felt herself fade away into the darkness. She felt at one with the black, and maybe, in her dizziness from the wine and the heat, floating on her back, maybe she was dissolving into the water. She let her eyes flutter closed. She felt like she was becoming one with the water, and the sky, and the stars; a dissolution of her body, of her existence.

THE NEXT MORNING, SHE AWOKE NAKED IN BED, THE AIR conditioning kicking on, and her phone bleeping with a text message from Nancy Gornick wondering why she'd skipped John's fiftieth last night. She slid the phone off her nightstand and replied something about not feeling well, but hoping it was great. Gavin was due home soon, she realized, so she rose from bed, pulled on shorts and a t-shirt, and make a fast pass through the house to make sure everything was picked up. She hadn't really dirtied much—mostly wineglasses.

She made a fast trip to Target to purchase the next volley of college things Kyle needed, and in the sheets aisle of the back-to-school dorm second, wondering if the sheets she was deciding between, tartan blue and white versus navy, and she sighed. This was where she was now, deciding between sheets for a kid who wouldn't even notice the difference. She felt a sudden rush of anger; why would she even spend time thinking about the fucking sheets if Kyle wouldn't even notice? She threw both back on the shelf and shoved her cart toward the exit. That was the story of all of her life now, all the thought and effort for nothing. For nobody who noticed or cared.

When her son and husband rolled up ninety minutes later, and Gavin entered the house carrying all the bags for Kyle and himself, she came to greet them. Ethan

Carlisle emerged from the car, took his duffel bag and backpack, thanked Gavin, basically ignored Kyle and wandered back across the street to his house.

Boys were funny like that, Amanda noted, even in the case where they'd just spent a few days together, Ethan could stop and shake Gavin's hand and be effusive in his thanks, and then to Kyle, just mutter an almost inaudible "later," and be gone. When Ethan left, Kyle immediately took off in his convertible, saying he had to go run errands. Before she could even ask, "how was it?" he had backed down the driveway and out into the street. She followed Gavin upstairs.

In their room, she thought about Phil again and pushed the thought from her head. Gavin wouldn't like it, wouldn't like him, so she banished it from her thoughts as if he could read minds. For a moment as he unpacked his bag and hung shirts in the closet, his big frame blocking the doorway, she felt as though she'd cheated, like she'd been disloyal in her fantasies about the neighbor. She felt guilty and moved across the room to him and wrapped her arms as best as she could around him from behind. What did she need to be fantasizing for? Everything she'd ever wanted was right here.

"Oh, hello there," he said softly, still hanging shirts. "You okay?"

"I just missed you," she whispered into his back. He turned around and kissed her on the cheek, and then reached around her for the next shirt. She blocked his arm and put herself between him and the bed. She wanted him, for her, to reassure her that he couldn't have known her emotional and fantastical indiscretion.

Somehow, she felt as though he could tell something was amiss, something was off, and that all she'd need to do was have sex with him to reset things to normal.

"Want to lay down for a little while?" she asked, reaching for his wrist and pulling him toward the bed. He smiled and withdrew his arm.

"Oh, sweetie I'd love to, but I'm wiped from the travel. I do want to lay down and take a nap though," he said, hanging his next shirt. She pulled on his arm.

"C'mon, it can be quick. You know what I want," she said, tapping her lips briefly as if to indicate what she'd do, knowing at least it would communicate it to him.

He shook his head.

"Maybe later, okay?" he said, folding his suitcase over and stowing it too in the closet. He whipped his shirt off over his head and she briefly tried to reach out for his hairy chest. He moved past her into the bathroom, clicking the light on as he went. He stepped into the shower and began running it, and she stood in the doorway, leaning on the jamb, watching him. He was a big man; the top of his head was higher than the glass enclosure.

"So how did it go?" she asked from the doorway.

"I think fine, we had some good conversations. I should really write up a quick report for the sales team."

"And how was the resort," she said, tamping down the bitterness in her voice.

"Fine. You know, pretty standard. Their camera system is pretty old, needs a big upgrade. Big job for our sales engineers, honestly."

She tried not to scoff—as if she cared about the camera layout—but she nodded along as if she did. He shut the shower off and stepped out, toweling dry his thick calves and his thighs. She let out a low whistle. He smiled, but shook his head, and kissed her again on the cheek as he passed the doorway.

"Later maybe, okay?" he said as he pulled some gym shorts on and a t-shirt, and left their bedroom for the office off the hallway. She followed a few steps behind him but stopped when she heard the latch of his office door close. She was crestfallen. After a whole weekend, how could he not want her? How could he not have missed her physically? She shook her head, as if to shake off these dark thoughts, and proceeded downstairs to the kitchen.

Some hours later, after she'd packed more of Kyle's college things in the *staging area* as she was referring to it in a corner the living room, he came back, and Ethan Carlisle returned with his swimsuit and a bag. She watched the boys as they floated in the pool, and for a moment she considered offering them beers again but held off. They'd likely had plenty to drink in Punta Canta, and her latent jealousy, knowingly misdirected at them seemed like a reason as any to avoid offering.

She came out and joined them, bringing a magazine and laying down on one of the lounges by the pool. It was hot still, that unrelenting heat, and she believed the local news reporting a severe drought. They'd only recently accepted the lexicon in their local forecast. In the weeks before, while the blistering heat smoldered on, the forecaster with the big teeth had used the phrase *drought-like conditions*, an expression now completely replaced with *drought*. *Such an ugly word*, she thought as she crossed the lawn, the grass crinkly and so dry, she didn't like that hard sound on the *ow* surrounded in harsh consonants. The word befit the definition, equally terrible.

Out at the pool, where the boys floated separately on their inflatable rafts, she thought back on when she was a teenager, how she'd lose her mind over a boy like Ethan, the forbidden sensuality of youth. She looked at Ethan's full lips. He was a handsome boy, she thought. He was growing older too, becoming a man, the stringiness of his arm muscles the herald of his encroaching manhood. He probably got lots of girls. She returned inside to avoid getting a sunburn, opened a bottle of white wine, and poured herself a glass.

THAT NIGHT AFTER DINNER, KYLE PROMPTLY VANISHED because he was *going out*—to where, she didn't have the firmness or precedence to ask. She made dinner with a buzz, grilled chicken, still drinking the white wine, serving the breasts on a bed of spinach with a side of mixed rice. Gavin too rose from the dinner table early, explaining he was meeting some of his buddies from the police at Reginald's, a bar downtown. She briefly thought about joining them, but decided against it. She didn't feel like sitting to the side, the only wife there as these flabby men—like Randy, his old partner, whose fat rolls hung off both sides of the chair—greeted her with a hello hug that lasted just a second too long.

She did a load of laundry—Gavin's from his travels —and opened a text to Nancy but remembered she was away overnight for further celebration of John's fiftieth and put her phone down. She thought about texting Phil, but Gavin was just down in town drinking and she shuddered at the thought of him catching her entertaining in his absence, and especially the black guy. She worried about him finding out they'd been hanging out, what happened then? How would she finesse that one? She'd probably never get to see him again. She shook her head as she folded Gavin's underwear and sighed loudly. There was something so grating about this chore, washing the dirty fabric that rubbed against her husband's sweaty crotch. Was this all she was left with now?

At nine o'clock, she was alone in the house and had moved onto the next bottle, another white, a Sancerre. She sat out back on the patio in the gathering darkness by the pool, drinking from the bottle. She stared into the pool as if a gazing into a crystal ball. Could the future be discerned by the pattern in which the leaves traced the edge of the pool, like tea leaves? She wasn't convinced it couldn't be.

SHE WAS OUT THERE WHEN SHE HEARD GAVIN COME home at eleven, and she went to greet him, kissing him long on the lips. He sloppily patted her on the shoulder, and also drunk, trudged up the stairs and keeled over on their bed, the center pegs creaking. For a minute there, she waited for him to move or to acknowledge her again. He didn't.

She returned to the kitchen. In the darkness, she moved slowly, her vision was slanting. The house was silent but for the hush of the air conditioning. She heard the slider door open, and her head turned slowly, hoping, praying it was Phil.

It wasn't.

It was Ethan Carlisle standing there, looking crazed. His eyes were wild, and he was breathing heavy. She took in his shape, he nearly filled the slider door, and for a second in the darkness, he could have been anyone, any man, any person.

"Ethan, what's up?" she said, crossing the space to him, her hand on the high stool to the island for stability. She could hear her words slur on their exit. She bit down on the words, had to make them line up, had to make them fall into place and be pronounced correctly.

At first, he didn't say anything. He looked around the kitchen, his eyes wide. A thin droplet of sweat rolled down his forehead and dripped off his eyebrow onto the wood floor. He didn't seem to notice.

"My . . . my," he started, "my bag. I left my bag here," he said slowly and with an audible gulp. She nodded, likely with too much force, and retrieved the black drawstring bag from the corner between the wall and the counter. When she turned around, he was nearer to her, watching her.

"You know," he said quietly. "Gavin cheated on you in the D.R."

The words barely registered an impact. It was like a

droplet somewhere in the ocean, creating a tidal wave across the planet. The information crashed like rolling waves. How could this happen?

Suddenly, she knew in the way she'd always known. It made sense. It was expected. This was why he'd left without her. This is why he took Kyle instead. This was what happened. She felt numb all over. She didn't cry, her eyes didn't feel hot, she just felt fire; flaming, raging, fire. She could feel her own muscles tightening and clenching. She would get retribution, she decided. Somehow.

"Here." She handed the bag to him, ignoring momentarily what he'd said, and he reached out slowly, his hand touching hers as he accepted the puckered mouth of the drawstring knapsack. They stood there a moment, and she could feel the sweat on his skin, on his hand, on his fingers, and she imagined licking them, salty. Briefly, she imagined fucking him to punish Gavin, to even the score.

Then as if exemplifying her fantasy, she felt him pull her to him, and he kissed her, and she found herself pulled into the kiss. It was long and slow, and powerful like a crashing wave. She pulled back, astonished, but God did she want it. She wanted it so badly. She let herself be taken with it; she hadn't been kissed like this in a long time. She kissed back, and she felt his muscles under his shirt. She pulled his shirt off over his head, his chest was hard too, and with a small copse of budding chest hair. He smelled of youth, of raw sex, of raw humanity, harsh animal sexuality. She wanted him, and he kissed her again, picking her up and setting her on the island counter, the cold granite under her thighs. She pulled her shorts down and fumbled with his belt, undoing his own shorts, reaching in the forbidden all she wanted. His fingers traveled between her legs, and she gasped, clasping her hand over her mouth, praying Gavin wouldn't hear.

ETHAN

SOME HOURS BEFORE, after he left the pool at Holbrooke's, he returned home. His mother was out, and Ethan took a shower to wash off the chlorine. His skin felt tight from the sun, and he knew he was in the pre-sunburn stages. He'd been feeling a little bit better about himself as of late, no doubt related to his imminent heroism on the lacrosse team. He left his phone ringer on while he showered, waiting for the text to tell him what time the party was underway at the Gornick's. Mackenzie's parents had gone away overnight for her dad's birthday, and she was having the entire lacrosse team over. Ethan had already tried to talk Kyle into going, but he had a competing party with some friends from work he'd rather hang out with.

At nine, he went downstairs and found an old bottle of merlot from the back of the pantry cupboard, definitely his mothers, purchased a long time ago and long forgotten. He slipped this into his big zippered backpack alongside the clattering big plastic bottle of Tylenol, or as he knew, Ecstasy. Dressed in a graphic T-shirt and a pair of khaki shorts, he was ready. He stopped at his door on the way out and thought about it, wondering if he should bring that caplet of Fever in case the opportunity arose, and he slipped the little bag in his pocket beside his phone. He crossed the street and walked down the evenly paved street to the Gornick's house, letting himself in the front door, which was open.

The wave of noise reached him almost immediately, a cascade of sound. The house was packed with people. It had to be most of his class from high school: jammed in the kitchen, sitting on the countertops, on the couches, leaning against the walls in the narrow hallway between the kitchen and foyer. He sought out Mackenzie and found her sitting on the hearth of the fireplace in the living room, surrounded by a small crowd of girls. He crossed to her, and she rose to greet him, her arms outstretched.

"You came!" she cried and hugged him briefly. He was surprised at this contact, but didn't reject it, and she pulled back. "You missed an incident at mentoring the other day. Danny and Caleb ended up actually physically fighting. Deb and I had to pull them off each other." Ethan pulled his head back, looking concerned. He set his backpack down and unzipped it, reaching in for the bottle of merlot.

"Oh, look at you bringing wine. So classy," she said, taking the wine from him and leading him back into the kitchen. "So, we had to separate them and call parents," she said, sliding sideways as they scooted through two girls from his pre-calc class the year prior, chatting.

Ethan swung the now-empty backpack back onto his shoulders.

"Jesus," he said as Mackenzie set the bottle down on the countertop with a clink.

"Hey, is Mike here?" he asked, peering around. He had to give this to Mike, the captain, so he'd remember to include him, so that he'd owe Ethan for helping make the sickest party of the summer. She nodded and rolled her eyes a little.

"I think he's out back smoking, I don't know," she said dismissively, pointing out through the slider to where a small group of kids stood. He wondered if they'd stopped hooking up, and briefly, he felt a rush of opportunity. Maybe if he could play his cards right . . .

"Perfect, thanks." He thought about that caplet of Fever. Maybe he should take it. He moved around her, still wearing his backpack, to the little bathroom and shut the door behind him. He dug in his pocket beside his phone and withdrew the pill. Beside the sink were little paper cups for mouthwash, and he put the pill on his tongue, swallowing it with one gulp of water. Now, to deal with Mike. He left the bathroom and headed out to the slider to the backyard. It was dark out there except for the bright blue glow from the pool light.

He pulled the slider open and was immediately greeted by the smell of pot. He slid it shut behind him and approached the circle of mostly boys, trying to reduce the swagger in his step.

"Hey, Mike," he said, and Mike turned around, handing off a joint to the next person.

"Carlisle. Hey."

Ethan looked around, as if it was illicit, the circle closing behind him, and Mike looking back wistfully. Ethan wished he could do this alone, but he'd never get Mike to go somewhere with him alone for a minute.

"I brought something to help get this night turnt," Ethan said, kicking himself for saying something as stupid as turnt. He took his backpack off, set it down and reached in for the bottle of Tylenol. He could hear the group of kids go silent, listening. The pills rattled as he lifted the bottle out of the bag and held it out to him. Mike looked around, confused.

"Is this some kind of weird joke?" he asked, looking around him to the surrounding people.

"What? No." He suddenly realized how ridiculous he looked, standing there holding out a bottle of Tylenol.

"This isn't Tylenol," he said quietly, embarrassed.

"Good, because I think I have some," Mike cut him off and the kids laughed.

"It's Ecstasy." The circle went quiet and they moved slowly to turn and look.

"What are you talking about?" Mike said, taking the bottle and pushing down on the cap and unscrewing to open the child-locked bottle. He peered inside, shaking the bottle slightly.

"That's Molly," Ethan said low, drawing in a breath for a speech he'd prepared all morning in his head. "I thought we could get this party started," he said with what he hoped was a confident grin.

"How did you, where did—" Mike began, his look changing from confusion to astonishment.

"I was in the D.R. over the weekend, and it's basically everywhere," Ethan said. "I just figured I'd do my part to help kick off this year right, you know?"

The circle was silent.

"Is this some kind of trick because you didn't make the cut, because I had nothing to do with that," he said, reaching in with his meaty fingers and withdrawing one tablet, and trying to catch it in the light from inside. The tablet was white and had a symbol printed cleanly on one side.

"Why are you doing this?" Mike began dropping the tablet back in, but his words faltered off as he realized why he was doing it.

"Because," Ethan said, finding it somewhere inside him to speak the truth. "This is our last year, we've gotta live this up as long as we can," he said, emphasizing the we, how lonely he felt. We, he thought. We can live this up. This is something I can participate in. "Because like, we're all outta here in nine months," he said quietly as the people around them began to return to their circle and the smell of pot. Mike stood up straighter and looked around at the people watching.

"Yeah, okay, thanks Carlisle," he said, stepping back. "Can you do me a favor and grab me a beer?" Ethan nodded without even thinking and turned back inside. Inside, he took time to maneuver to the fridge to open it and find the box of Coors Light, the cardboard torn open on the top, and he reached in and closed his fingers around one icy cylinder. He withdrew it, and as he closed the door, he noticed Mike come in. Ethan maneuvered around the kids and held the beer out to

Mike. Mike turned to him, and took a sharp breath, put his hands on his hips, and bellowed his reply.

"Thanks Carlisle. You're dismissed."

The party around him burst into laughter, and Ethan felt his face grow hot. He wasn't some fucking servant, waiting around to grab beers for people. He thought he was doing him a favor. He retreated, but everyone around him seemed to be laughing at him.

"Run along now." Mike gestured with his hand, opening the beer with a hiss and a pop. The laughter continued. Ethan was mortified. Why the fuck would he do that? What did that mean? A scowl crossed to his face, and Powell began to laugh. He could feel his face flushing hot. He needed to get out, get away. His vision was buzzing, the edges of his vision rippling. He took a step backward, bumping a coffee table, and the laughter increased again. He staggered, turning around suddenly and moving quickly from the room. He found Mackenzie in the hallway, almost charging past her.

"Hey, hey, hold up, what's going on?" she said, reaching for his forearm and grabbing it. He stopped and pivoted towards her. In the harsh hallway lighting, lined with framed photos of her as a little girl, he suddenly realized how beautiful she was, how she had dimples and a wide smile, and eyes that upturned in the corner. In that moment, he felt like kissing her, like sweeping her away.

"Did you really just do that?" she said quietly, her eyes darting around the hallway. "That was really cool of you, you know," she said softly. Her hand was still on his arm, and he felt goosebumps rise, hoping she didn't notice. Her hand on his arm felt so loving, so delicate, so gentle. He wondered if the pill was kicking in. The urge to kiss her was imminent now, required. He couldn't stop himself. He leaned in, in that packed hallway, and kissed her on her perfect red lips.

She pulled back immediately. He moved in to kiss her again, and she turned away, turning her mouth away from his. Why was she doing this? She wanted him too! Why else would she touch him?

"Ethan! What are you doing!" she cried out, and the chatter in the hallway around them stopped. The silence moved like a virus, spreading rapidly, it was silent now in the living room, people peered into the hallway, looking to see what all the fuss was about. He leaned in again to kiss her. *C'mon*, he thought, that was a misunderstanding. She had to know how he felt about her. He closed his eyes, and she shoved him back.

"Ethan stop," she said loudly, and next he could see Mike and another player, Jim entering the hallway. They moved on either side of him, and he felt like he was floating, as they dragged him away from her, and to the front door. He couldn't remember the next day if he was actually tossed out like a cartoon, or if they just pulled him out to the lawn and left him there, shutting and locking the door behind them, but he came to his senses on the grass, standing there, under the expanse of stars.

The grass was burned, and he felt the urge to lay down on it and roll around, to feel the crinkliness against his skin. He remembered he'd left a bag at Kyle's house earlier, so he charged across the street to the dark house, his head tilted forward. He slipped in the door in the fence, and crossed the dark yard, pulling the slider open. The kitchen was cool in the hot night, the air still. He slid the slider shut behind him and suddenly turned to see someone. It was Amanda, Kyle's mother standing there in the darkness. Without light, she didn't look like a mom—she looked young and perky, her blonde hair pulled back into a ponytail. She had cheekbones like Mackenzie.

"Ethan, what's up?" she said, but he could barely hear her, his heartbeat was pulsing hard in his head. She moved toward him, and he focused hard. Why was he here? As she approached, he could smell her, it was beautiful, something sexy. He was sweating, his armpits were damp.

"My . . . my . . ." he started, trying to remember why he was there. "My bag. I left my bag here," he said slowly, and suddenly he noticed her nipples were erect under her shirt. She looked good, and he gulped. She nodded slowly and went to the corner of the kitchen, where she'd moved his bag when she discovered it that afternoon.

He eyed her as she leaned over to retrieve the bag. She still had a good body for someone in her forties. He wanted her. What could he say to her? He suddenly remembered the girl in the Dominican Republic, the girl who Gavin had let into his room.

"You know, Gavin cheated on you in the D.R.," he said gently in the stillness of the dark kitchen. Her eyes, bloodshot and glassy, barely registered this. It was like she knew already.

"Here." She handed the bag out to him, and he

reached out too. He wanted to touch her, even for a moment. His hand made contact with hers, and her skin was warm, and he felt an electric sensation course up his arm and into his body. He wanted her, right now.

He pulled her to him and kissed her hard on her lips. She didn't resist like Mackenzie had, Amanda leaned in, and when he pulled back, she reached for his face and kissed him again, this time sloppily forcing her tongue into his mouth. Her hands moved over his sweaty shirt, pressing it to his abdomen. She started to pull his shirt off, and he lifted his arms to ease it up. She kissed his chest, between his pectorals, and he lifted her chin and kissed her again. He wanted to fuck her so bad, he just wanted that touch, that human hot touch. He lifted her up—she was so light—and put her on the counter. He undid the button on her shorts, and she let them fall to the floor. She struggled with his belt and reached in, he felt like he would burst something. He pulled his pants and boxers down, and climbed up on the island, entering her with a gasp. Christ that was what he fucking wanted, what he fucking needed. He went slow, and she exhaled and inhaled in sync. Finally, not long, he felt the surge traveling through his body, and she clawed at him, as if to pull him closer to inside her for it, and it happened.

They stayed there a moment on the island counter, his face on her shoulder, damp with sweat. Suddenly she shoved him away, her eyes panicked.

"You have to get the fuck out of here," she said quickly, and he clambered down from the counter, scampered to pull his pants up, not wanting to get thrown out again. He grabbed his shirt off the floor and headed for the slider.

"Go!" she hissed, pointing away from the slider as she buttoned her pants, and Ethan, shirt half on, ran across the dark street toward his house.

CHAPTER 9

SATURDAY, AUGUST 23 - SUNDAY,
AUGUST 24

NEIL

THE DAY after his business pitch failed, Neil texted Tony again, hoping for a response. He switched on the read-notifications before he wrote to him so he could see when Tony read it. He tapped out the reply carefully from the leather couch in his living room. Outside the window, the clouds rolled over gray and thick, and for a moment, Neil watched intently, as if it was going to rain. He checked the weather app on his phone, but it showed merely clouds, no rain. He was reminded of the Sting song: heavy cloud, but no rain.

He returned to compose the message to Tony.

Hey, you give any more thought to my proposal? Simple, clean, it made the most sense. He clicked send and watched as the bubble moved from his text field to the channel of chatter, mostly brief messages. He waited a minute, watching for the minute font under the message to change from *Delivered* to *Read,* but much like the rain, it didn't happen. He set his phone down, turned his ringer on loudly, and left it on the counter. He had the day ahead of him, and he thought he'd find something to do. He opened another text window and composed a message to Sarah.

You around and want to hang?

He always kept his messages vague with her, messages obtuse and not easily perceived in case Jack, who he'd decided was definitely her husband, saw her phone. He was probably listed in her phone as Aunt Jeanne or a friend from work, likely a female name, someone innocuous so if he spotted it, she could brush it off. "Liz wants to hang out, but I don't have time, and I'd rather spend time with you," she'd say sweetly, and he'd buy it.

She hadn't called him Ben in forever, the alias he'd used the first time they met. It was like the veneer had dissolved. She'd been to his house twice, she had to have spotted his name somewhere. It was okay if she knew his name, he determined. Who cared? He didn't. She probably had figured out he wasn't really married, albeit, he was less interested in addressing that with her, that lie remained free of presumption. He ascended the stairs to his bedroom and stopped at the landing, looking through the glass over the door.

Out on the smooth pavement, a white Dorset PD cruiser rolled slowly. It came down the street, turning around in the cul-de-sac deftly, and then driving back down and out. It was shiny and clean, and he wondered how recently it had been washed. For a second, a wave of nervous energy washed over him. Was this a regular patrol? Was this the sort of thing he hadn't noticed before, police cruisers driving through a couple of times a week? He briefly seized up at the thought of someone turning him in, and he realized he was becoming like Tony. Were the police really monitoring his laptop? Probably not. Even still, he hadn't had the heart to delete the proposal files yet, out of hope Tony would change his mind. Maybe Ethan had gotten caught with the pot or the booze he'd sold him.

Maybe—he wondered as he checked his phone and saw that Sarah had opened his message, but apparently elected not to reply—maybe he was too rough with her, and she reported him for drug possession. *No no*, he warned himself, this was how people became paranoid, they lose their sense of reality. He shook off the panic and felt an exhaustion set in around his shoulders. Suddenly, his unmade bed looked appealing, and he looked around guiltily, as if he wasn't supposed to be napping and climbed into bed and closed his eyes, and swiftly fell asleep.

When he awoke some hours later, it was dark; night had fallen over Staniford Drive, and the lights were on in the nearby homes. He was briefly disoriented by his dark bedroom, and the lit screen of his phone burned too bright, stinging his retinas in the dark. Sarah still hadn't responded to him; she likely felt jilted after he'd kicked her out so unceremoniously days prior. Tony had read his message, but also didn't respond. This gave him a queasy feeling in his stomach. He felt like writing back something snarky—*I know you can see this*—but his mild fear of Tony made him decide against it. Neil climbed out of his platform bed and stood up, stretching. He should probably eat something, he thought as he moved across his bedroom looking for his shirt, and found it on the floor by the window. He bent over to retrieve it, and when he stood back up, he could see a car coming down Staniford Drive slowly, its headlights on. It passed his neighbor's house, the lights displaying the bold, slanting font on the side of the car. It was another police cruiser.

Neil suddenly felt a panic creep over him and roll through his muscles. All the calm from his nap quickly dissipated like the smoke from an extinguished candle. That was the second police patrol in the same day, and who knew how many went by while he was napping. Something was up, and he began to worry they were watching him too. Suddenly, Tony's warning didn't seem as crazy, didn't seem as irrational. He was seeing it.

It could have been anyone, he reviewed; Ethan busted with drugs gave him up, Tony getting arrested for something else entirely and the police obtained his phone, Sarah feeling jilted and angry at being deceived throwing him under the bus with an anonymous tip. He suddenly realized the doors to the house weren't locked. He pulled his shirt on quickly and left his bedroom. gripping the railing as he descended the stairs in the main foyer rapidly, checking that indeed the front-door was locked, and then proceeded to the back door. The slider wasn't, and he slid the bar down in the track, pulling the drapes across the glass to hide it. He moved quickly to the door to the kitchen from the garage, flipped the lock, and breathed a sigh of relief.

What was he going to do if he'd found someone in

his house, anyway? How could he defend himself? He felt his vision tightening. He was probably on a list somewhere. He was probably about to be investigated. He suddenly had an idea; he needed some kind of emergency defense protocol. He needed a gun.

He suddenly remembered something from when he was in high school. When his elderly grandfather, a World War II veteran had passed away, he remembered cleaning out his ranch in Waterbury with his father, before he'd gotten sick. The boxes and boxes of things: maps of France and Germany, where his grandfather had landed twelve days after D-Day in Marseille. Gigantic brass shell-casings from tank anti-aircraft fire, the shells looking like regular bullet shells, just twelve inches long, and four inches wide at the base. He remembered his father standing on his tip-toes to reach the top of the closet in his grandfather's bedroom, and retrieved a small wooden box. It seemed heavy, and his father called to him.

"Would you get a look at this," he said quietly, turning to sit on the quilted bed. Neil stopped boxing up home-made cassette tapes of Matlock and turned to look.

"What?" He moved to sit beside his father on the bed. His father slowly flipped the lid open, and inside the box, inside a red sponge-like foam, which smelled like dust, was a gun. It was black, with brown handgrips, and he for a minute thought it looked like the gun James Bond used.

"Jesus Christ," his father said, lifting the gun from the foam and waving off a cloud of dust. "He wasn't supposed to have this," he said, turning the gun over in his hand. "You need a permit." He set the gun back down and flipping the lid closed. "The old man probably thought he was a veteran, and the permit rule didn't apply to him."

"What are you going to do with it?" Neil asked. "Are you going to turn it in?"

His father shook his head.

"I can't do that. I'd never see it again. This was my dad's sidearm in World War II. This is a piece of history. I'm going to hold onto it and see if twenty years from now I can donate it to a museum." He never would, of course. Three years later he'd begin displaying the early signs of Alzheimer's and Neil didn't remember him ever referencing the gun again. Come to think of it, Neil though, his hand on the counter, he'd never even seen the gun again. What if, he thought, what if the gun hadn't moved with him? What if he'd forgotten it was there? Briefly pushing away that maybe forgetting about it showed that his cognitive recall was slipping earlier than even he realized, Neil had an idea. He left the kitchen and crossed into the cool foyer, climbing the stairs slowly. At the landing, he turned into a guest bedroom, and opened the closet, seeing the hatch in the ceiling to the attic.

He pulled the cord, and the short ladder descended down into the closet. He tested it for a minute, the wood wobbly and unsecured, and for a second, he imagined falling and hitting his head on the tight walls of the closet. He started to climb, and as soon as his fingers were around the edges of the crawlspace entrance, he lifted himself up and in. The attic was dusty, and roof sloped on either side, and the air was a muggy, thick fog of summer heat. He looked down and saw the beams like a grid across the floor, fluffy pink insulation between them. He stepped across the gaps of insulation until he found a section of the floor that was covered by a wide, flexible piece of plywood. If he remembered correctly, he thought, standing on the plywood, and crouching down. Between the rafters under this piece of plywood was where his father would hide gifts for as long as he could remember.

Neil took his watch off, flexed his fingers, and reached through the cotton-candy like insulation and reached under the plywood. His fingers grazed a hard object, and he closed around it, pulling. It was heavy, it felt like a wooden brick, and sure enough, from under the plywood, he pulled the wooden box that had contained his grandfather's pistol.

For a minute, he felt a swelling feeling in his chest. The last person who had touched this object was his father. What else did he have like this? For a second in the dusty staid attic, he felt his eyes grow hot, but remembered he couldn't touch them, as he'd just shoved his hand through insulation. He tucked the box under his arm and continued across the rafters, back to the hatch and the wobbly ladder and down back into the chilly, air-conditioned house, sniffing down the ladder.

DOWNSTAIRS AT THE KITCHEN TABLE, HE OPENED THE wooden case on a little hinge and found not only the gun, but a clip, which looked like it had bullets in it. Both were very heavy. He slid the clip into the gun, and it made a refreshing *click*. He was surprised at how pleasing that sound was, and he put the gun, now loaded, back in the box. He flipped the lid closed and rose from the table.

Across the kitchen, as he stood with his hand on the fridge door, he realized how much the box looked like it had a gun in it. He worried what it would look like if the cops came back again. He moved to the island counter and reached under to the recycling bin and found a shoebox, with crumpled tissue paper inside. Yeah, this would be better. He transferred the gun into the shoebox, closing the now empty and still surprisingly heavy wooden box and moving it into a drawer of assorted other junk beside the stove.

He returned to the fridge, but found himself staring back at the shoebox, sitting on the counter innocently.

CARLA

THE MORNING after Carla and her new friend Jen drank too much wine, Carla woke up determined to set things right. Phil was gone from the bed, which wasn't like him; he was usually the late sleeper, usually the snoozer long past the alarm while she was the earlier riser, getting in a run before making breakfast. This morning, though, it was Saturday, and they both should have been sleeping in. She, still surprised he wasn't there, rolled out of bed and pulled sweatpants on. Downstairs, she could hear the TV on, it was early morning news, reporters speculating if Hillary Clinton was running for President again. Phil was at the kitchen table, surrounded by notes and some books. His laptop was open, and he smiled at her as she came down the stairs. It seemed all was forgiven in the light of the morning.

"Hey," he said, as she crossed the space to him, smiling. She kissed him once on the cheek, and he hugged her around the midsection from his seated position.

"Coffee's on," he said, throwing a thumb over his shoulder.

"God, you're the greatest," she said, perhaps too enthusiastically as she crossed to the coffee maker. She lifted the carafe from the holder, and called behind her, reaching for a mug.

"Doin' a little work this morning?" she asked as she poured it, reaching into the fridge for the half and half.

"Yeah, I have an idea, but I want you to sit down first before I tell you." She froze at this. *Interesting*, she thought, adding one spoonful of sugar and stirring it into the white mug. She sat down beside him, and he lowered his laptop lid melodramatically.

"Fire away," she said.

"Well," he said pausing for a gulp. "I think I'm going to open my own practice." This was indeed news and a decent idea. Phil was a good lawyer, he was smart and kind and listened so well, he could do very well doing wills and trusts and divorces in town. She briefly worried about the capital base they'd need—renting a space, furniture—and they weren't super liquid at the moment; she'd only gotten one official paycheck from Yale thus far. Still, this was something. This was a good idea.

"Oh sweetie, that's a great idea," she said, leaning in and kissing him again.

"You think? I mean, you really think it's a good idea?" he asked, scanning her eyes, his eyes full of concern. She smiled at him comfortingly.

"Of course! This is a great idea! You can do like

wills and trusts and divorces," she said, vocalizing her thoughts.

"Absolutely. Starting, hopefully with Amanda Holbrooke," he said softly, the sounds falling off at the end of that sentence kind of like he felt bad for bringing her up after last night.

"I'm browsing commercial properties in town right now," he said, opening his laptop lid again. There was a page of listings, storefronts in the supermarket plaza, converted houses downtown. The rents looked high, and Carla tried to hold onto the smile.

"Couldn't you just work out of the house for the start, you know? Until you've got those retainers rolling in?"

"I doubt anybody would take me on if I didn't have an office somewhere," he said quickly, continuing to scroll. "This one looks nice." It was one of the converted colonial houses, downtown by the coffee shop.

"Well, you could get in on like a consulting capacity, you know? Like, just sort of do ad-hoc work until you've got your sea-legs," she said, leaning in like she was interested, trying not to let the sky-high rents affect her facial expression.

"That's not how this works honey," he said with the hint of an edge. "You need a proper storefront, that's why it's called hanging a shingle, you know?" The last syllables were tossed off with an air of apparent obliviousness, and was she detecting condescension? She couldn't be. He didn't have a job for chrissakes. This was a last resort.

"Well, darling," she began harshly and then revised her tone, scaling it back. Not now, not again, she wouldn't let them argue again. "We need to look at the finances because I know we sunk a lot into buying the house," she said softly, putting her hand on his wrist.

"I'll get a small business loan, it's no big deal," he said with a shrug. "People do that all the time." *And what will you put up as collateral*, she thought, her mind racing. *Our equity?*

"Well," she said again, that word being used over and over again to start their dialogues, as if to pad the impact. "Look at all the options and let me know," she said, scooting back in the chair and rising, walking back toward the kitchen.

"I did," he said plainly. "This is what I'm doing," he said, sounding distracted. She froze, her arm in the cabinet reaching for the frying pan. Since when does he have unilateral decision making power? They did nothing unilaterally. Every decision—even when she was the one in the position of power; it was her being offered the position at Yale, even when she was the driver—she brought the decisions home, back to the table so they could discuss them together and make a plan. Together. They never acted independently on things like this. Even the house: they saw it together, viewed all the houses together, and refused to pull the trigger until they were in agreement. He was really pushing back this morning—but no, no she wouldn't take the bait, she couldn't. She gave up in the cabinet, despite finding the handle of the frying pan and stood up.

"Well," there it was again, "let me know how much you think all this will be, I've gotta go do a few things."

He murmured an acknowledgement, and she turned toward her office door, picking up her laptop bag from the banister as she went. She opened it to the stagnant smell of a room with a door rarely opened. She crossed the room to the blinds, and twisted them open, letting bright sunlight slant in, highlighting all the dust that hung in the air.

She sat down at her desk, plugged in her computer, and tapped the keyboard twice, and the screen awoke. She decided to write an email to all of her students enrolled for the fall, welcoming them to the class and sending the syllabus. She popped it open and began writing. Near the end, summarizing her expectations, she wrote a closing line, but stopped. What tone did she want to use, she wondered, now that she was at *Yale*. Was she supposed to be tonally different? Less informal? She deleted the line about *looking forward to meeting and getting to know each of you,* and revised it to be *looking forward to diving in to these texts and this material with you.* She stopped and looked at that again. Did that sound like she didn't know the material herself and would be learning alongside them? No no, she decided, she needed to immediately command the material, but also indicate she was friendly but firm. A sudden idea struck her and she typed quickly.

I'm looking forward to showing you all the parts of this course and these texts I love and find interesting, and learning what texts and concepts inspire you too. Enjoy the last few weeks of summer.

Yes, that'd work nicely, she thought as she hit send.

AMANDA

THE TEARS CAME, of course, as they always seemed to, in the shower.

After Ethan ran from her house, she found herself standing there frozen, in shock at what she'd done. She felt a sudden crushing wave of panic as the hormones in her body charged through her. What had she just done? She had just had sex with a kid. With one of her kid's friends. He was seventeen. She felt dizzy. She stabilized herself on the chair. The world was coming into harsher focus in the dark, the shapes more defined, the fuzziness around the edges bleeding away to crisp lines.

She crept upstairs slowly, avoiding creaking on the stairs, taking each one delicately, each one slowly as to not make noise. She slid into her bedroom, where Gavin was snoring, long, deep grunting snores. For a moment, she pitied him, this pathetic man, asleep there, fat, repugnant, repulsive. She wondered briefly if she could put the pillow over his face now, if she could hold on while he flailed, while his arms and legs kicked out, his body screaming for oxygen. He'd deserve it.

She snuck past him to the bathroom and locked the door. For a minute, she stood there in the darkness of the bathroom, breathing. The space felt claustrophobic in the total darkness; dense, the air stagnant, but she closed her eyes and took a breath. She belonged to the darkness now. She reached for the light switch and pressed it, clicking the overhead on, putting the marble bathroom into focus. She squinted while she disrobed and cleaned herself with some toilet paper, before running the shower. The hush of the steam and the heat felt good from the chill of the air conditioning, or the cold of the marble shower wall on her bare behind.

For a moment in the shower, before the tears came, she stood and tried to pretend like this was a regular shower, like she was there for hygiene or comfort reasons, like it was a cold day in January and she needed to warm up.

Suddenly, and without warning, the tears came hot and fast. They shuddered up and surprised her like a hiccup, echoing up from somewhere deep within, the saltwater forced its way up, through her eyes, down onto her cheeks. Her sobs sounded like gasps, and she retreated to the floor of the shower under the beam of water.

Jesus Christ, how could he, she thought, now finally processing. How fucking he could he, for everything she did for him, for everything she let him do to her. For what, or with whom? Was she younger? Was she pretty? Was she Dominican? She'd never know now because she could never talk to Ethan again, that was for sure. She couldn't be in orbit of him anymore. She couldn't be around when he was, she couldn't face him. In a way, she thought through tears, it didn't fucking matter who the other woman was, only that it had happened, and she had suddenly sought retribution.

Did she deserve to be so angry? She'd gotten revenge; they were even, he fucked someone else, so did she. A part of her thoughts felt righteous, she reclaimed this, but that part was shouted down quickly, Ethan was just a boy, he was seventeen, a full almost thirty years younger than she was. She hadn't taken a high road. In fact, she'd probably broken the law.

She was in the shower a long time, before she returned to her bedroom, dressed, and went to sleep in the guest room.

IN THE MORNING, SHE WATCHED THE SUN COME UP through the trees, sleeping very little. Giving up the fight, she went downstairs and made herself some breakfast, but the egg on the plate didn't look appealing. It looked revolting actually, and she wasn't sure she wasn't going to be sick. She needed to talk to someone, but she couldn't. She wanted to talk to Phil, hear his voice, hear his steady calm, but she couldn't incriminate him too. Nobody could know. This secret wore on her, dragging her down, but was hers alone.

She threw the egg away, and moved to the liquor cabinet, pouring vodka into a glass, and adding orange juice. She moved out to the pool and sat down on the patio, her thoughts her only company.

Gavin left for the day, saying something about needing to go run errands up in Hartford. Kyle, too, called a goodbye and started his car going somewhere, anywhere, did it matter? None of it did. When she finished the roughshod screwdriver and the rest of the orange juice, she moved to the wine rack and grabbed a bottle at random. She uncorked it through the foil, she didn't care, and took the bottle with her out to the pool. She sat out there all day, in the heat, working so hard not to feel, trying so hard not to exist, trying so hard to undo what she'd done, undo what she'd learned.

She couldn't, of course. She couldn't forget it. Every time she closed her eyes, she felt him, she smelled him, and it was good. But every time her mind remarked on how good it felt, there was a deep wrenching feeling in her gut, knowing how wrong it was. He was just a boy; she was a grown woman. She stifled tears again. Not this time, not again. She wouldn't fall prey to the leaking of her eyes again.

Outside on the pool deck, there in the heat, she thought beyond Ethan and Gavin. Was this all her life was reduced to? She had literally nothing else; a checking account with forty dollars in it, a son who virtually ignored her, and a husband who hated her and had even cheated on her. What would she be remembered for? Certainly not for her career, that was for sure. Or her marriage. Or for raising a particularly brilliant kid; Kyle, academically, was at average at best. Or, she feared, would she be remembered as that bored house-

wife who fucked the high-schooler. It was this epithet
that made her feel like she'd swallowed ice cubes
whole. She'd never be able to live this down, her life
was defined by five feverish minutes, mere seconds of
human contact. She'd have to move, pack up and leave
this place if the news ever got out. She prayed it never
would. What would her son think? Her husband? She
shuddered at the thought.

The sky darkened, and the sun set. She went inside
and ate some bread, not even bothering to slice it,
tearing it free from the end of the loaf, and returning to
the chair by the pool. At some point, she dozed off out
on the patio, her head drooped down, and was awoken
when someone came home and flipped the pool
light on.

"Mom?" It was Kyle. She startled and jumped up.

"Hey, hey," she said, wiping her mouth, and running
her hands through her hair.

"Are you okay?" He said, and she nodded. "Of
course, honey, are you hungry?"

"Nah I'm okay, we just got fast food. I just figured
I'd let you know, I'm going to a party, I'll be back
later."

"Are you driving?" he asked, knowing that was
something she should ask, but not remembering why.

"Ethan's going to drive me," Kyle said, turning to
the slider. Ethan. That name immediately made her heart
plummet. She remembered how he felt inside of her,
how flexible and young he was, how smooth his skin
was, how soft the hair on his chest was. How he smelled
like sweat, like sweet, pungent, erotic sweat. For a

moment, she thought she was going to be sick again. She sniffed hard.

"You okay?" Kyle said from the other side of the slider.

"Yep, I think I'm coming down with something," she said, turning away from him and wiping a tear from her left eye.

"Well go to bed, and sleep, I don't want to get sick," he said with a slight chuckle as he shut the door and she tearfully nodded. She returned to the chair and wiped her eyes on her T-shirt, reaching for the bottle of wine on the stone between the legs of the chair.

GAVIN'S CAR PULLED UP WITH A SCREECH SOMETIME after eleven. The car's lights were still on, and she startled awake with the sound of the tires. She heard him struggle with the keypad for the garage door; she heard the decline code three times before finally the doors rolled up, and he pulled the car in, bumping the rear wall of the garage as he shut the car off. She heard him trip on the way up the steps from the garage and the low rumble of the slider opening, like a storm off in the distance, a warning.

"You're still out here?" he asked. She turned her head to look at him. He was drunk, visibly, leaning on the door jamb, and slurring his words.

"Yeah, I'm still fucking out here," she said, turning away, looking back at the green-lit pool.

"Is this what you did all day?" he said, stepping onto the patio, crossing his arms.

"Where the fuck have you been, huh? What about that?" she asked, reaching under her chair for the wine bottle, but her hands found it turned over on its side, long emptied. Her fingers grazed it, and it rolled a few inches toward the pool.

"I was at Reginald's with my friends," he said dismissively. "You know, friends? A concept you don't seem to fucking understand anymore."

"Who was there?" she asked, baiting him. She wondered if she'd just set off an alarm bell in his head. Probably not, stupid piece of shit that he was. He was too stupid to realize what she was implying.

"Some of the guys from the force, you know," he said softly.

"Any women there, Gavin?" she asked, rising from the chair, pulling her hair back in a ponytail. She reached for an elastic on her wrist, but there wasn't one. She let her gathered hair fall again and blinked through it.

"I don't like what you're implying," he said clearly, moving towards her slowly.

"I know what fucking happened in Punta Cana," she said quickly, taking one step backward, toward the pool.

"And what was that, out of curiosity? That I had a nice time because you weren't fucking there, bringing me down and laying around in fucking pajama pants all day?"

Her eyes burned. How dare he. How dare he spin this so it was somehow her fault. How dare he make her feel bad. She put a bullet in the chamber.

"No, I know that you fucked someone else. But it's

okay, darling," she said, her tone now pleasant, laced with hatred, a delicate patronization. "Because, I evened the score, and I had sex with someone else too," she said, a maniacal smile across her face, her eyes wild. Her vision was slanting now, distorting, Gavin was a blur stopped in his tracks, his face in the green light of the pool shocked.

"How did you . . ." he started, but seemed to catch himself. She suddenly was gripped with a panic; why did she do that? Why did she reveal that she'd cheated too? Why did she give him this point? She could see his drunk mind doing the math right then, if she'd just left it, just told him that she knew he'd cheated, she'd be fine. If she'd just fucking stopped talking, she could have probably gotten him on defense, forced him to admit to his sins, forced him to be better, to do better, but it was over now, she'd compromised this.

"You what?" he said slowly, and she could see his teeth gritting, his fist balling, he was ready to strike. "Did you just say you fucked somebody?"

"Only because you did, so we're even," she said, taking a step back again, evening her tone. This needn't to get dangerous, she thought, trying to stay flat, trying to return the equilibrium. *You had a second piece of cake, so I did as well. Now we've both done it, we're even.*

"Who was it?" he blurted all of a sudden, the noise taking her by surprise. She stepped back, her heel hitting the wine bottle, sending it rolling another inch. She bent over and picked it up, keeping her eye on him, her fingers around the neck of the bottle.

"It doesn't matter," she said calmly, evenly. "Just like it doesn't matter who it was in Punta Cana." She saw the fury developing in his eyes. She saw the fire, the hatred.

"I know who it was," he said suddenly, his face splitting into a wide, sick smile. She knew what he was thinking, she knew what he was about to say.

"I've seen it on the cameras," he said, pointing to one in the corner eaves of the house. "I've seen how often he comes over. You let him swim in the pool, pour him lemonade."

Of course, she thought sadly. He'd switched the cameras on at some point to watch her. There was no audio, but he could see her. Pity for him, he was wrong.

"It was," he said softly, his eyes wild. "It was Bishop, wasn't it, that fuckin—"

"Stop. Don't you dare." She could feel her own anger now, coursing through her veins, searing up and down her arms, firing goose bumps through her nerve endings. He wouldn't. She wouldn't let him. He'd been watching her, fine, but Phil had been all she had, Phil had always been there for her. "Don't you dare say it," she said through gritted teeth. He smiled again, and raised his eyebrows, daring.

"That fucking ni—" he started, and she shrieked and hurled the bottle in a sidearm throw, her fingers releasing the neck in the direction of his head.

ETHAN

ETHAN STAGGERED out the sliding door of the Holbrook house, aflame.

He could feel everything, his arms cutting the muggy air, the wind on his chest hairs, tickling him, sending goosebumps shot up his arms and back to his head. He could feel everything, even the ground seemed to have give, and while he ran, he tried not to jump and bounce, as if he might drift off the surface of the planet, like gravity was looser. When he reached his yard, he kicked off his sneakers, feeling the burned grass between his toes. It was a bright night, the moon was nearly full, casting a white glow over everything, and for a moment, he stopped and stared at the stars, as the noises from the Gornick house and the party he'd just been kicked out of raged on, and the wind in the trees, and the sound of tree-frogs and cicadas, and the clicking and whirring of the night.

. . .

IN THE MORNING, WHEN HE CAME TO, AT FIRST, HE remembered very little. He was dirty, covered in sweat, still in his shorts and T-shirt in bed, his hair plastered to his forehead. In his fury last night, he hadn't switched on his fan before bed. His phone told him it was 10:04 AM, and he rose and stretched. It was strange, he realized as he flexed his torso, and heard cracks and pops from his spine, he didn't have a headache like he would have if he'd been drinking.

He needed a shower. He wandered down the hallway to the bathroom, yawning as he went. What went on last night, he wondered. The last thing he remembered he was at Mackenzie's house, and he gave the Ecstasy to Mike.

In the bathroom, he started the shower and undid his belt, and the buckle made a clattering noise as it disconnected, and suddenly he remembered. That was the noise it made last night when Amanda Holbrooke, Kyle's mother, had undone his belt. He suddenly felt a spasm of panic as images from the night came flooding back to him. He took Fever in the bathroom at Mackenzie's house, and suddenly, she looked even better, she smelled even better, and he tried to kiss her. He got thrown out, he went back to Kyle's to get his bag, and Amanda was there. She must've been drunk, but she looked good too. He realized that he'd told her about Gavin, and then, she undid his pants. He remembered the feeling of the countertop under his knees, he remembered her nails scratching his shoulder. Was this some kind of surreal dream? For a minute, he prayed it hadn't happened, that he hadn't done that. There was only one way to know.

He pulled his shirt off over his head and turned around in the mirror. There were scratches there—red ones, angry and inflamed. His face felt hot. Suddenly everything felt hot, and he felt his mouth get sweaty, his saliva producing at a massive rate, and then, finally, he got sick over the sink in the bathroom.

His mom rapped at the bathroom door.

"Honey, you okay in there?"

"Yeah, I'm okay," he said in a trembling voice. "I just puked, I'm okay, I'm going to take a shower."

"Okay, you sure?"

He was annoyed. Yes, he just said that he was okay.

"Yeah I'm fine," he said, wiping his mouth off with a handful of water. He stepped carefully into the shower and thought hard about what had happened. He'd given Mike the tablets. He'd taken Fever, because Mackenzie had been giving him signals—she had, hadn't she? He kissed her, and he smiled faintly at the prospect, that did feel good, but then she shoved him away, she didn't want it, didn't want him.

He closed his eyes and stood under the water until the trembling stopped. He rinsed his body, toweled off and returned to his room, pulling a pair of gym shorts and a t-shirt on. He left the room and headed downstairs.

His mother was at the table with a cup of coffee.

"Feeling better?" she asked sweetly.

"Yeah, much. Puking just startled me, that's all."

"Sit down, Ethan," she said firmly. He froze, his hand on the fridge door and turned slowly.

"Okay," he said slowly. He slowly slid a chair out from the table and took a seat to her right.

"We need to talk."

"Okay," he said again.

"I know you were out drinking last night. I heard when you came home, and I heard you throwing up just now." He tried not to shake his head; how little she knew.

"I wasn't drinking," he said. Not a lie, reasoned. She looked at him incredulously, and he fought to avoid looking guilty.

"Did you drive?" she asked slowly, leaning in to the table in a near whisper. "The punishments are so serious for someone underage, you'd lose your license forever if you were arrested for drinking and driving under twenty-one," she said quickly.

"If you heard me come home, you'd have heard the car, wouldn't you?"

"Please don't be obstinate," she said coldly, and for a second, school psychologist Mom was seated beside him.

"I was nearby. I walked." Again, not a lie.

"I'm worried about you," she said, reaching out and putting her hand on his. He fought his impulses not to retract his hand. It felt weird being touched by his mom after last night, as if somehow his own mom holding his hand was equally criminal, equally sexual.

"I think you're struggling with the lacrosse thing, and I don't think it's just about not making the team," she said, taking her hand back and placing them face down on the table, leaning in over her elbows, shrinking her shape. This was called, he knew from her, *nonthreatening body language*; a trick to make the other person feel at ease.

"I think you probably lost some friends when you didn't make the cut, and I know this changes things for college. We probably can't count on lacrosse scholarship money,"

"And my grades aren't good enough to make a difference," he added quietly.

"You have a lot to be proud of in your grades," she said softly.

"Like my cumulative 3.09? Yeah, Mom, that'll get me into Princeton, or should I focus on Yale so I can be nearby?" he said bitterly, and immediately regretted it. His mother's face withdrew, she looked hurt.

"We'll figure out how to pay for school," she said softly, looking away from him. He felt stung by the lie. They couldn't afford it, he knew, even with loans, and then what was he going to do? Become a world-famous lacrosse player to pay down his loans? That wouldn't happen either. She wouldn't look at him. He suddenly felt horrible for his mom; all she'd tried, all the effort she'd made, they still fell short because of him. He spoke.

"I'm sorry. I just . . . you're right," he said, eager to wrap this discussion up and to move on. She didn't really get it. Of course, some of it he knew he was feeling, but she couldn't have known. She didn't know the whole picture, how all of these events were sending him hurtling in a direction he'd never though he'd be heading in, and now without college in the future, what was his destiny? The uncertainty felt like someone was squeezing his intestines.

"And now you were out drinking last night, and I can't help but wonder if this is connected to you going to the Dominican Republic with Kyle." He suddenly froze. She couldn't know, could she? He waited for her to speak again.

"You just . . . you started drinking there because it was legal, and now you're here, and you figure why not continue, right?" she said, and his nervousness faded, his worry vanishing like fog burning off in the morning sunlight. She really didn't get it. He couldn't tell her, of course. It would incriminate her. She'd want to report Amanda as a predator when it was he who had initiated, because of the Fever. He couldn't risk that.

"Mom, I'm really tired," he lied. "Can we talk about this some other time. I'll figure it all out, okay?" he said, and he meant it. He rose from the table, and from standing, his mother looked so small, and he was struck with a sudden sadness.

"I just want you to be careful," she said softly.

"I know," he said quietly, looking out the window to the street. A thought bubbled up in him, the weight of the secret now suddenly too heavy for him to carry on top of everything else. He had to say it, had to come clean about this at least. "I'm sorry I let you down by not making the team."

"Oh, Ethan," she said softly, and she stood up too.

His eyes began to run now, and she moved quickly to him.

"I know how much me playing lacrosse meant to you, I just feel like, I—"

"Oh Ethan," she said again. "You didn't let me down."

"Sure I did, Mom," he said, putting his hand on the wall, bracing himself as the tears were coming now, the muscles in his cheeks tightening. "You've been so into it for years. I know what this meant to you."

She smiled at him and wrapped her arms around him, her little frame, her stringy arms wrapped around his thick torso and he closed his eyes as his tears fell into her hair.

"Honey, I was only ever into it because you were so into it," she said into his chest as she rubbed his back. "I only cared about it because you did so much. It was because of you. I just wanted to support you."

At that moment, it was like the lighting of a candle in the dark. Everything around him had been spiraling out of control. He'd lost his bearings, he'd lost his cardinal directions, up versus down, east now paralleled south, and here, in all this maelstrom of confusion, and the shame and anger he was flush with, his mom, his wonderful single mom lit a flash of brightness in the darkness. He felt the tension at the edges of his eyes and his head start to lessen. He sniffed.

"Are you serious?" he asked.

"Of course, I am," she said. He felt her squeeze him tighter, and he let out a long exhale.

"Thanks, Mom," he said, and he felt her arms release him.

"I was just speaking my truth," she said with a smile, her psychologist mannerisms creeping back in.

"Oh-kay," he said, rolling his wet eyes with a smile, and she chuckled.

"Go lay down," she said mildly and pointed at the stairs. "Go rest, take a nap. I'll wake you up later on. You're going through a lot, you should rest."

He nodded. Boy was she right without even knowing. He moved through the kitchen, back to the stairs and back up to his room.

From his bed, he felt a sudden tightening in his chest and wondered if Kyle had found out about him and Amanda. He had to know. He composed a text to Kyle.

Hey, he began.

Hey, Kyle wrote back quickly.

You hear about what happened last night? he typed, figuring it was best to be vague and see what he knew.

No, what?

Ethan breathed a sigh of relief. Kyle didn't know. Now he could be veiled in his honesty.

Well, I tried to make a move on Mackenzie, because I thought she was giving me signals, but she was definitely not into me, and I got kicked out from the lacrosse party.

I think I told you those guys were douches, Kyle wrote back quickly.

I shoulda listened.

He sent back a little picture of a thumb and forefinger touching, the universal *okay* symbol.

Always trust in Holbrooke, Kyle replied, and for a minute Ethan's stomach spasmed at the thought of Amanda again. How long was this going to happen?

Yep, he wrote back resignedly and set his phone on his bedside table, crossing his elbow over his eyes to block the midday sun. His phone plinked again.

There's a party tonight over on Maple if you're interested. I doubt it's anybody from the lacrosse team or their fanboys. Ethan knew who that meant would be there; Chelsea. Still, he needed to get his mind off the events of last night.

Will Chelsea be there?

Oh shit, probably, Kyle wrote back and followed it up immediately. *Boy son, you're two for two eh?*

Three for three, Ethan corrected in his head and felt his stomach twist.

It's fine, I'll go, he admitted.

Great. Want to give me a ride?

Sure. Want to get beer?

I can do that. I'll swipe some from Gav, he wrote back. *9PM.*

Ethan replied in the affirmative.

THAT NIGHT AFTER HE PICKED UP KYLE, AND THEY drove down Staniford and out onto Cliff Road. They drove along the guardrails that looked out over the ledge, that long precipice of mountainous rock that dropped straight down, sixty feet to the rocky forest below.

They drove down the hill, the road bending, his

headlights on in the fading light, the sun almost completely set. Kyle provided instructions and indicated he should slow down suddenly. Then he instructed him to pull over. Ethan, confused, stopped, but didn't put the car in park. They were pulled off the road onto the pine-needled floor of the forest, the road bracketed by thick trees. It was quiet in the gathering darkness.

"This is it." Kyle fished out a pack of cigarettes from his pocket. He jammed one in his mouth, and flicked the clear plastic lighter, catching it. He put the lighter and pack back in his pockets.

"This is what?" Ethan said, confused. Where were they going?

"It's in here, here, c'mon." He held his phone up like a compass, and Ethan could see the standard maps app was open, and in the center of the map was a purple dot, and along the bottom of the screen was a distance gauge. Nine-hundred feet.

"It's this way," Kyle pointed with his hand side-ways, vertical, like he was shaking hands with nobody. Even Ethan needed to admit this was cool; they must've picked a spot in the woods and shared the GPS coordinates to everyone. This was genius, more genius than having it at someone's house. Ethan smiled a little bit and lifted the box of Coors from the backseat, locking the car as he went.

"Wait hold up," Kyle said. He reached in and opened the flap on the box, pulling a beer out. "You want one for the walk?" Ethan nodded, and Kyle opened them both, handing him one, and they started into the woods.

The night was warm and dark, the air humid around him. Carrying the box of beer, Ethan climbed through bramble and brush, guided by the light of Kyle's phone. Leaves and pine needles crunched under his sneakers. He sipped from his thin can, the beer still cold despite the heat of the night.

A few feet out, Ethan could see light flickering from between the trees, and as they approached, he saw it, a raging fire, roiling in a ditch in the middle of a clearing, sending sparks and smoke skyward, ashen lit cinders floating to join their cousins sparkling into being above.

There were at least two dozen kids there, the smell of smoke from the bonfire and pot wafting as Ethan and Kyle stepped into the clearing. Kyle's friend Charlie—Chuckles, as he was known online in their gaming team—approached them and gave Kyle a brief pat on the shoulder.

Ethan finished his beer and dropped it into the gaping black maw of a lawn and leaf trash bag by a cooler atop which a Bluetooth speaker blared techno into the night. He opened a second beer and stood by while Kyle engaged in a conversation about the latest update to the game and how they game developers had reduced the impact of one of Kyle's favorite guns.

For a minute, standing as a passive observer, drinking his beer, smelling the mix of the smokes—fire, cigarette and weed—Ethan started to feel relaxed. Maybe it was the beer working, a secondhand high, his mom's honesty earlier, or a combination of the direction the day took. But he felt a little lighter, the draining ache down below somehow a little less painful, like after the ibuprofen would kick in after he'd hurt his back at practice. For a minute, as the first waves of feeling from the beer washed over his mind, he relaxed a little bit.

The pain wasn't completely gone, though, and neither were any of the other problems he'd found himself in. He still probably wasn't going to college. He'd still committed what he figured was a federal crime, and was waiting on that to pay off, for the team to remember to include him, not to let him be forgotten. He'd still been high as a kite and fucked his friend's mother, a memory which made him tense all over.

Taking stock of everything though, standing there by the fire, tuning out the conversation, the relief he'd felt momentarily was burning off. He swore he felt the pit in his stomach burrow just a little deeper, the dread spreading just a little bit more, just a little bit worse, the poison of darkness infecting him a little more, becoming more part of him.

CHAPTER 10

SUNDAY, AUGUST 24 — MONDAY,
AUGUST 25

NEIL

THE PARANOIA WAS CONSUMMATE NOW. It was all-encompassing. Neil spent his time worrying and nervously pacing, locking and re-locking the doors, justifying that they weren't really locked properly. He paced the downstairs, walking from one end to the next. Were the cops onto him? He wasn't sure, but he had to be careful, had to take precautions.

He paced the house in a fury until after dark as he watched the sun settle down below the tree line, casting a radiant orange glow over the neighborhood from his bedroom. He couldn't sleep, he knew that. They could break in while he slept and bust him on possession charges. Couldn't let that happen. He had to stay awake. He made himself a drink, and then another one, each one progressively stronger until he was pouring the vodka directly into the tumbler, skipping the tonic completely.

He hadn't figured out where to put the gun, yet. He'd left it in the shoebox on his dining room table.

343

He'd loaded the clip, made sure a bullet was in the chamber, locked the safety down and put it back down in the box. It wasn't safe, he knew that, but it wasn't like he had toddlers tottering around the place, grabbing things, lifting them, squeezing a trigger. It was fine for now. He needed a place where he could access it anytime, anywhere.

After dark, he watched as a giant red pickup truck, Tony's, drive down Staniford and park in the driveway. What was he doing here? Tony moved quickly up the walkway at the front of the house and knocked rapidly at the door.

"Yo, you gotta let me in," Tony said quickly, his voice muffled through the door. "I have to talk to you."

Neil moved to open it quickly and Tony stepped in, nodding to him as he sealed the door shut, locking it.

"What's up?" Neil asked once they were inside. Tony nodded as he closed the door, the weather seal closing with a squish, and locked the door with a *click*.

Tony's speed surprised him, as Neil was slammed up against the wall, a framed picture (a mountain he and Vanessa had hiked years ago) falling off in the impact from the back of his head. He struggled against it, but Tony was strong.

"What the fuck," he gasped against Tony's forearm pressed against his chest.

"Did you fucking do this?" he asked slowly, his eyes glassy and wide, slowly swiveling his head.

"Did I do what?" he gasped.

"Did you fucking do this, I asked," Tony asked again, calmly, slowly pronouncing each sound. Tony dug his phone out of his jeans, and for a moment, almost comically, Neil wondered how Tony could retrieve a phone from pants that were that tight. He held it up on an article, the headline big and in bold, filling most of the screen, it was from WTNH, the local news network; *Dorset High School Student Arrested for MDMA Possession.* Neil couldn't believe it; how could this have happened? There's no way. Suddenly, he remembered Ethan asking for them. It must've been Ethan. It had to have been him. He cursed the boy briefly, damn him, getting caught like this.

"I didn't do it," he gasped. "I swear." Tony let him down, and he fell forward slightly, catching himself, and wheezing. Tony paced the foyer.

"Then who the fuck did, because I gotta tell you, this fucking looks like you're taking what I sell you and handing it off to fucking children."

"You never gave me Ecstasy. you said you couldn't get it," Neil implored, his eyes wide. How could he be blaming him for this? He knew he wasn't the one supplying them.

"So, I'm supposed to think this is a coincidence that two days ago, you ask me if I can get you Ecstasy of all things, and now, there's an article in the paper about some seventeen-year-old being arrested for possessing MDMA? You don't think this adds up?" he said, again, pacing. He rubbed his face quickly, harshly, and Neil began to wonder if he was on something, if he was twigging out because he was high, his paranoia increasing because of whatever chemicals were coursing through his system.

"Tell me how this doesn't link back to me? Tell me how," he said, stopping pacing and putting his hands on his hips.

"I didn't get Ecstasy for anyone," Neil said slowly. "I have no idea who that kid is."

"How am I supposed to believe you? You literally gave me a fucking presentation about how we could bring drugs to the suburbs, about how much money we could make, and then something like this happens, and you try and tell me it isn't related? It isn't you trying to horn in on my business?"

"That's not what's happening, I swear," Neil said, nervous now. He needed Tony to leave. He needed him to exit and never return. This was getting hairy. He could feel his pulse in his ears, a swelling pressure behind his eyes. He could hear his pulse.

"So how long until one of these kids cracks under police pressure and throws you under the bus, eh? How long?" Neil opened his mouth to speak, but no words came out. He took a careful sidestep toward the archway to the dining room. Tony was back to pacing now, walking steadily back and forth across the wooden floor.

"And then, how long until you rat me out, and then they're coming for me next, huh?"

Neil took another step, this time backwards into the dining room. He put his hands up. The gun was in the box on the table, and just four or five feet from him.

"Tony, I don't even know your last name."

Tony advanced on him quickly, and Neil stepped back again, closer now, even closer to the gun.

"But you have my fucking number in my phone,

don't you? You don't think they can look that up?" He took another step, and Neil bumped against a chair pushed in around the table. The gun was right there now, all he had to do was get the box.

"So, tell me, Neil, how the fuck doesn't this lead back to me, eh? How doesn't this get tied to me?" Tony put his hand over his eyes, and turned away, looking like he was thinking of something he didn't want to, deciding to do something he felt like he shouldn't. Neil knew what he was thinking. The only way this didn't lead back to him, was if he wasn't in the picture anymore. He saw his window as Tony turned away from them.

"So, what am I supposed to do? I don't want to have to do this," Tony said quietly, facing away from him. Neil spun around and flipped the lid of the shoebox open, snatching the handgun and flicking the safety off. He spun around again and pointed it at him, squaring his stance, using his left hand to brace it, like he'd seen in movies and TV. For a moment, he worried if it would even fire, sixty years later, not that he expected to have to pull the trigger. No no, he couldn't do that.

In the flurry of activity, Tony turned around, and his eyes went wide at the sight of the gun.

"Get in your car, and get the hell outta here," Neil said slowly, even though his voice was shaking. The gun was heavy, and he felt his arm shaking too, as if his nervousness was traveling along his muscles and bones, like a tightrope, or power lines, stretched to tensile strength.

Tony's eyes shrunk, a look of disgust fixed on his face. He took one step closer.

"Don't, don't, please, don't come any closer. Okay? Just go, get in the car and leave," Neil said, stuttering.

"You pulled a gun on me?" Tony said, surprised, angry. He slapped his own chest on *me*, the sound loud and firm sounding like a drum.

"You're a lot more stupid than I fucking thought," Tony said, stepping closer. "You know what, I don't think you're man enough to do it. I think you're a piece of chicken shit. Too scared to actually man up and defend yourself. Isn't that your problem, Neil?" Neil could hear his pulse in his head, his pounding, he had gritted his teeth. He wasn't going to be fucking lectured to by a drug dealer. No fucking way.

"Don't come any closer. Just go," he said loudly. "Last call."

"Or what? You actually think you're going to shoot me? Do you even know how to fucking use that?" He took another step toward him, and Neil flinched, his eyes snapping shut, and squeezed the trigger.

The whiplash was intense, his whole arm felt jarred from his body, like he'd just grabbed the handlebars of a passing motorcycle, or been pulled from standing by a charging dog on a leash. The feeling traveled up to his core, shaking him. The sound of the bullet in the contained space was like a collision, the sound echoing off the walls, reverberating through the chandelier for a millisecond after. Tony cried out, and there was a splatter of blood on the floor behind him, Neil had missed, of course, hitting him in the center of his left shoulder. Tony clapped his hand to his shoulder and roared and charged at him. Neil retreated and tripped, Tony punching him across the jaw, and he felt the gun slide out of his fingertips.

The blood was pouring out of his shoulder now, and Tony swung again, this time breaking Neil's nose. He could feel the hot blood run down his face. Neil shoved up at him, trying to get Tony off him, but he couldn't. Tony was too strong. Neil's breath was coming in ragged breaths now, and Tony swung again, blocking the light, this time sending his vision careening, disorienting him, briefly, and then he stopped. He heard Tony pick up the gun off the floor, and Neil began to pant.

"No, no, no, please no," he heard himself begging, and Tony pulled back on the chamber load, releasing each bullet in the clip, ejecting them, one after another each one landing on the floor with a clatter like dropped marbles.

"Now, I need you to learn," Tony said, still holding his shoulder, "why you shouldn't fucking have a gun." He shifted his grip on the gun, holding it by the barrel, and he brought the handle down, that heavy steel handle, onto the back of Neil's head.

Neil stopped feeling pain, of course, soon after the second impact. He stopped worrying too. For a while, while Tony smashed his head in with the butt of the pistol, he was awake but absent, like he was elsewhere, like he was at sea again, like when he was with Vanessa. Finally, when Tony determined he'd had enough, he rose, holding his shoulder and stood over him. His vision was slanting and fading, his eyesight tunneling.

"I'm sorry it had to end like this," he said coldly, his words distorting and echoing, before dropping the gun on the floor with a clatter and a splat, there was a pool of blood from somewhere, Neil wasn't sure where. Tony moved to the light switch and flipped it off, plunging the foyer into darkness. He unlocked the door and stepped out into the night.

For a while, his consciousness slipping away from his destroyed cerebrum, Neil lay there on the cool floor. His thoughts grew dissonant, disconnected thoughts, things that didn't make sense, or didn't have bearing. He briefly wondered if he'd need a vacation day for Monday, if they'd fix the printer at work. He wondered when Vanessa was due home, she'd be mad there was blood all over the foyer. He was freezing, and crawled, by his arms across the floor to the door slowly. It was warm outside, it had to be, it had been so hot lately.

He tried to get the door open, tried to reach for the handle, but his hands were too slippery to get the handle to work. He tried wiped it off on his shorts, another blood smear, and pulled down on the handle, opening the door.

He felt a wave of heat from the outside air, like coming in from a snowstorm, and he exhaled in comfort a small smile. He thought of Vanessa, of how happy she looked, how contented and happy, even that slight smirk, he missed that most of all.

The hot night air felt good, and then, nothing more.

CARLA

SUNDAY, 9:10 PM

SHE STARTED her run that early evening, heading down the hill, back toward Staniford, hoping to do one last quick loop of the cul-de-sac before turning in. Sometimes, when she was out here, she'd see Amanda Holbrooke running and give a friendly wave. Now, since they were friends, they'd need to talk to each other. Phil would insist that they coordinate their runs, and then she'd be forced to race this lady in a series of passive-aggressive contests.

"You're down for another mile, right? There's a great trail up ahead it's a perfect loop," Amanda would suggest all easy and friendly. "Just one?" she'd reply with a breathless laugh. "Let's do another three!"

She was glad they didn't do that. She didn't like the jealousy she felt toward that white woman, but there was an inherent discomfort she felt with her attachment to Phil. Oh sure, she acknowledged as she increased her speed for the hill, Phil was in love with her. She knew, of course. She loved him so much too. But still, Amanda had a fascination with him, almost like because he was her only counsel, like she had an ownership—a claim—to him. The way Amanda acted when she was around, Carla felt like Amanda was proposing that her relationship with Phil was somehow equal to her legal and intimate bond.

That was ridiculous. As she rounded the corner and began down Staniford, she reminded herself Amanda was just in a loveless marriage. She's drawn to Phil because he's amazing, and he's sweet, and he's kind, and he's so good looking. She didn't blame Amanda. If the situation were reversed, Carla would probably have made moves on him by now. She briefly let her mind wander to a fantasy place where she and Phil were illicit lovers, torn apart by society, by warring families, forced to have sex in secret, forced to share their love in handwritten letters. She finished the loop and reset the timer on her watch. She was a little slower than normal. That wasn't good. She cleared the screen to try and forget.

In the house, she called out her entrance, and she spied Phil at the table in the kitchen still working. She smiled.

"Hey," he called without looking up. He reached his hands over his head and stretched, the muscles in his shoulders and upper arms stretching, tight firm cables, and she stood in the doorway, taking in what a good looking man her husband was, and despite her sweatiness from the run, and the heat outside, she wanted him.

In the foyer, she slid out of her sneakers, setting them by the doormat, and shimmied out of her yoga pants, leaving them and her socks on the floor. She pulled her tank top off and unclipped her sports bra. She even took her watch off. Then, completely naked, and trying to repress a smile, she padded into the kitchen, and to the table. She pulled up behind his chair and wrapped her arms around him. He smiled and made a contented noise.

"Scoot back," she whispered in his ear.

"What?" he asked.

"Scoot back from the table." She released him, and he did as he was told, pushing back, and she stepped around him, naked, swinging her legs over him to straddle him. He laughed out loud, and she laughed too.

"I was not expecting this," he said with another chuckle, and she demurred. He pressed his face between her breasts, and she reached down and undid his jeans. He lifted himself up and shimmied them down. He was ready in seconds, and she straddled him again and felt him ease into her with a low groan. Christ, it felt good. There, on the chair, in front of his open laptop, pads, and pens, they had passionate sex, whispering loving comments, goading each other on. He pulled his shirt off over his head, and she threw it across the kitchen.

When it was over, and when Phil went stiff and moaned and pressed his sweaty face against her sweaty chest, they stayed like that a while, kissing gingerly, delicately, she, hoping their biology would collide, and an embryo would happen. When they finally separated and disentangled, she took his hand and led him up to the shower.

Under the stream of hot water, in the humid bathroom, the mirror above the sink already fogged, they held each other.

"Thanks for that, by the way. I'm sorry I've been so distracted today," he said softly, the water running off the tip of his nose, running down his lips.

"It's what I really needed, you know," she said, standing on her tiptoes and kissing him. "I'm glad you're finding your way back to your old self," she said, and he smiled.

"I think this is really going to work," he said calmly, speaking about his own practice, but she liked to think he meant their marriage.

"I think so too," she said, vocalizing a sense of confidence she didn't actually have.

They left the shower, donning sweatpants and t-shirts and ordered a pizza. It came, and they ate it at the island counter, pouring glasses of domestic pinot noir, too much, but they laughed while they drank it. It was nice, she thought to do things like they did before, to order in a pizza, and stand together, getting a little drunk, kissing one another every now and again. Phil had, it seemed discovered a renewed vigor. He suddenly had a plan; it was what he'd needed all this time. It was the solution to all of their problems, or at least to his problems. No, she corrected herself, they were her problems too. Success or failure, rise or fall, they were in it together. They'd make it, she thought.

They retired to bed around eleven, and she fell quickly asleep from the wine and the bloaty pizza, undoing, she determined as she pulled the sheets up, any of the good she'd done on the run. She closed her eyes, felt Phil's arms around her, and she quickly fell asleep.

SOME HOURS LATER, SHE FELT HIM STIR, AND SHE AWOKE on her side, her eyes fluttering open. There was a bright light shining from Phil's side of the bed. He was on his phone. She closed her eyes again, trying to fall back asleep, but Phil rose now, standing and finding some clothes. She could hear him dressing in the dark. From behind her long eyelashes, she could see he slid past her, and stood in the doorway for a moment, as if he was watching her for a second from the doorway, then he gently closed the door behind him.

On his way down the stairs, she heard his voice, low and muffled. He was talking to someone, probably someone on his phone. She sat up. What was going on, she wondered, giving up on sleep, as she slid out of bed and opened the door onto the dark hallway. She heard the back-slider door close, and she descended the stairs, slowly, the house still and undisturbed in the dark. She was careful in rounding the corner of the stairs and gripped the banister. Outside, from the glass panels on either side of the door, she couldn't see anything, it was pitch black. She padded down through the foyer, past her discarded running clothes to the kitchen. Nothing seemed out of place, but where the hell was he going? He wasn't in the backyard, the yellowed grass almost white in the light of the moon. She had half a mind to call him, but her phone was upstairs, charging on her bedside table.

Suddenly, out on the street, she heard sirens, loud, wailing agonizing sirens, and she left the slider and ran to the front of the house. A police cruiser flew up the driveway of the house next door, but it curved out of view of her window. She leaned as close as she could, flattening her forehead against the glass trying to see more, but their house was pulled forward, and the neighbor's house was tucked back.

It was there, pressed against the glass when her stomach fell out beneath her, and she staggered back.

She heard one loud gunshot ring out.

It was loud enough to even be heard inside her house with the windows closed and the air conditioning running.

She gasped and pressed her hand to her lips.

AMANDA

GAVIN DUCKED, of course. He dodged, jerking his head to the right as the bottle sailed over his shoulder, bouncing off the siding of the house but shattering on the patio, scattering green glass everywhere. She couldn't believe at first that she'd missed; the bottle left her hand like a thrown paper airplane, drifting lazily, slowly through the air toward her husband, her disgusting, horrible husband.

After it smashed, they both froze, not believing what had just happened.

"You're a fucking drunk," Gavin said angrily, turning back to the house. "That's it, I don't think you need a fucking allowance anymore if you're just going to use it to get loaded." He yanked the slider open and stepped through.

"Fine," she shrieked. "I don't want your fucking allowance like I'm a fucking eleven-year-old." For a minute she felt satisfied, but suddenly she realized, if he was taking the money she had left, he'd find the new credit card she'd just gotten. She dashed across the pool deck, scattering glass as she went. Gavin was stalking around the kitchen, searching for her purse. They spotted it at the same time, hanging off the edge of one of the chairs at the island counter. She ran for it and reached it at the same time he did, he plunged his hand in and withdrew her white leather wallet, unzipping the brass zipper.

"Stop it, don't touch my fucking—" she started, reaching for the wallet, the pads of her fingers just grazing the leather side of the wallet before he shoved her away hard.

It took her by surprise as she impacted a low cabinet, her elbow breaking through the side, cracking the veneer. She heard wood splinter as she crumpled, panting.

He suddenly froze and turned to face her. He was wheezing.

"WHAT. THE. FUCK. IS. THIS." He lifted her credit card out of her wallet. She said nothing, convulsing with anger and fear. Her shoulder hurt. She wanted to kill him, wanted to hurt him. She spotted the knife block on the counter. It was too far away, and he was between her and it anyway. He held the card up in his hand, between his fingers, and bent it, folding the card into a plastic triangle. He unfolded it again and folded it on the same axis again until the plastic snapped.

"YOU KNOW," he said, wheezing as he threw the broken plastic pieces in the sink, "YOU KNOW YOU AREN'T SUPPOSED TO HAVE THIS." He stepped towards her, where she still sat on the tile of the kitchen floor, her back against the dented cabinet.

"You're gonna pay for this," he said calmly, and stepped closer to her again, planting his feet, spreading his legs, and she saw an opening. She kicked up, hard with her foot, and shoved her heel as hard as she could into his crotch. She felt the soft membranes of his dick, his delicate testicles compress, and she struck again for impact. He gasped and stumbled backward, clutching his crotch, falling back onto his ass between the counter and the cabinets, and she saw her window. She leaped up and ran from the kitchen, past the living room, and dug her phone out of her pocket, the screen cracked from the impact of her fall, but still working. She dialed 9 and 1. . . but stopped. Gavin was friends with virtually all of the Dorset cops. They would never believe her. She instead opened messages as quickly as she could as she scampered down the stairs. She selected Phil and typed quickly. She heard Gavin roar from the kitchen and his heavy footfalls following.

Help! Gavin is trying to kill me, please, please help, she sent, shaking hard as she descended the stairs to the garage, pulling the door shut behind her, realizing it locked from the inside. She popped it open again, as Gavin's footfalls increased, she flicked the lock, knowing it would only delay him a minute. She descended the steps again and regretting she hadn't gotten keys to either of the cars in the garage. She folded herself up low behind his car and slid herself under it like she was a mechanic. It was tight, and the metal undercarriage scraped her shirt, tearing it as she slid under the car, pulling her legs and feet behind her.

She heard Gavin at the door struggling to pull it open, slamming his fist on it, and then fumbling with the lock. In that moment, adrenaline pumping, she was thankful he was as drunk as he was. The door sprung open though, and Gavin flicked the overhead lights on, and she suddenly sucked in and held her breath, praying he wouldn't see her.

She heard the massive garage door rolling up on itself, and the hot, humid night air broke up the stagnant garage. Her heart was pounding, and she whispered an unspoken prayer that he couldn't hear her heartbeat. She heard him pound past the car, and charge outside into the driveway.

"Where the fuck are you," she heard him growl, a low, angry growl, charging out into the hot night. She heard him shoving his hands through the bushes, panting as he stomped past again.

"Where could you have fucking gone?" he said menacingly, limping.

For a minute or two, she heard him stomp off through the front yard, and she breathed a sigh of relief. Her elbow was aching, and she'd scraped her other arm as she'd slid under the car. She waited, listening carefully, and heard him stomping around from the other side of the house. He'd done a lap, his steps fading away and then came back. For a minute, he stood in the mouth of the garage, breathing heavily, and she sucked in a breath, holding it.

Suddenly, he grabbed her foot and began dragging

her out from under the car, her chest and face scraping along the cement floor, along the undercarriage. He dragged her out, and she sat upright and put her hands up. Her heart was racing. This was it. This was where she was going to die, she thought.

"Don't, don't, don't do anything, I give up," she said, raising her hands. He didn't care, and launched himself at her, shoving his meaty hands past hers, to her neck. She grabbed his wrists, and he lifted her to her feet, against the wall of the garage, squeezing her wind-pipe. She tried to suck in a breath, but it burned, she started to panic, her vision began to swim before her, pinpricks of light began in her vision. This was it, she told herself, she was going to die.

Suddenly there was a loud thud, and his hands weakened, and she sucked in a breath, coughing, a cold breath of air, and she slid down, her limbs crumbling under her. Over Gavin's shoulder, she could see Phil in the darkness, holding a fireplace poker, and Gavin spun about to face him, and Phil swung the poker again, catching Gavin in the chest. She was dizzy, she was sweating, her underarms soaked, her hair matted against her head, Gavin swung a punch and Phil ducked it. From the street, she could see blue and red lights flash-ing, loud sirens so loud it felt like it was shaking her brain in its fluid as a police car pulled onto the burned lawn, the door springing open.

Then, it happened.

Gavin swung another punch at Phil, and the officer, a man she couldn't tell who it was, he was backlit by the red and blue, leaning on his car door, withdrew his gun.

"Freeze!" the cop shouted.

"Help! He's attacking us!" Gavin screamed back, sounding pathetic, she thought, as Gavin swung another punch at Phil which landed, cracking Phil across the jaw. Phil spat blood, drew up to his full height and stepped closer to him.

"DON'T YOU EVER TOUCH HER AGAIN," he roared, hoarse like an old man, as his muscular arm wound up and swung the poker one final time like a golf club, catching Gavin across the face. There was a sudden crunch, and her husband's eyes went slack, he fell backward.

Simultaneously, there was a loud crack that she swore pierced her eardrums and a sickening splatter. In the headlights, of the police cruiser, she could see a spray of red blood from Phil's head as he too collapsed. The officer had fired, and Phil crumpled beside the metal poker and her now-dead husband.

IN THE WANING SECONDS BETWEEN WHEN HE'D FIRED and when she passed out, the officer holstered his gun and ran to Gavin and felt his pulse. She suddenly realized it was Randy, his old partner. He shook his head and called Gavin's name, shook him, felt for a pulse. He quickly moved to Phil and did the same but for a much shorter time, like he'd known he was dead already, a pool of blood had formed around Phil. He ran to her next, his face white with panic, his eyes watery, scanning hers, as he crouched down beside her.

"S'okay Amanda, s'okay, just," he started, stammering. She leaned over and became sick all over his pants. He snatched his radio from his hip.

"I need an ambulance and back up immediately," he said quickly, but she was losing consciousness rapidly, and she could hear his words as if he was in a tunnel far away, just echoing sounds.

"Amanda, Amanda, I need you to stay with me," it sounded like, but she was being spirited away, far from the garage, away to unconsciousness.

ETHAN

AT THE PARTY, with the fire, the same night, as the low feeling of dread spread throughout his body, traveling along his bloodstream, he finished his second beer and opened a third when he noticed her.

Chelsea was there, across the party, turned away from the fire, her back to him. He felt the muscle in his chest clinch; he felt everything tighten. She'd obviously seen he was there, and he had an urge to talk to her. He wanted to fix things, needed some contact with someone his own age. He wanted to be accepted by someone in a way more than the passive tolerance of Kyle's relationship with him.

He had no illusions about that. He knew he was a backup singer to Kyle's lead performance. He began to chug the can of beer, stopping every few seconds to burp. He'd need to be pretty drunk to confront her, but damnit, he was going to say something. He needed to apologize. When he finished the beer minutes later and crushed the can in his fist, he dropped it with an aluminum clatter against the other cans in the bag, grabbed another one, and he began to walk toward her.

He could hear his own pulse in his head, every step felt like it was toward his destiny, and finally, when he was close enough behind her, he said her name.

"Chelsea."

She halted conversation with some other girl, someone with thick eye makeup, smoking a joint. The other girl's eyes widened in curiosity, but Chelsea wouldn't turn around. It was like she was steeling herself for something, and for a moment, he felt panic. He felt another burp well up inside of him, and he stifled it quietly with his hand. Chelsea turned around.

"What could you possibly want from me," she said loudly, and Ethan immediately began having flashbacks to the night before, Mackenzie's cries to stop, her shoving him away, and he took a step back. The back of his heel hit a round log, positioned by the fire, as a seat, and he suddenly remembered his mother's non-threatening posture. He slowly crouched down and sat, trying to shrink the size of his body mass. Chelsea's tone immediately shifted.

"I really meant it when I asked you to please leave me alone," she said softer now, looking around and finally at him below her. He looked up at her, saying nothing for a minute, and the haze from the fire and three downed beers swam in his vision for a moment.

"I wanted to say I'm sorry," he said quietly. She looked around for another log by the fire, found one, and she too crouched down and sat down across from him. Her friend looked bored and wandered with her joint away.

"Want a beer?" He offered the unopened Coors, tab first toward her and she waved her head.

"No, no, no thank you," she said calmly. He opened it with a hiss and a pop and took a sip of the froth. He felt another burp rise, one he didn't stifle as well, and he swore he saw her trying not to smile as she turned away from it.

"You definitely need more beer," she said rubbing her face to definitely conceal a smile, he determined.

"I'm sorry. I didn't know what I was doing. I didn't know what I was feeling."

She looked at him slowly, sadly. "There are days I feel really bad for you, Ethan," she said and looked to the fire, flickering orange on the clearing and on their faces. "You can't seem to ever be able to tell people how you feel, or admit to anyone that you have feelings or are more complex than you appear to be."

He closed his eyes and listened to her words. She wasn't wrong. Manhood was that, in a nutshell, he realized. It was pretending you weren't who you were, for fear of being ostracized. It was pretending you were emotionless. It was pretending you didn't have interests, or you didn't care about most things. The indifference was the key, it was the selling point, and for a minute, he too felt bad for himself.

"I had feelings for you, you know," she added quietly. "I can say that, see? I found the way to do that. I can admit it. You still can't. What we did meant something to me, and obviously it didn't to you, and you got spooked."

For a minute, his brain fuzzy with cheap beer, he realized how right she was. That was exactly what happened.

"I thought you'd give a shit, like I thought it wasn't just something physical. I know you don't reciprocate feelings, that's fine," she said defensively, like she'd rehearsed this line for ages. He didn't have the words.

"I like what we did," he said slowly. She looked at him incredulously.

"Of course you did," she said, shaking her head.

"No, I mean, I'm glad it was you," he said with brutal honesty.

"What does that mean?"

"I'm glad my first time," the words were like rusted gears, each millimeter of rotation scraped and squealed to form the words, "was with a friend of mine, was with someone I know and like." She seemed shocked, unable to look at him. He realized she hadn't known it was his first time.

"Why couldn't you have said any of this after? I tried to reach out to you, I tried to be friends with you still. I would have respected whatever boundary you'd created."

"Because I was scared because I didn't have feelings back," he said suddenly, and perhaps louder than he planned. Chelsea looked around and stood up, dusting off her behind as she did. As she rose, and the firelight caught her eyes, shiny, he felt another sting of guilt.

Had he, unloved, uninvited, unincluded Ethan Carlisle been her Mackenzie Gornick? Had she fantasized and romanticized him, but kept her distance to respect their friendship? At that moment, he knew exactly how she'd felt. He'd been there, no, he'd lived there, that was the space he occupied, the body he inhabited, the feelings and sensations and longings and the tormenting dreams where you fall asleep and wish you'd wake up beside the person. He nodded, and in the moment it all became clear.

"God, Chelsea, I'm so sorry. I never, I didn't—"

"You didn't think anybody could ever want you like that?" Chelsea prompted as she stuck her hands in the pockets of her shorts. Looking at her now, this girl, who already had figured him out, had assessed him and diagnosed him before he could even understand it, was turning to leave.

"And that, Ethan Carlisle, is why I feel bad for you. I think we should give each other space, okay? Thank you for explaining and apologizing." She took a step back.

He didn't want that, he wanted her to stay. He wanted her to sit next to him at the fire, and smell the smoke, and taste the beer, and in that warm night, maybe he could feel her lips again.

"Chelsea, wait, do you think we, we could . . ." But he stopped as she shook her head rapidly.

"No, no, I can't," she said with an edge, and his face, drunk, must've shared how he was feeling, and her tone shifted before she spoke again this time softly. "At least not right now, not tonight okay. I need some space, and some time for now."

His hearing suddenly dialed in on a phrase being spoken, no, read, across the clearing.

"...schooler arrested today for possession of the club drug MDMA, also known as Ecstasy," someone said elsewhere, and he suddenly was clenched with panic. What was that? He jumped up. One girl was on her phone, the screen bright in the dark. He crossed to her. Her name was Katie, she'd been in an art class with him some years ago.

"What-what's that?" he said now, his words scrambling.

"Oh, the cops arrested someone from school for possessing Molly. An athlete apparently."

His ears suddenly perked up. He knew, without knowing, he knew. But he had to confirm.

"Who was it?"

"They're not saying. It could be anybody," she said, looking back down, scrolling again. Suddenly phones all across the clearing began lighting up, some green text messages bouncing in to tell people, some got news alerts, but one by one, each phone ignited brightly, casting white beams toward the sky all around the fire.

"It's Mike Powell!" one girl cried. He suddenly felt gripped with panic. Mike would give him up in seconds to save himself.

"Yep, he was arrested after lacrosse practice this afternoon, taken in for questioning and charged a few hours ago," somebody said. Cries of *holy shit* and *wow* rung out through the clearing. He suddenly felt like he was going to be sick, the heat of the night and the heat of the fire were too much. He leaned away from the clearing and staggered a few feet into the woods before getting sick all over the downed leaves. He couldn't see it in the dark, but he could hear the splatter.

Suddenly his phone vibrated, and he yanked it out of his pocket. It was a random number—a 203 area code, someone from Dorset calling. He slid the slider over. It was a man's voice.

"Hello?" Ethan said shakily, his hand on a tree to steady himself in case he got sick again. The line disconnected. He felt himself tremble. It had to have been the police. Mike had sold him out. They were coming for him.

Suddenly, off in the distance, blue and red lights flashed through the trees, as if confirming what he thought, and he heard footsteps running and crumpling through the footage.

"It's the cops! Run!" somebody shrieked, and he bolted, running away from the flashlights now bouncing between the trees, the sirens loud and raucous, the kids screaming and running. The police were yelling something, loud and stern deep voices, something he couldn't hear. He tripped over brush in the dark and rolled his ankle briefly, searing with pain in a little ditch, and he yelped, but got back up and continued limping away.

Holy shit, he thought as he emerged from the woods, about ten feet from his car. He doubled over, the pain in his ankle, and in his head throbbing. He bent over and got sick again, mostly water this time, painful cramps and yanking pain from below his ribcage. He was sure he'd pulled something there too. He fumbled in his pocket for his keys, and struggled to hit the unlock button, he re-locked his car twice, before finally getting it and sliding in behind the driver's seat. He didn't have time to wait for Kyle. He couldn't. He had to save himself.

He jammed the worn key into the ignition and started it up. He was too drunk to drive, this he knew, but he didn't have a choice. If the cops caught him for partying, they'd figure out he was the supplier for Mike, and he'd be in federal prison. If they found his car, they would find his mother, it was registered in her name. He pulled back onto the road and started toward home as quickly as he could, the road in his headlights slanting to the right and left. Suddenly on a long open stretch of Route 80, he saw red and blue lights far behind him. Fuck no, he thought, they wouldn't catch him. He just had to lose them. There was no way they could get his plate number or make and model in all this dark. He veered left down Cliff Road without signaling, speeding through the corners.

He cruised left over the river overpass, and the lights were still following. He sped up the hill toward Staniford Drive. If he could just make it home and put the car in the garage, strip down and climb into bed, he could play innocent. They wouldn't catch him. The lights through the trees and the sirens were growing in volume, they were getting closer. Right before the mouth of Staniford, he swerved to avoid an oncoming giant red truck pulling out of Staniford at too high a speed. He slammed on his brakes and yanked the car to the left to avoid getting hit.

The road was covered in dust and pebbles, and his tires lost their grip.

He heard the squealing noise, and then the deafening crunch from his hood. The car tore through the guardrail over the precipice, bending it backward, as the station wagon was launched from the cliff. It happened too quickly; the car was airborne briefly, and Ethan felt liberated, there in the blissful altitude. For a split second, he could see above the tree line before the two tons of steel fell, his stomach dropping out from beneath him like a roller coaster ride. The car rolled over and over down the cliff, through the rocks, crushing the car, denting it, airbags deploying, the rocks smashing the windows, the jagged points tearing through the roof and with it, the driver seat, and the driver.

WHEN THE CAR FINALLY STOPPED TUMBLING AT THE bottom of the cliff, it looked less like a car, and more like a pile of sheared and smashed metal. The police stopped at the top of the cliff, their lights projecting a warning, and as the officer quickly scampered down an inclined area toward the wreck, the boy they found behind the wheel was dead.

CHAPTER 11

MONDAY, SEPTEMBER 8

CARLA

11:38 AM

TWO WEEKS LATER, under cloudy skies, two professional moving trucks were parked outside Carla Bishop's house. She, inside, directed teams of movers, young men, tall and big as to which rooms should be loaded.

"Be careful with that couch," she directed as they angled the living room sofa out the front door and down the burned grass. She didn't mean it, of course, nothing mattered, really anymore. She hadn't even found a buyer for the house yet, she just wanted out. She couldn't be here anymore.

THAT NIGHT, WHEN SHE'D HEARD THE GUNSHOT, SHE knew it was Phil. She felt it, that monumental disruption in the equilibrium of the universe, that seismic shift, like her footing was suddenly uneven, planet's surface suddenly at a slant. The second she heard the shot, she knew her husband, the person she loved more than any other on earth was gone. She ran out of the house in her pajamas, across the burned grass, the dead lawn to the cop car with the flashing lights. The officer was tending to Amanda, who was ghostly pale and unconscious on the driveway. Phil lay face down on the ground, a pool of blood and brain matter around his head. His brain, his perfect, beautiful brain—the brain that had been everything, that had done everything, that had fallen for her, that she loved and committed to forever—was spilling out over Staniford Drive.

She howled, a painful, agonizing howl, an unbelievable guttural noise. She ran to him, and the officer leaped up to stop her.

"Ma'am, please, please," the officer held her, and she shrieked and flailed, screaming that it was her husband, that was her husband, she needed to see him. She had no idea in that moment that that was the man who had slaughtered him.

Amanda made some sounds, the officer, alone at the scene, released her, and Carla stood still for a moment as the returned to attend to Amanda, and she ran to Phil, putting her hand on his arm. He was still warm, his skin still slick with sweat from the heat.

A second and third police car, and an ambulance followed up, and another officer pulled her off him as Amanda was loaded onto a stretcher and taken away. Phil, her Phillip, would get no stretcher. No ambulance. They already knew he was dead.

Beside him, his head bent at an unhealthy angle, was Gavin Holbrooke, lying on his back, his cheek blooming bright red. His eyes were open, but he saw nothing.

They took her to the station and asked her some

innocuous questions; there were no answers, nor did she feel like she owed them any. Amanda awoke at the hospital some hours later and told them the story, a story they now repeated to her. Gavin was trying to kill his wife, that Phil stepped in and saved her life, and killed Gavin, and when the police arrived, the officer, not understanding what was happening shot and killed Phillip. *It was all a misunderstanding*, was a phrase that had been used by some social worker, something she couldn't hear, couldn't understand, the words coming at her like a loud high pitched tone, like the buzz of static lurked just on the periphery of her hearing.

THE NEXT DAY, CARLA RETURNED HOME AS SHE MADE the phone calls, and the tears came, each time renewed, each time more profound and somehow different. She felt so alone, even if her family was on their way up from Jersey. How could he leave her like this, so alone?

At the kitchen table, her cell phone in her hand, she had a sudden thought. What if Phil hadn't left her? What if she had gotten pregnant that last time they'd had sex? What if right now, she was carrying Phil in the form of their child. What if she'd gotten lucky? Maybe, just maybe, she was carrying a piece of him right now, a little boy with gray eyes she could look into and see Phil. What if it was happening? She knew where the pregnancy tests were, she knew she could take one, but she wanted to wait. She almost didn't want to find out.

. . .

FOUR DAYS LATER, IN THE SHOWER, HER PERIOD CAME, and she began trembling, another fresh wave of tears charging up from deep within her, and she slid down the wall of the shower and sat on the floor. That was when she decided to go home, when she decided she needed to leave Staniford Drive, leave Dorset. Now there was no reason for her to stay here.

She called the department chair, and explained her situation, explained what had happened. The chair, patient and kind the old woman, of course understood, told her she'd do whatever she could to have Carla start teaching next semester. Her parents wanted her to come with them, back to their little raised ranch in suburban New Jersey, the house in which she grew up. She could go back there while she healed and, in the spring, come back to New Haven.

But never again to Dorset.

AMANDA HAD CALLED TWICE TRYING TO REACH HER, looking for some closure, trying to tell her that Phil had saved her life, that she wouldn't still be here without him, that she owed her life to him. Carla bitterly deleted the voicemails, wishing that Amanda had traded her life for his. Then he would still be here, and Amanda would be the one cremated, ready to have her ashes buried alongside her grandparents in Virginia.

AS THE MOVERS SHUFFLED AROUND THE HOUSE, CARLA went door to door, being sure that every box had been found and packed. She was in a daze, a trance, going through the motions. In one cabinet in the kitchen, she found the box of packed baking tins. The box still had tape on it, and Phil's handwriting in sharpie. It had never gotten unpacked in the month they'd lived here. She pulled it out of the cabinet and held it in her arms for a second, the box dusty and the cake pans inside clattering against one another. This thing, this was something she knew he'd held, something he'd signed, something he'd touched with his soft hands. She'd never unpack it now, she vowed. This was a memory from the before, from the time before Dorset, before this stupid house and this stupid street. She'd take this one herself in the car. She couldn't trust the movers with it.

A voice called out from the foyer, and Carla set the box down.

Amanda poked her head around the front doorway as the movers moved past with a coffee table. She stepped around them and in. She was in running clothes: bright sneakers, yoga pants, a neon tank-top. The bruises around her neck were barely noticeable now.

"Hello?" she called into the emptying house, as Carla walked around the corner and leaned on the arch, looking at her, nodding to her. *What could she possibly fucking want?* Carla though savagely. She thought she made it clear she didn't want to talk to her.

"Wow, so, you're moving," Amanda said, innocently looking around. Carla nodded.

"I wanted to see if you got my messages, about," she sucked in a breath, "about Phil."

"Yeah, I got them," Carla said coldly. Amanda

379

looked hurt. She softened her tone, but pushed on. "If you don't mind, I've only got the movers for another few hours, and we've got a lot more to do."

Amanda nodded and turned like she was leaving but stopped.

"Listen, I need you to know, your husband saved my life. He saved me from Gavin. He was so brave. He . . . risked himself for me, an acquaintance."

"He gave himself for you," Carla corrected, and her face felt hot. Amanda's eyes grew glassy too.

"I just want you to know what an incredible man he was," Amanda said on the verge of tears, and she looked at her feet. "And I wish the best for you, for whatever's next. I'll never forget you, or Phil." She sniffed hard.

Carla tightened her grip on the box of cake tins. Who was this woman lecturing her about her own husband? Didn't she know she knew he was the greatest person to ever exist? Didn't she know he was the kindest, the sweetest, the most incredible human being ever? She was married to him. She slept next to him. She held him inside her body. She vowed to forever with him. Who was this woman telling her—of all people—that he was great? She felt the tears coming. Nobody knew it fucking better than she did.

Tears were rolling down her cheek now, splashing on the wood, and Amanda began to cry too. She turned to head back out the door, and Carla felt bad briefly for the anger in her thoughts. Amanda really thought she was somehow bringing her closure. She thought she was doing right by Phil. She shifted the box of cake tins again. It felt heavy.

What would Phil have wanted her to do? He would have wanted her to be nice to her, Carla admitted. He would have said something like:

"Oh, come on, she doesn't have anybody left, she's home with that kid of hers all day. We have to be the good people. We have to be the bigger people, be nice to her."

She wiped her eyes, thinking of what he would have said. He'd have pulled her close to him and kissed the top of her head. For a moment, she swore she could feel his lips there, in the part of her hair. *Okay, you lousy do-gooder*, she thought, *I'll be nice.*

"Thank you, for that," Carla said slowly, sniffing and wiping her eyes. Amanda, already in the doorway, stopped, turned, and looked back at her. She nodded, and these two women, now alone again, locked eyes, and Amanda turned out the door and walked across the grass.

CARLA MADE ONE FINAL PASS, THE MOVERS HAD PRETTY much everything, and she grabbed the box of baking tins, this relic from him, and tucked it under her arm as she crossed the foyer to the front door. She didn't bid farewell to the house, as she pulled the door closed, locking it. She didn't want to forgive this place. She didn't want to validate it.

In her convertible, she set the box with Phil's scrawling writing on it gently on the passenger seat beside her and started the car, backing slowly down the driveway out onto the cul-de-sac and looked around one last time.

As she drove down Staniford, she slowed as she passed Jen's house, the little cape with the overgrown grass. She, too, had lost everything. Her son had died in a car accident the same night Phil died. She heard about this, but couldn't bring herself to call her, even though she was experiencing the same thing. She thought for a second to stop, but she took her foot off the brake and began to roll away toward the main road. She suddenly heard a shout of "hey!", and in the rearview mirror she saw Jen standing there in the street behind her car. Carla put the car in park and popped open the door.

Jen stood there, in the street, as the clouds hung thick and dark over the forested neighborhood. Carla looked at her, scanning her. She looked thin, tired; she probably wasn't eating either. She approached her, and Jen put her arms out slowly, and Carla did the same, and they embraced.

There, standing there, on the cul-de-sac, her engine running, alone, she held her friend, the only friend she made in these short weeks.

"Carla, I . . ." Jen said, burying her head in her hair, and Carla couldn't hold it in any longer. The dam broke loose, her eyes running, sobs shaking her body, Jen's own body shaking, both women quaking as a low rumble sounded off over the trees. The wind picked up, and they both released looking around, and Carla wiped her eyes. Jen did the same, with a loud snort.

"I'm going home for a while, and then I'll be back, at least to New Haven, back to teach for next semester.

Call me then, okay?" Carla said quietly, suddenly looking around. A cool wind blew a leaf over the street, and Jen nodded.

"I will, I promise." They hugged again, briefly, and Carla got back in her car. Jen retreated back to her own driveway. She waved to her from the driver's seat and turned to leave.

On the window, beside her, she suddenly spotted it, a handprint, just five pads of fingers, and for a second, she lifted her own hand, hovering over it. It was much larger than hers. She suddenly felt a wave of emotion. This was Phil. This was all that was left of him, a handprint on the inside of a window. *Enough*, she thought. Enough.

She wiped her eyes, shifted the car into drive, and headed out onto the road, and away from Staniford Drive forever.

AMANDA

12:09 PM

AMANDA HAD PLANNED on setting off for her run immediately after she caught Carla, but somehow she found
herself returning home to check on Kyle. She watched
from the glass beside the door in her house as Carla
carried one box out to her car, set it into the passenger
seat, and started to drive away. She was glad she got to
see her before she left; when she noticed the moving
trucks roll up that morning, she panicked, realizing she
may never have a chance to tell her how she felt. As she
watched Carla's Audi convertible pull out of the driveway, she breathed an exhalation she'd been holding in
for two weeks. *Okay*, she steeled herself.

She found Kyle where he was before, on the couch
in the living room, wrapped in a blanket, watching TV.
The air conditioning was chilly, and she'd suggested he
turn it off, but he didn't. She sat down beside him. He'd
deferred a semester at UMass, the shocking death of his
father two weeks before classes would start was as good
a reason to defer as any.

"How are you feeling?" she asked, as if he was physically sick. His eyes were puffy; he'd been crying again.

"I just," he started and sniffed. "I'm so, so sorry," he said for what was possibly the thousandth time. She hated that the most, she thought, that somehow, her perfect baby boy thought all this tragedy was somehow his fault. He blamed himself for his father's abuse, for Phil Bishop's death.

"No, no, no," she said again, as she had so many times before. "This wasn't either of our faults." She pulled him into a one-armed hug. It was just them now. It was on them to figure everything out. She felt heart-sick for him; in one night he lost both his best friend and his father. This boy would be forced to grow up fast, become an adult sooner. He'd be different now than he would have been in everything had stayed the same. He'd be a different man. It's events like this that permanently change them, that warp them, that twist them into different people. Still, she was so thankful she had him. He was all she needed.

SHE REMEMBERED ETHAN'S MOTHER, JENNIFER, WHO she barely knew, at the high-school memorial service. She looked like a ghost, white, disoriented, guided to where she needed to be seated by the Principal. She was still in shock. When Amanda heard the news at the hospital that night, the news that Ethan had died in a car wreck, she almost fainted with relief. Nobody would know her secret now. Nobody would ever find out.

Then, she felt repulsed at herself, disgusted for feeling that way. She felt complicit somehow in Ethan's death.

She cried for him, at that service, more tears than she'd cried for Gavin. For Gavin, it was the death of the man he was ten years ago, the death of the person he was before. Who he was in the unfolding years was like a distortion, a fun-house mirror of the man she'd fallen in love with so many years ago. She didn't mourn him long. She felt grief for Phil longer. She still did, and poor Carla, lost without him now. She worried about her too.

That wasn't all the death, in the days following she read the news and heard that there was a fourth, a random murder across the street. She'd never known the man who lived there, but he was found in his foyer, the door open, his skull bashed in. Triple killings in suburbia, the headlines read. She could barely read anymore.

IN THE HOSPITAL THAT NIGHT WHEN SHE FINALLY CAME to, she demanded to see the police officer, and she explained everything, she demanded it be on the record that she was not pressing charges, and that Phil Bishop had saved her life before he was killed. They took statements, and she dictated them all through the next morning until Kyle arrived, picked up by the police at some party in the woods or whatever, she didn't care, and once the police learned who his parents were, they skipped the lecture.

She stopped in the doorway, looking back at him. He already looked older. Already looked weathered and worn. He already looked like he'd been through hell and back, that he'd seen the fire up close, and made it through, scorched and burned, but alive. This poor boy.

"Watch something funny, okay?" she said quietly from the doorway. He nodded, wide-eyed, still fixed on the TV.

She padded down the stairs, stretching her arms as she went, flexing her muscles. Okay, now she'd do it. She really did need to run. She re-laced her sneakers at the bottom of the stairs and let herself out the front door, and began a steady jog down the driveway, and out onto Staniford Drive.

As she ran, synchronizing her steps with her arm movements, she focused on her breathing—her inhalations and her exhalations. As she finished a lap of the cul-de-sac, she felt a cold wind blow through, and she shivered slightly at the relief from the stagnant heat so present and so overbearing for the last six weeks.

She felt a sudden tingle on one spot on her upper arm. It felt like being stung. Like some tiny insect bite. Then another. Then another. The feeling was almost foreign on her skin, and she stopped. Amanda closed her eyes and turned her face toward the sky to feel it on her cheeks, on her eyelids, on her lips.

All around her, on the dark pavement, spots began to appear, and a low noise rumbled off in the distance over the trees.

It began to rain.

ACKNOWLEDGMENTS

I'm not sure how to say thank you to the absolute tribe of people who made this book possible, but I'll try.

First, I want to thank Nicole Tone at Magnolia Press for taking a risk on an unknown nobody writer and for believing in this work, even when I didn't.

I want to thank some incredible educators who made all the difference; Beth Micciche, Maura Coughlin, Janet Dean, Martha Kuhlman and Terri Hasseler, I would never have written this without your guidance, love and support during and since my education. These five incredible friends helped me discover that writing was really a thing you can do as a career, and supported me in it every step of the way.

I also want to thank Sonya Huber and Hollis Seamon, I learned such important lessons from these brilliant writers, especially how to live the life of a writer, and for this I can't even begin to thank you.

Thanks to Andrew DiPrinzio and LaRue Cook for being such patient readers and feedback-providers, talented writers unto themselves, and good friends through this process and back in grad school.

From and especially my forever workshop team and best friends I could imagine; Maria Marmanides and Mary Lide for reading so many sections (and eventually a whole draft!) of this novel, and always being a true think tank.

To my Boston network of people who loved and supported me through writing and publishing this, thank you; Wendy Frawley, Amy Bronson, Sarah Speltz, James Bransford, Robin Panella, Sarah Parise and Jeff Cruikshank who never once wavered in their confidence in me as a writer. I couldn't have done this without you all.

To all my absolutely amazing beta-readers; Rachael Cina, Marty McGannon, Steve Ishihara and Danielle Jenkins, I can't thank you enough for your feedback and support in reading some pretty rough drafts of this crazy novel.

I also want to thank the greatest pair of writing mentors that could ever exist, Rachel Basch and Karen Osborn. Since the beginning, Karen and Rachel have supported me and my writing, and been coaches, cheerleaders, editors, idea machines, and forever supporters, whether I was writing a terrible first novel or this one; Rachel and Karen were constantly there for support and confidence in me, especially when I didn't have it. Thank you.

To the most amazing friends in the world who supported and celebrated with me, the highs and the lows and who put up with all of my nonsense and helped provide all of the wine consumed in the process of writing this; Ariel Scalise, Alex Burns, Dan Branco, Mark Fusco, Shawna Marks Campbell, Ian Campbell, and Brian Hardeman, thank you, thank you, thank you. To Alex Catullo, who from the beginning has always had the clarity to see as if through a vase, or a plate glass window that this work is what I'm meant to be doing, thank you. Thanks to my family, my aunts Monica, Christine and Sheila, and my Uncle Tim, my grandfather Carmelo, and my brother in laws Eric, Steven, and Jay for all the love through the years, and of course, all the books.

I couldn't go without thanking all of my amazing siblings, Natalie, Samantha and Thomas for always believing in their insane older brother with his weird dream of being a writer. I also wanted to thank my mom, Ellen, for being my first and the best critique partner in giving thorough feedback on all of my pieces over the years, and my dad, Rick, for always being so proud of everything I've written, good or bad, but never of the condition of my vehicle. I love you all so much.

Finally, I can't even find the words to thank my absolutely incredible wife, Lisa for literally everything. You are the first person who reads everything, the person who inspires me every single day, my perpetual adventure partner, the Spock to my Kirk, and the human who I owe all of this to. There were times when you carried me through my daily life, helped me stand upright, even when you yourself weren't standing, and for always, always, always helping own my dreams and take responsibility for them. What did Kurt Vonnegut write; "I never knew a writer's wife who wasn't beautiful?" I'd say thank you, but even those words don't feel enough for all you do every day for me. I love you always.

...and to you, human being, holding this book in your hands and reading it, without you, I wouldn't have had the push to put this into the world, so thanks to you too.

ABOUT THE AUTHOR

Nick Mancuso is an author and essayist based in New England. His work has appeared in Gravel, The Esthetic Apostle, the Anthropoid Collective, The Huffington Post, and Spry among others. He holds a B.A. in Literary and Cultural Studies from Bryant University, and an M.F.A. in Creative Writing from Fairfield University. He presently lives in southern Maine with his wife, and their dog. Fever is his first novel.

You can visit www.nickmancuso.net for more information, or follow along on social media at @mancusonr

CPSIA information can be obtained
at www.ICGtesting.com
Printed in the USA
BVHW031306270819
556941BV00001B/4/P